Hellraiser

Mother Jones: An Historical Novel

Jerry Ash

*Dedicated to strong women
then and now*

Contents

If history repeats itself, and the unexpected always happens, how incapable must man be of learning from experience ~
George Bernard Shaw

Irish playwright and co-founder
of the London School of Economics

Preface

This book is a work of fiction, a novel based on the long and remarkable life of the iconoclastic Mother Jones. During her time — the most ruthless period of America's Industrial Revolution — capitalists often referred to her as "the most dangerous woman in America." Likewise, in our time, this novel could become the "most dangerous *book* in America." The parallels between "then" and "now" are both frightening and powerful. The lessons are vital to our present and to our future.

I first became acquainted with Mother Jones in 1976 when I was chosen to co-author the book *West Virginia USA*. The other co-author, then Associated Press feature writer Strat Douthat, was given the assignment to write the chapter titled, "Fussin' and Feudin'."

Not only did that chapter touch upon the famous feud between the Hatfields and McCoys, it told of a tiny old Irish woman who was, in her day, alternately referred to with reverence or hate as Mother Jones.

Strat's chapter told only of a small part of her work in West Virginia, but her story was much bigger than that. Across the country, during the late eighteenth and early nineteenth centuries, Mary Harris Jones faced threats and jail terms, bullets and bombs to defend the American worker — men, women and children — against the greed of robber barons and, more broadly, to defend the promises of democracy from unrestrained capitalism.

She battled injustice and economic servitude from New York and Washington, D.C., across the Midwest to Colorado, up to the Pacific Northwest, and down Mexico way.

Her fight began during the latter years of the Civil War and ended upon her death in 1930 at the height of the Great Depression — an epic of more than 65 years.

She was the counterpoint to the icons of the American Industrial Revolution — Ford, Rockefeller, Carnegie, Morgan, Vanderbilt and others. These men still stand tall in the history of the United States and the minds of most of its informed citizens, but the significance of Mother Jones is fading fast. Over the past few years, my casual mentions of this writing project largely brought looks of puzzlement. Apologetically my listeners mostly admitted they weren't sure if they'd ever heard of Mother Jones.

Many fine historians have written tens of thousands of pages on the facts of her life and legacy, but unfortunately these tomes are not in the mainstream of popular books. In the fashion of Mother Jones, I wanted to bring back her message, not just to the few — the historians or history buffs or political wonks among us — but to the most of us, and so I have chosen the historical novel as my framework.

I have also chosen to use *first person* and *present tense* as much as possible to retell this story in the context of today. In first person, Mother Jones tells the story and in present tense she guides you as if you are there with her as the thought-provoking episodes unfold to finally meet up with the here and now.

Telling the story through Mother Jones required me to get inside her skin, climb inside her body, see through her eyes, think through her mind, feel through her heart. The result has been a personal epiphany that has enlightened me, if not turned me around. I want to share with you a little bit of the impact the telling has had on *me* before you run the risk of having something like that happen to *you* as you experience the life of Mother Jones.

In 1979, three years after the publication of *West Virginia USA*, I was elected to the West Virginia State Senate. I was a registered Independent until I surprised myself, and especially others, by becoming a political candidate.

As a journalist, I had thought it was important to be neither Democrat nor Republican and that's the way I behaved as editor and co-publisher of *The Preston County News*, located in the little mountain town of Terra Alta, West Virginia, not far from the Maryland border.

Suddenly I was in the State Senate. Since, as a candidate, I had re-registered in the Democratic column, organized labor also expected me to be in their column. I refused to swear my allegiance to either labor or business, and that didn't set well with the United Mine Workers of America or the AFL-CIO. Since I wasn't "for" them, they assumed I must be "against" them. And so they put me in their bad guy column.

Business didn't know what to think.

I was okay with that. I liked being nobody's man except my constituents'. It was a difficult path, but I managed and I made my way up in the ranks of the Senate hierarchy without owing my soul to any special interest group.

As I look back on it now, I probably looked at organized labor as some kind of mindless cult and, frankly, I didn't really know much about why there *was* such a thing as organized labor, even though my father was a coal miner and the union had been of benefit to my childhood.

Now, 34 years later, after all the research I've done on the life of Mother Jones; after helping her tell her complete story again in a different way, having experienced with her the natural conflict and history; after gaining a better understanding of the nature of the differences between the motivations and behaviors of business and labor; and between the goals and objectives of capitalism and democracy … well, I can only say that Mother Jones and I think alike.

I didn't mean for this to happen. When I started writing, I intended only to retell the story of Mother Jones in a more complete and readable way. As it turns out, Mother Jones has retold her story in a more up-to-date and meaningful way.

I'll be surprised if you come to the end of the book without a new perspective on the past and the present. I sincerely hope so.

Jerry Ash
September 2013

Prologue

I listen to a mother cry. It reminds me of another young girl I met one hundred years earlier in a makeshift jail in southern West Virginia.

After all this time, it's happening again. What they say is true. History repeats itself.

Mother Jones
2013

Chapter One

Pratt, West Virginia ~ February, 1913

I'm talking to that long-ago mother now.

"Stop saying that, child," says I. "You're not bad and you don't deserve to be in jail any more than I do. We're all victims of the situation here."

We're fellow inmates.

Sarah James is barely seventeen years old. Arrested for child neglect and prostitution. She was accused of seeing men to earn money after her husband was killed. For that she was declared an unfit mother. Her baby boy has been taken from her and sent to Charleston, West Virginia, to be raised by a foster family.

"But it's true, ma'am," says the disheveled urchin sitting on her haunches in the corner, arms wrapped around her white, spindly legs. "I love that baby with all my heart, but they're right. I am an unfit mother and little Jacob deserves a better chance at life than I can give him in this coal town."

I doubt that. In my fights against child labor I have seen just how the foster family system works in this country most of the time. I'll leave that to your imagination for now, but what I'm gonna tell Sarah later will be worse than anything you can dream up.

"I'm saying it again, Sarah. Stop saying those things and stop thinking that way. What you're saying just isn't so and I'll explain it to you as soon as I have a minute. Then we'll set about putting matters straight."

—◆◆◆—

But for now I have to think and plan my next moves. For at this moment I am in the center of the biggest battle of my life, leading my boys against the tyranny of American capitalism at its worst.

Unlike Sarah, the rest of us in this makeshift jail are under arrest for the parts we played in our women's march on the Baldwin-Felts guard headquarters at Mucklow, West Virginia. We were protesting the cowardly machine gun attack on sleeping men, women and children at the miners' tent colony at Hollygrove.

Baldwin-Felts is the so-called detective agency hired as mine guards by the coal mine owners and operators to bully the workers and their families.

The cowardly attack on Hollygrove happened without warning on a bitter cold February night and the cowards were not only the hated mine guards, but the state militia and the local sheriff's gang. It was glorious luck that only one soul, a coal miner who was standing guard for the tent colony that night, was lost in the Hollygrove attack.

Eleven of us women are in jail, accused of inciting the vengeful riot at Mucklow a couple of days later. Our march on Mucklow was non-violent, but in the end, sixteen of Baldwin's hired thugs were sent to their places in hell. All together, there were fifty arrested during our protest. I was arrested later in Charleston while leading a group of men to deliver a petition to the governor to protest the attack on Hollygrove.

We are either miners, their wives, some of their children, and then there's me. The children who were involved weren't arrested of course, but taken instead to stay with families in and around Pratt.

All fifty of us adults are crammed in temporary jails. The men are suffering bitter cold in boxcars and the women are stuffed in this ramshackle two-room shanty with one sagging bed plus extra mattresses strewn all over the plank floor. No other furniture. A small coal fire burns in a homemade iron stove hooked up to a flue in the corner of the first room.

None of the Baldwin-Felts thugs is in jail even though they fired the first shots at Mucklow.

I'm gonna tell you the whole story a little later. But any how, they took us all to the various lock-ups at Pratt because the regular jail was already full of prisoners who were sent there mostly because it was far enough from Charleston to be out of sight and mind. Poor Sarah, who had nothing to do with our war, was already in the shack when we arrived.

Sarah repeats herself. "Ma'am, I love my baby; but I am an unfit mother."

"Don't say that," I say again. "You are a child yourself but you have the heart of a wonderful mother and the both of you deserve a better chance at life. You need each other. You and little Jacob have a bond between you that must not be broken, whatever the cost."

That cost has already been high, and Sarah's story is typical of the human tragedy that politicians and the press call the Industrial Revolution.

She was born in 1896 into a West Virginia mining family and raised in a coal camp deep in the Appalachian Mountains, just a few miles – as the crow flies – from the state capital.

Her father works in low coal twelve hours a day, six days a week. Every day except Sunday he descends a sloping underground shaft into a dark network of veins dug by hand only as high as the coal itself, four or five feet at the most, sometimes lower.

Day in and day out he crawls into one of those veins, kneels down, adjusts his miner's lamp, and with a pickaxe little bigger than a hammer proceeds to dig coal.

He drags it in boxes to the main shaft where he loads the coal in a waiting hopper car, said to hold two ton. The weigh-man tells her father at the end of his shift how much the total weight is for that day, which is then recorded on a slip. Sarah's father knows the weigh-man's figure is a lot less than the actual weight, even accounting for slate and shale that may have gotten in. But her father has no way of proving it. He signs the slip and lets the fraud pass. It is what it is.

Unlike many other miners, at the end of his shift he bypasses the makeshift saloon on his way home. The saloon was established early on by a few miners who had a way of getting moonshine in. But the company outlawed the practice, took over the saloon, and began to sell cheap commercial whiskey at twice the price. The company says it is to the miner's benefit because this way they can spend scrip on the whiskey.

Scrip is like credit slips which is the only way the company pays a miner. No greenbacks. And if a miner has any kind of real cash, he is prohibited from spending it while on company property. With no way of getting to and from town, what little money he has is useless.

Truth is, there is very little real money around. Some of the drunken miners have very little scrip to spend at the saloon or when it comes time to do business at the company store. And so, they buy everything on credit against the next payday. And the next. And the next.

At home, Sarah's father spends most of his off hours curled up on his cot because his body is permanently bent in that shape. While swinging his pickaxe in the lowest of the coal seams, he often lies down on his side in a fetal position.

Sarah's brothers, ages ten and twelve, help out by working for very low wages ten hours a day above ground as breaker boys. They perch alongside the conveyor belt that leads into a processing plant called a tipple. Her brothers are part of a host of boys whose responsibility it is to pick slate and other refuse from the raw coal.

They squat precariously on a perch alongside the conveyor. Over the years several of the breaker boys have fallen onto the belt, losing feet, legs, arms and hands to the tipple's mechanism. As soon as they reach fourteen, they are allowed by law to go to work underground where the jobs are actually a little safer, if you can call that safe! And, they earn a somewhat higher, but still inadequate, wage.

Some of the older-looking children lie about their ages and get in the mines sooner. Their parents claim they're fourteen because the family needs the money. Sometimes the father takes a child to work just to help him load the coal on hoppers and that way the father gets paid for more tonnage. The child isn't really working for the company and therefore, technically, isn't an underage employee.

The company happily looks the other way. Or the company accepts a false claim of age in the absence of a birth certificate if the child is going to be on the company payroll. A birth certificate probably doesn't exist, so who's to say?

Together, the three males in Sarah's family barely earn enough to make payments on the family debt to the company store and still keep a meager supply of food on the table. Even at that, they always come up short, the debt gets bigger and the family is even more beholden to the company.

Sarah's mother contributes to the household by working for the company cooking, cleaning, sewing and doing odd jobs. Sarah has always helped out as much as she can, but mostly she is a non-contributing consumer of the family resources.

—◆◆◆—

So when a polite twenty-year-old miner asks Sarah's father for permission to marry his fifteen-year-old daughter, her father consents and Sarah says "Yes," even though she only remotely knows the man. What she does know is that it will help her family when she moves out of the house.

And so she graduates from coal miner's daughter to coal miner's wife.

Sarah says to me, "He was a good man, a religious man, an obedient worker. He never complained. In fact, he never talked much at all. Just went about his business. I never thought much about whether I loved him. Until, that is, the day he died in that roof fall. Then it came to me that I did love him and he did love me, though we never spoke of it.

"And he was a good father. I could see it in his eyes, which were almost always without much expression except when they fell upon the baby. Then he smiled this sweet smile that made me feel so happy every time I seen it. He nicknamed the baby 'Squirt'."

Says I, "I know that feeling. My Mr. Jones was a lot like that when it came to talking personal, but when it came to talking about the union, his voice came alive."

"Mr. Jones," Sarah repeats the name. "Was he your father?"

"No, child, he was my husband."

"Tell me about him," she says.

"I can't tell you that story without you knowing what my life was before I met him," says I. "His memory and the memories of my children are part of what drives me now."

—◆◆◆—

Before I can go on with the story, a rap comes on the door. "Ladies, a young boy is here with your supper." It is one of the two military guards. "Stand back now and no funny stuff."

The door opens and a blushing boy delivers a bucket of soup, some spoons and a couple of loaves of bread. "I'll be back to get the bucket later," he says. There are no bowls. The ladies begin eating out of the community pot and pass the loaves of bread around.

"Son," says I in a whisper as I block his escape, "do you think you could bring me some paper and a pen when you come back? I would very much appreciate it."

He looks down at his feet. "I'll try, ma'am."

"That's a good boy," says I. "Be careful not to let the guards know."

When he comes back to fetch the bucket, he has a scholar's notepad with lines on it, a straight pen and a bottle of ink.

I begin writing my letters. First to a reporter I know at the *Argus*, a socialist newspaper in Charleston. Then to a reporter at the *Charleston Gazette*. I figure these men will get the word out in Charleston and it will spread quickly to the rest of the state and the country that Mother Jones is being held captive by the West Virginia State Militia, facing a court-martial trial on a charge of murder.

Once I finish my letters, intending to send them off with the boy on his next visit, I continue telling Sarah some of the things that led me to become Mother Jones.

I suppose injustice just naturally brings out the fight in me, whether it's social, political or economic injustice. I was born in the city of Cork, Ireland to a poor family around 1830. I'm not telling the exact year because I've lied about my age most of my life.

Not the way you probably think.

Unlike most women, I claim to be a little older than I am. It started when I got a reputation and my public image became one of a sweet-looking old woman up against robber barons and their hired thugs. My age was first exaggerated by a newspaper reporter. Since then, cartoonists have had a great time with the old woman image!

Just imagine how it stirs the emotions and sympathies of people all over the country, me a woman near her eighties in jail, this time in West Virginia, unfairly accused in a military court for inciting men to take up arms with the intent to murder. Little old me, a frail "Danielle" in the lion's den.

But my physical image has always been an issue from the time I was a young school teacher, and my physical stature is still a factor this very day. I have always been … well, cute as a button. And short. As a young girl just out of Normal School, people thought I looked more like a schoolgirl than a schoolmarm. People still think of me as cute as I get older, so they are flabbergasted when they see me fighting for the rights of the working class.

They especially like it when I scrunch up that sweet little face of mine into an expression of rage! And they're surprised when my voice drops to a low rumble rather than the high pitch they might expect.

People no longer look at me as a naïve school teacher. The capitalists see me as just plain dangerous. And they don't know what to do about it.

Publicity has always been the major weapon in my arsenal. Unless I dramatize the terrible things that are going on up here in these hills and hollers, the world will not know the truth and there will be no pressure to fix the problems. And so, my persona is my strategic advantage and I make the most of it.

—◆◆◆—

Anyway, my family fought for Ireland's freedom from the British for generations, and we were hungry right along with everyone else during the potato famines of the 1830s. So I know what it's like to be starving poor.

And I know violence. When I was just a young girl, I watched British soldiers parade through the streets with the heads of Irishmen on their bayonets. My father was an Irish freedom fighter. His father, who was also a freedom fighter, was hanged and my father was forced to come to America to escape a similar fate.

He got a job as a laborer on a railway construction crew and saved his money so as to bring me, my two brothers and my mother to America. Just after he became an American citizen he sent for us. Soon after we arrived in America he got a job laying track for a railroad company up in Canada and that's where I finished my growing up.

We weren't rich up there, but we weren't poor either. I was able to finish what they called Common School and then attended Normal School with the intention of becoming a school teacher.

I got a teaching certificate and took my first teaching position at a convent in Monroe, Michigan. My job was mostly bossing little children around, much less teaching. They were orphans, you see, and it was I who got the education. That is to say, I learned how the most unfortunate of young souls were treated in America.

I quit, of course. And I quit teaching too. Right away I went to Chicago and opened up a dressmaking business. My mother was a wonderful seamstress and she taught me well.

Still, I felt guilty for wasting the education my father had worked so hard for. And I didn't like making dresses for the rich lords and ladies of Chicago. Word came out that there was a desperate need for teachers among the poor people of Memphis, Tennessee. I closed my shop and headed south. There I met the man who made me Mrs. Mary Harris Jones.

"It was such a happy time," I tell Sarah. "When I knew I was with child – my first – I once again quit teaching. George was a trade union man and a skilled laborer. He made a decent wage and he was able to support me as the proper wife and mother of his children."

"What do you mean by proper?" Sarah asks.

"Well," says I, "I mean a wife's proper place is in the home. And a husband's place is to provide a decent home where their children can be properly raised. But I also believe a wife sometimes has to stand by her man outside the home. She has to care for the things her husband cares about."

In Memphis, I felt it was my job to support George's efforts to organize shops and recruit men into the Iron Molder's International Union.

Chapter Two
Memphis, Tennessee ~ 1860-1867

"Oh George," says I. "I am so glad you're home. I've been up all night with Terence. He's complaining of a stomach ache and he's running a bit of a fever. They say that's the way the yellow fever begins. Would you please go fetch Doctor Johnson?"

George has worked night shift and I know he is dead tired, but I barely get the last words out before he dashes back out the door.

We have had such an incredible seven years of marriage. We were in love with each other every minute and I bore a child for him every year of the first four years. Then we decided that was enough and we avoided our most passionate lovemaking when I was in season.

We shared everything about our lives with each other. I even went with him to meetings of the Iron Molders Union and got other union wives to look after my children so I could travel with him sometimes when he went about visiting men in their homes to talk about the benefits of union membership.

Now we are about to be partners in tragedy. Our fairy tale life is about to take a bad turn. I fear this night that the good times will end. I have no idea how total that will be.

—◆◆◆—

Before I met George I was so unhappy with life in Memphis. Coming here, I had thought, was a mistake. I spent all my free time thinking out where in the world I should go next. It wasn't the teaching job this time that repelled me. It was the place, the teaming city, the stench from the stagnant swamps filled with sewage and the damned mosquitoes. Even the streets were fouled with garbage and sewage. And the heat and humidity that thickened the air with dust and dirt! It was hard to breath and my nose ran from the day I got off the boat.

I was living in a boarding house for women in a section they called Chickasaw Bluff, which was well-known as the unhealthiest place in town. It was also where many of the Irish lived.

The boarding house was owned by a fellow who bought up properties at bargain prices during the yellow fever epidemic of 1855. He did not spend a dime on those properties. Instead he rented them out in any condition, especially in Chickasaw Bluff where he got low rent from people with little money —— and kicked them out into the filthy streets the moment they missed a payment.

My room was very small. I had a single bed the size of a cot. It took up two-thirds of the space. A plain-faced wardrobe stood in the corner and there was a chest of drawers decorated with carvings that were scarred or partly missing. There was a small window, which I had to keep closed as much as I could to keep the mosquitoes out.

The matron who ran the boarding house and cooked the meals did the best she could. She served the kind of food that gives comfort and sustenance but gets boring after a few weeks. Definitely not Irish.

—◆◆◆—

I met George at a church social. Neither one of us was very religious, but it was about the only entertainment either of us could afford. He was a tall, handsome man in spite of a scarred up face that made him look a little scary, like he was mean. But he couldn't keep his eyes off me and when I passed close to him, I saw kindness and hope in his eyes.

He was apparently also shy. When I looked toward him, he looked away. And went away. Disappeared!

At the next church social he was there again, and I still caught him looking at me every time I looked.

"I've had enough of this," I said to myself. "He may think I'm a Jezebel, but I'm going to break the ice."

And so I did. I walked right up to him and said "Hello."

He said, "Hello."

Then nothing.

"Do you mind getting me some lemonade from the table?" I asked.

"Don't mind at all," he said, and came back with two lemonades.

"Thank you."

"You're welcome."

Silence.

"You don't talk much, do you?" I said.

"I don't know what to say," said he.

"Well, how about telling me about yourself," said I. "I'd like to know about you."

"There's not much to tell" he mumbled, and looked away.

Sounded to me like he would be happier if I just went away. And so I started to.

"Oh, miss, please don't go." It was a plea, I tell you, I couldn't resist.

"Okay, I'll start first. I'm a talker. I'll tell you my story," and I did. I started with my name and where I was born. Halfway through I unfurled the blanket I'd brought and we sat. That was a lot easier on my neck, you see. He was nearly six feet and I was barely five.

While I told my story his eyes never left me. He listened with an intensity I'd never experienced before. When I finished, we both fell silent for a time. Then he said, "My story's not so special as yours, but I'll tell it if you like."

"I like," I said.

He'd had a much simpler life than me. Born and raised in Memphis, his father was an iron molder and that got George into the Iron Molder's Union at a young age. He had worked in the foundry in various positions as a helper and finally got the chance to pour molten metal. His face was scarred because the metal sometimes splashed during his early training and bits of fiery metal pocked his face. An injury rarely happened now that he was a skilled worker.

We were together a lot from then on.

He was good at signing up new union members, but his recruiting proposal to me was as backward as his way.

By and by he said, "I think we oughta get married."

"I think we oughta too," said I. Thus I became Mrs. Mary Harris Jones.

It was the happiest time of my life. As I said before, we had four beautiful children: Catherine, Elizabeth, Terence and Mary. It was George's idea to name the last one Mary because I was Mary, and so were my mother and grandmother before me. Our daughter would become the fourth Mary in as many generations.

We lived modestly but well. We rented a house in Saint Mary's Parrish even though it was one of the poorest neighborhoods in Memphis where most of the Irish workers lived. The water from the community well was always brown, and most of the dwellings were rickety shacks. But our house had been here long before the shacks were built and George kept it in good repair. We wanted for nothing.

I was able to be a full-time wife and mother and I loved it. I could not imagine ever being anything else.

—◆◆◆—

Most of the first four years of our married lives were also years of Civil War. In the beginning, George sometimes had cuts and scrapes on his face when he came home from the foundry. There were lots of arguments and fistfights among the workers in support of either the Union or the Confederacy. The men he worked with were about evenly split on allegiance to the North or South. Some of them quit their jobs and joined one side or the other. George supported the North and at first the foundry was busy turning out weapons of war for the Union. George thought that was his part in supporting the North. Then Tennessee seceded and production switched to support the Confederacy. I thought there for a while George was going to quit his job and join the Union Army.

But at the same time George and a few others were busy recruiting other iron molders, regardless of their allegiances, into the Iron Molders Union International and they were working toward starting a chapter in Memphis as soon as they had enough members. That's where George's true interests lay and he eventually managed to hide his war loyalties in order to talk with men on both sides about joining his labor union.

At first, I didn't quite understand why George was so hell-bent on labor unions. "I've heard of unions," said I. "They had 'em in Ireland. But I was too young to know much about them." George gave me his recruiting message, just the same as if I were a potential member of the Iron Molders Union. He got *my* support!

My mother was my model and she always supported my father in everything he did. I did the same for George, even with his work as a recruiter for the union. In fact, he really needed me. He was an eager recruiter but his sales proposal was a lot like his marriage proposal. "You oughta join the union," he would say.

I was the talker in the family and so I thought I should go with him on some of his recruiting missions whenever I could. Some of the other recruiters' wives also believed in helping their husbands and so they would take turns looking after my children so I could help George and sometimes I would take care of theirs.

The two of us visiting families together turned out to be a good thing. It meant a lot to other couples who would see how enthusiastic we were about the benefits of the organized labor movement, which was just getting started in America. The Iron Molders Union International was one of the first unions to organize on the national level.

I learned too.

The owner of the Memphis Foundry did not mind that George was involved in organizing his shop. In fact, the owner was secretly in support of it. You see, he was a benevolent owner, but he was also smart and understood he would get more support from his workers as union members.

He was in agreement with most of the things the union stood for. For instance, workers worked an eight-hour shift in his shop and got overtime pay for longer hours. The owner told George that if all the foundries in Memphis were unionized — and if his competitors had to pay a decent wage for decent hours — it would make for fairer competition. Of course, those competitors would be real mad at George's boss!

The boss' attitude gave George the freedom he needed to build a membership quickly in a friendly workplace. His goal was to get enough members to form a chapter of the iron workers in Memphis.

I also learned about the condition of the workers and their families. We visited people who were living in such poverty that two and sometimes three families lived in one shack. In one case, the families said that in the daytime they spread out in the well-to-do parts of the city to sort through rich folks' trash for scraps of food. Their children had no time for school.

"My heart breaks for you," said I. "How can you put up with this? Why do you stay here?"

"Ain't got no other place to go, ma'am," one man said. "Pouring metal is the only thing I know and I hear it's the same all over."

"Well, why don't you go to work for the Memphis Foundry where George works?"

"Cain't. The place I work is owned by a big company up north. They have foundries all over the United States. And they know how to hook a feller. There's a general store over there at the plant where employees can get credit. Over the years we've run up a big debt to the company, and we cain't leave 'till the debt is paid. Which will be never, because we don't make enough to make ends meet and so we need that credit and we need the company store."

"That's slavery," said I. "They can't make you stay because of a debt. You'd be better off going where the pay's fair and with the extra money you could pay the company off."

"I don't know, ma'am. I don't know."

"We're afraid," his wife added. "We're afraid to quit the job. And we're afraid to join your union. We're afraid to make the big bosses mad. We just cain't do it. I'm sorry."

Against these kinds of odds George and his friends were able to establish Local 66 of the Iron Molders Union by 1867.

—◆◆◆—

"Yes, Mrs. Jones," says the doctor. "You're right. It's probably yellow fever."

I sob.

"No one knows how you catch this fever or how it spreads," he says. "The disease might be in the air, or it might be spread from person to person. We don't know and we don't have a cure. But the good news is young children are more likely to survive than adults. I guess their young bodies are stronger."

"There's nothing we can do?" George asks.

"Just give the boy plenty of water so he doesn't dehydrate when he gets to the vomiting stage. Keep him clean. Keep a cold cloth on his forehead to keep the fever down. Make him as comfortable as you can. And pray. The Good Lord saves some of them."

We do all those things but Terence isn't strong enough. First his eyes, then his skin become yellow. His vomit comes up with blood and by the second day he is bleeding through every opening in his body — ears, nose, mouth, bottom, even his pores. On the third day his yellow skin gets black splotches and by the fourth day his vomit turns black. Before the end of that day, he is gone.

There is no time for grieving, though. George and I prepare the body for burial and some of his union friends come to carry the boy away for a proper ceremony. That is more than most victims are getting. I can hear the death cart passing in the streets day and night. I am sure those corpses go to their graves without the proper words said.

At the same time, two of our girls begin showing early signs of the fever and they follow the same path and die. Then little Mary begins to show signs of illness. We do all we can for her, but four days later George and I are childless. Finally we have time to grieve together and we do.

We are still not allowed to leave our home even though our family epidemic is over. The health officials say there is a possibility that George and I still are contagious, so we stay put. Two days later both George and I begin to show the same symptoms. At first we try to take care of each other, but soon George is too sick to take care of me. I am still able but it takes all my strength to take care of myself.

Some of George's union brothers and their wives visit us often throughout the whole ordeal. They stay outside our door and ask what they can do. Then one of the brothers' wives receives permission and comes through that door, commencing to care for both of us. She has survived the fever earlier and the doctor guesses she might now be immune to the disease. The doctor also tells her he understands it helps to bleed the patients some, and so she does that for us.

George is failing faster than I am, and by the third day he is gone. In addition to being ill from the fever, my heart is broken. I could have just given up at that point, but I knew I would be a fighter to the end. Just a few hours after George's body has been cleaned up and taken away to be given a high ceremony and funeral by the union, I begin to get better. Maybe the bleeding is working for me. In a few days I am well enough to be on my own and I want to be by myself.

I stay in our house. I mourn my losses for three days. I cry. I scream. I curse God. And I still hear those damned death carts passing by and the wails of mourning all around me. Finally, it comes to me that my mission in Memphis is not over. Now I am probably immune just like our friend. So I go to the health workers and volunteer to help people fight the disease until the epidemic is over. It is several weeks.

Chapter Three
Pratt, West Virginia ~ February, 1913

"So you see, Sarah, I have personal reasons to feel the way I do about the preciousness of innocent children," says I. "You will regret it for the rest of your life if you don't fight for your child just as I fight against child labor wherever I find it."

"All right," Sarah says. " But I don't know what to do."

"Well, the first thing is to raise hell," says I. "That's always the first thing to do when you're faced with an injustice and you feel powerless. That's what I do in my fight for the working class."

"But how can I fight when they have me in this jail?" she asks.

"Being in jail is one of the best places to carry on a good fight," I say. "One of the ways for me to get people's attention is to get myself arrested and then put out the word that a sweet old woman has been thrown in a horrible jail because she fights for the rights of men and women and children who are being used like slaves to pour iron, build railroads, dig coal, weave cloth, sew clothes, and produce every product that comes from America's factories."

Another of my fellow inmates, Addie Thompson, speaks up in her manly voice.

"Well, I'm not too thrilled about being in jail. I don't see how this is getting us anywhere. You talked us into having a women's march on Mucklow and then the fighting broke out and now everyone is in the hoosegow."

Addie Thompson was my volunteer lieutenant who led the women's march on Mucklow while I went to Charleston to fight on the political front. She and her husband came to West Virginia from Colorado where her husband was a coal miner. Since I have spent a lot of time organizing labor out there, I recognize her Western background as soon as she says "hoosegow" which is an American pronunciation of a Mexican word meaning jail.

Tall, slender, with straight brown hair to the middle of her back, brash as a Western girl can be, Addie is very bright and has enough education to be trouble when she wants to be. And she wants to be now. That's why I picked her to be my lieutenant at Mucklow.

"Addie," says I, "I'm surprised you are so easily defeated."

My words redden her already ruddy complexion. She is enraged and her tough eyes show the born fighter in her. I grin at her: "I swear they arrested you just because you scared 'em to death!" It was the truth. They say when the deputy grabbed hold of her, she struggled like a she-cat.

Addie grins back, pleased with the thought. "That's why they call me Addie, not Sweet Adeline. But in truth, I haven't been a fighter 'till now; I've been a victim long enough! My husband and I gathered what little money we had and bought a small ranch in Colorado. We figured with hard work we could annex more land and be successful raising cattle.

"And we were on our way, too, until the drought came and we could no longer make payments to the bank. My husband went to work in the mines to make ends meet and I went on running the ranch.

"He used his scrip to buy groceries and I went up there once a week to haul those groceries home. Of course, it wasn't enough to feed the ranch hands and so I began hauling home more food than my husband's salary would cover.

"Soon we were hopelessly in debt to the coal company, and so on the last trip I had both the groceries and my husband under the tarp. His shift wasn't over, but he staggered out of the mine so tired he could hardly move.

"We were desperate by then — hopelessly in debt to the company and my husband was working himself to death. We heard there was work in West Virginia and so we decided to come here for a fresh start. We dug up a tin can we'd buried, abandoned the ranch and used the money to get us to West Virginia. There was not much use here for ranch hands, and so we moved into the coal camp. Now we're even worse off. So don't tell me I'm easily defeated. I'm just damned frustrated and mad!"

I apologize for my thoughtlessness.

"What I don't understand," Addie says, "is why these coal operators do such rotten things to the very people who are giving them honest work. My husband is a hard worker and glad to do it."

"Well, honey, it's capitalism that brings out the meanness and greed," says I. "Our founding fathers did a decent job of framing our democracy. They wrote the Constitution and added a Bill of Rights that intended for people of all classes to enjoy the freedoms the Constitution offers. But capitalism came along without a constitution or a bill of rights and the industrialists grabbed unrestricted power. The capitalists wrote their own 'Declaration of Capitalism'.

"Democracy is supposed to be 'of the people, by the people and for the people'. Capitalism is 'of the capitalist, for the capitalist'. Period.

"The government lets the capitalists get away with murder because the politicians are as greedy as the robber barons. Many of the politicians *are* robber barons. As long as capitalism drives the Industrial Revolution and makes the country rich, politicians don't mind if some people get filthy rich while most people are left dirt poor, even starving.

"But the Bill of Rights says everyone's equal," Addie said. "How comes that don't mean anything to the capitalists?"

"Honey, it isn't democracy that runs this country. Capitalism rules. It does no good to reason with the capitalists or their politicians. This is a class war. We have to stir up the American people, the lower class. Some of the better-off lower class do show some sympathy for us when they're smacked with the facts. And when they voice themselves collectively, good things happen."

"Sounds to me like democracy and capitalism don't mix," says Addie.

"You got that right," says I.

"What's all this have to do with me?" Sarah asks. "Why would you bother with me or with one child, when you have so much bigger business on your mind?"

"Sarah," says I, "you are a perfect example of what the abuse of power, of labor, of whole families, can cause. Your life is a tragedy from start to finish, and people will be outraged when they hear about it. You were a child forced into marriage and motherhood by necessity. You were forced into prostitution to survive. And you were forced to give up the only good thing that ever happened to you in your short life — they forced you to give up your child.

"Now you sit in prison. You are a dramatic example of what an unchecked Industrial Revolution, backed by the government, is doing to the people. Don't you fret, Sarah, we'll get this word out and it will help you and the labor movement as well. And we'll get your child back before he is put on an orphan train bound for the Midwest and servitude on a farm."

"But they said he would grow up with a foster family," Sarah protests.

"Sure," says I, "and the company promises it'll raise wages as soon as it can."

Addie, who had been following this conversation, asks, "How did you get so smart?"

"The hard way," says I. "Memphis was just the start of my education, but I had much more to learn before I could become a danger to the capitalists."

—◆◆◆—

It is time for me to write another letter. "Dear esteemed guardian of the press, let me tell you a story about the grief that follows the greed in the coalfields of West Virginia."

Chapter Four
Chicago ~ October, 1867

I stay in Memphis until October when the epidemic is finally over.

As long as I keep busy helping other families in their crises, I can avoid reliving my own by thinking of something else.

But as soon as I am back in my empty home, day and night, I begin remembering the events of my own loss over and over again. I become angry at whoever carried this disease to us, at the doctor who didn't know how to cure it, at the God-forsaken city of Memphis, at God himself. "Why me, God?" I ask.

My sobs turn into screams. I hate life. Even the wonderful seven years I had with my family becomes a nightmare in my mind because the good times were just setting me up for the bad. I scream at God: "Why did you do this to me, God?"

Then I wonder if it's all my fault. Did I do enough to save them? Should I have sent for another doctor? What had I done to anger God? Should I have taken my family to Mass more often? Was I a good enough wife and mother? If only I had done this or said that.

Finally, I become so depressed I can hardly get out of my bed. What food is left in the house goes begging. I begin to worry about what to do next.

At that moment, a letter is slid under my front door. It is from my dear friend back in Chicago, Jenny Flynn, whose family brought her to America from County Cork, same as me. She is my age and so we have a lot in common.

We have corresponded often since I've been in Memphis. A letter from her came in the first days of our quarantine. She was very concerned about our situation.

When I wrote to say I had lost my husband and all my children she begged me to come back to Chicago. She wanted us to become partners in a new dressmaking business, saying Chicago had grown fast since I had left with the number of rich people who could afford to hire a seamstress to sew fancy dresses more than doubling. She had more business than she could handle.

Now, I decide that's what I'll do. I need to make a living, and I need to get past my grief. I go to the graves of my husband and my children and make my peace. I promise my family I will always carry them in my heart and I promise George I will make him proud of me when he looks down from Heaven. I also make peace with my God.

I take passage on a steamboat up the Mississippi and eventually transfer to a train, the same course in reverse I had followed when I moved to Memphis. But I am a different person now. I have plenty of money to make the trip and pay my share in starting the new dressmaking business. George's union has taken up a collection to help me, his widow, start a new life. It is a considerable amount, a fortune to a woman who has lived hand to mouth her entire adult life. Which, come to think of, my life isn't over. I am now only thirty years old.

—◆◆◆—

Jenny is easy to spot as the train pulls into the station. She is jumping up and down like a jack-in-the-box. Her manner of dress is about as comical as the clown in the child's toy, but in place of a tinkling tune, she is screaming at the top of her lungs. I guess she is happy to see me. In spite of my still-heavy heart, I have to smile.

When I reach her, she hugs the breath out of me and kisses my face all over. We each carry one of my bags and she talks non-stop for ten minutes, then stops dead in her tracks and says, "Oh, Mary, I'm so thoughtless. Here I am bubbling over about you being here and I know you must still be grieving over your losses. You know I share your pain as best as any friend can."

"I know," says I, "and your enthusiasm is just the tonic I've been needing. I'm still clearing my head of the darkness and your cheer is what the doctor ordered.

"Thank you, Jenny. Thank you so much. If it weren't for you, I don't know how long it would take me to gather my wits about me. Thank you." And I hug her as hard as she had hugged me. Only this time, tears ran down both our cheeks. Mine were actually tears of joy. The best way to wash away the tears of despair I thought, but did not say.

"Where did you get the idea for that colorful outfit?" I ask. "It looks like you're ready for a New Year's Eve party."

"Exactly. I made it for this rich lady who insisted she was a size smaller than she really is. When it didn't fit her, I tried it on and liked what I saw in the mirror. So I kept it. Now I'm wearing it for our new year's party, a new beginning for you and me."

Jenny finds a small store building on Washington Street in the warehouse district near Lake Michigan and right on the edge of downtown. There is a sleeping room in the back with a small cook stove. Jenny has hung a curtain hiding the chamber pot in one back corner. A communal outhouse stands out back, which serves several establishments. All that is left is enough room for one bed. But we were like sisters and Jenny intends for both of us to sleep in it.

The bigger commercial buildings are made of stone and masonry, but most of Chicago is a wooden city and our shop is no exception. The outside walls are clapboard, painted a cheery yellow, and the rafters are wood with slats that support cedar shake shingles. There is a small covered porch across the front and windows on each side of the front door. Two more windows on each of the other three sides provide plenty of natural light.

The sign in one of the front windows reads "Flynn & Jones, Dressmakers."

"Oh, Jenny, you've done a great job," says I. I've taken the money to pay for the shop from the funds the union boys collected for me. The property is titled in my name now that I am here to sign the papers. Jenny has paid for the supplies and the two treadle sewing machines.

In addition to the usual bolts of cloth, boxes full of threads, needles, pins and such, she has bought ready-made dress patterns. They were developed by a man named Ebenezer Butterick during the time I was in Memphis. They come with drawings of the finished products and they can easily be adjusted to different sizes.

What a change from the past when a seamstress had to draw her own patterns from pictures or tear apart old worn-out dresses and trace them on butcher paper. Sizes depended on extensive measuring of the customer or resizing self-drawn patterns.

What makes these commercial patterns even more appealing is that they are said to be the latest Paris fashions!

"Jenny," says I, "you're a genius!"

But I am equally genius at getting the word around and attracting customers. I start putting placards in the upper class sections of town announcing "Flynn & Jones, Dressmakers — For the Latest Paris Fashions." In a matter of days, we have more orders than the two of us can fill. And those rich ladies are willing to pay twice the price for those fancy Paris fashions. Those same patterns make it possible for us to turn out double the number of dresses in a week. We are very successful capitalists and Jenny, it turns out, is a very shrewd businesswoman.

"Capitalists!" I am a little uncomfortable with the idea of being a capitalist. My thoughts about capitalism were founded on what I learned from George and the union in Memphis and capitalism didn't seem so bad then. My experience with organizing and collective bargaining was very positive in Memphis. It was mostly carried out in a civilized manner, although words sometimes got rough.

Nevertheless, now in Chicago, I'm thinking of capital and labor as "them and us" and the process is like a battle. When I recollect my earlier days as an independent dressmaker, I thought of myself then as one of the laboring class. This partnership with Jenny seems to put a different face on it. We are businesswomen — capitalists — even though we are also the only labor we have. Still, I puzzle about it.

—◆◆◆—

My work often puts me in the mansions of the barons and baronesses of capitalism along Lakeshore Drive. Fittings and alterations take all day sometimes, and I keep looking out the plate glass windows of those mansions at the steady stream of poor families trudging along, going who knows where or for who knows what.

In the dead of winter it is bitter cold out there, while the insides of the mansions are heated to tropical condition. I can't help thinking about those unfortunates outside who are either out of work or being paid slave wages by the very people I'm working for.

It comes to me that I actually haven't left all of me behind. Certainly fighting on the side of the working class is still very much in my heart. I could give up capitalism and return to the labor movement sooner, but my life is again about to be struck by tragedy, the Great Chicago Fire.

Chapter Five
Chicago ~ October 8, 1871

The smell of smoke awakens us soon after we go to bed on October 8, 1871. We think nothing of it since many people burn wood in their heating stoves. But then we look out our window and see a red sky long after the sun has set.

"There must be a terrible fire somewhere," says I.

"Yes," Jenny says. "It looks like it's a long way from here, though."

"It does," I agree. "Let's go back to bed. We both have a hard day's work tomorrow."

The night before there had been a similar fire in the distance and the fire department apparently put it out. But we have been reading in the newspapers for weeks that the summer's drought has turned Chicago into a tinderbox. Still, we are a long way from tonight's fire and we are located right here on the Great Lake with its limitless supply of water. We are safe, we think.

But this fire, unbeknownst to us, is marching north at a fast pace, consuming everything in its path and heading straight for the heart of Chicago which contains the business district and our little dressmaking establishment and home.

Jenny and I go to bed, satisfied that the fire is way off somewhere. Then in the middle of the night someone pounds on our front door. We listen for another knock, but none comes. So we get up and both of us go to the door. When we open it, no one is there, but in the distance we see a wall of flame reaching maybe one hundred feet into the sky. Hundreds, probably thousands, of people are running past us toward Lake Michigan, most of them wrapped in blankets to keep warm.

One says, "Better hurry, ladies. The fire travels fast. It will be here in just a few minutes. Dress warmly and bring some blankets."

The horror of it hits us and we quickly do as the man says, except instead of blankets we carry bolts of flannel along with scissors, thinking we can share with those who do not bring blankets. As we arrive at the water's edge we can see heads bobbing in and out of the water, everyone dodging the sparks and fireballs falling from the sky like snow. But this isn't the white stuff. It is colored red and orange and yellow and it is deadly.

Each time I surface for a breath of air I glance over at our dress shop. First the sparks and fireballs are landing on the shake roof; the next time I surface there are little fires all over it; a few bobs later and I see the little building explode in flame as though it has been bombed.

The heat from the wall of fire is like a blast furnace. I think about George and what it must have been like for him standing in front of those iron furnaces back in Memphis. This fire seems to create its own wind, as if it plans on boiling us all right there in Lake Michigan. But the water remains cool and the fire and wind die down quickly. On shore I can make out little bonfires and debris as far as I can see, but the wall of flame is out and the air is clear of burning debris.

Once I've gathered my wits, I start looking for our building. It is gone, of course, and I really can't identify the spot where it once stood.

It is usually quite cold in Chicago in October, but the air is still warm from the fire as we all make our way back from the chilled water of Lake Michigan. People, adults and children, men and women alike, each contribute to a keening I will never forget.

Humans of all description are wandering around, stunned. Some are without blankets and Jenny and I begin cutting off pieces of cloth from the bolts we had carried into the water. "Hurry," I say. "Take this cloth where there's a small fire and dry the fabric out as fast as you can. Also, dry yourselves by the fire. You don't want to be wet when the cold air returns. The heat from the fire will soon be gone and the air will turn very cold."

Much later it occurs to me that there is no social class in the wake of the fire. You can tell by the clothing they wear which are of the upper class and which are not. But in that moment, we are all equal and amazingly most are not just grieving but caring for one another regardless of class, offering sympathy, sharing a blanket, huddling together, giving words of encouragement. I myself make no distinction between class as I cut off pieces of cloth for those in need.

The night passes and at first light a few begin milling around, wondering what to do next. Myself, I have no doubt. This is bigger than the horror of the yellow fever in Memphis, but not as devastating to me. In Memphis I lost my entire family of course, but here my loss is only of material things — a building, a bed, a business. I quickly put those things out of my mind and begin tending to the survivors of this new tragedy as I did in Memphis just a few years back.

—◆◆◆—

My focus remains on helping Chicago recover, helping the poor, while Jenny sets about recovering our business. As I've said, Jenny is the business head in our partnership and she quickly finds the resources not only to restore what we had — two women and two foot-treadle sewing machines in a small cottage — but now she begins turning our little enterprise into a veritable factory. Soon it will be staffed by several other seamstresses.

Providing warm clothing for the thousands of burned-out citizens of Chicago is considered an essential service and so

Jenny is able to grab as much of the recovery money flooding into Chicago as she needs. The city gives us two new sewing machines to help clothe the homeless. We set up temporary shop in a church that stands unharmed outside the path of the fire.

Meanwhile, our new factory is being built on the approximate location of our old cottage. Several volunteers work shifts on our machines, which frees me up to take garments to the needy.

After our obligations to the City of Chicago are filled, Jenny lets me be myself, tending victims. I visit her at the new sewing factory from time to time. We are still partners, but I really don't feel that way because I'm not contributing much.

So, one day, I say "Jenny, it's not fair to you, my not helping."

Jenny says, "Mary Jones, hush! This is still Flynn & Jones. You are one of the founders and the only thing that has changed is you aren't drawing a salary because you aren't working here. But you still own half and when we start making a profit, half of that profit will be yours."

"Oh, fiddlesticks," says I. "All I own is what we started with. You're taking it beyond two custom dressmakers to a clothing factory. That's all of your doing and I don't deserve anything from it."

"Oh, fiddlesticks yourself, Mary Jones!" Her face wrinkles up and her eyes take on a hard look. "Let's just change our agreement. We'll say that you are now a silent partner in the Flynn & Jones enterprise and you will receive one-half of any profit that's made. You deserve that as a founder and investor. But if it will make you feel better, use the money to do good work for the poor people and the working class."

"All right, Jenny, I'll take my fair share if the workers in our factory get their fair share. When the factory starts making a profit, I say we divide it three ways — a third for you, a third for me and a third for the workers."

"Absolutely!" Jenny shouts. "What a grand idea!"

And so it is that I am freed up to complete my humanitarian work in Chicago.

Chapter Six
Pratt, West Virginia ~ November, 1912

"Oh, Mary," Sarah says. "You tell a story so well. I feel almost like I was there, and I feel so sad for you and those poor people in Chicago."

"Well," says I, "it was just another tragedy for me at the time. But as I look back on it, the fire was midwife to a rebirth of Chicago and of me. During the recovery days in Chicago, I got back into the labor movement. There is still much to tell about that, but my head is here now, here in West Virginia, and my heart is with those who suffer from the attack at Hollygrove and the battle of Mucklow."

—◆◆◆—

Sarah James is the only one among us who did not experience the recent events at Hollygrove and Mucklow that led to the arrest of dozens of victims. But she has experienced the conditions that led to what is now being called the Coal Wars.

By 1902 the United Mine Workers had gained some recognition in southern West Virginia, which was then the largest coal producing area in the state. I was there then as I am now. The UMW was the first coal miners' union to organize in the state. In 1903, the coal producers responded by forming their own "union" or association as they called it — the Kanawha County Coal Operators Association, the first such organization of its kind in the state.

The coal operators hired private detectives from the Baldwin-Felts Detective Agency in Bluefield. They weren't really detectives.

They were thugs who posed as mine guards, not to provide security for the mine properties but to harass union organizers and protect the scabs who would be recruited when the regular employees went out on strike.

—◆◆◆—

On April 18, 1912, the coal operators reject a wage increase demanded by the miners on Paint Creek in Kanawha County and the miners walk off the job. The miners on nearby Cabin Creek, who have lost their union, join the Paint Creek men and also walk off the job.

They demand the right to organize, the right to free speech and assembly, an end to the blacklisting of union organizers, alternatives to the company stores, an end to the use of mine guards, accurate scales to weigh coal and the right of unions to hire their own check weigh-men to make sure they aren't being cheated.

Right away, the operators send Baldwin-Felts thugs to evict strikers from their company housing even though the tenants have paid their rent. These homeless families set up tent colonies and makeshift lean-tos at a place just outside the mine property called Hollygrove.

All of this leads to violence. But it isn't the first violence I have experienced as an advocate for working people. In fact, I have been seasoned by violence during events that took place in other parts of the country long before Hollygrove and Mucklow.

You'll see.

Chapter Seven
Charleston, West Virginia ~ October, 1912

By October the striking miners on Cabin Creek have all but given up.

As the fall leaves begin to turn, spreading a beautiful but deceptive blanket over the hills, I return to West Virginia.

I have heard that efforts to organize miners in mines not far from the state capital have failed, the miners have been fired and replaced by scabs brought in to break the strike. The miners are now living, cowardly I think, with their families in tents and lean-tos and cabins as the cold mountain winter sets in.

Giving in is unacceptable to me. It is unacceptable not only in the heart of West Virginia coal country but unacceptable as it affects the entire union movement across the country where I have also fought.

I recall the old Knights of Labor slogan, "An injury to one is an injury to all." In West Virginia, a failure here is a failure for organized labor everywhere as far as I am concerned. This defeat cannot stand. I am back in West Virginia.

I arrive by rail in Charleston where I am met by some local railroad men I know from some of the railroad battles I've been in. They get me a free ride to Eskdale, a small town just outside the control of the coal companies.

I call together three trusted men, true leaders, and ask them to go up the creeks where the mines are located. I instruct them to get the word out that I want the miners to come to Charleston to a prearranged place on Tuesday afternoon.

"Be sure to tell them I don't want them to bring any clubs or guns to this meeting," says I. "But tell them I plan on leading them right up to the capitol steps."

The men from the camps come out in full force, but they are quiet, sullen, heads hung low. Defeated men. I could use words to help them restore their spirits and self-respect, but instead I simply say, "This fight isn't over. We are going to march right up to the capitol and demand to see the governor. Are there any chickens here who don't cotton to that?" No one speaks.

Then I lay out the plan and emphasize that we will be gentlemanly, orderly, but firm in our demonstration.

"I asked you not to bring guns or clubs," I recall as we reach the capitol. "We are not here to cause violence. This is an exercise in free speech. That's all. I trust none of you has a weapon on you?"

No one says "yea" or "nay."

But it is useless to try to stop *threats* of violence. A group of protesters has brought its own banner objecting to a certain Baldwin gunman who is particularly hated, saying that if he were not out of town by tonight, he would be hung on a telegraph pole. I hold my tongue.

Then I tell them to follow me as I hold one end of our own banner that reads "Nero Fiddled While Rome Burned." In this case "Nero" is the governor who fiddles to the tune of the moneyed interests while the people of the state are being enslaved and then cast aside like yesterday's garbage.

We march through the streets of Charleston and then gather on the statehouse grounds. "You boys wait here and behave yourselves while I go in and talk to the governor," says I.

The West Virginia Statehouse is a converted building in downtown Charleston. It has only been a bit over thirty some years since western Virginia was made a separate state during the Civil War and they haven't got around to building a real capitol building yet.

My black miner's boots echo under my long black dress as I walk alone through the halls of the temporary statehouse. The walls near the governor's office are hung with oil portraits of the few governors the state has had.

The portrait of the current governor, William Ellsworth Glasscock, hangs just outside the big doors leading into his reception room, which is big enough to hold our entire delegation of miners. There are lots of plush couches and armchairs around. No one is sitting in them.

"I am here to speak to the governor," says I to the receptionist who is sitting off to one side of the room at a desk that looks big enough to be the governor's.

"Whom may I tell him is calling?" the receptionist asks.

"My name doesn't matter," says I. "Just say I'm the representative of a large group of out-of-work miners gathered out there on the capitol grounds."

She picks up the telephone. "Sir, there's a little old lady out here says she represents a bunch of coal miners milling around out on the lawn."

I guess she is talking to the governor.

"He will be out shortly," the receptionist says.

I'm disappointed he isn't inviting me into his office. After what I'd seen of the hallway and reception room I am curious to see the trappings in the lion's den.

A man comes through the governor's door and I can tell by his bearing and from the portrait I've seen that he must be the governor. As he walks toward me, the state trooper who has been standing outside the door follows close.

"You're Mother Jones, aren't you," says the governor.

"That's what they call me."

"What is your purpose today, Mother?"

"Sir, there's a lawn party going on outside. It's made up of a large number of your state's finest citizens, the producers of its wealth, and they would like you to join them."

"Mother," says he, "I can't come with you but I want you to know I am not as bad as you think I am. I'm just not able to do as you ask at this time."

I can see in his eyes that he really wants to come, but protocol and politics stop him. Or maybe it is that the almighty powerbrokers of industrial tyranny who stop him.

He turns to leave and I grab him by the coattails.

"Come," says I, and the state trooper steps toward me. The governor motions him back. But then he just shakes his honorable head and stands there looking down into my eyes. I see a scared child. I feel sorry for him. He is a man without the courage of his convictions. A good man, but a weak man who cannot measure up to the position he holds, a position that calls for great strength and leadership.

I realize there is no point in pressing further. I go back outside and mount the statehouse steps to read a document we have drawn up requesting the governor rule against the use of private thugs like the Baldwin-Felts guards. It asks the governor to re-establish the American principles of freedom and prosperity in West Virginia.

Then I call for the committee made up of the three men who have helped me organize this march and ask them to carry the document into the statehouse and place it respectfully on the receptionist's desk. When they have departed on their mission, I turn and speak to the crowd. "Go home now," says I. "Keep away from the saloons. Save your money. You are going to need it."

"What are we going to need it for?" asks a voice from the crowd.

"For guns and ammunition," says I. "Go home and read the words of the immortal George Washington which he spoke to the colonists. He told those who were struggling against the imperialists of England to buy guns and fight for life, liberty and the pursuit of happiness."

The crowd leaves peacefully and buys every gun in the hardware stores of Charleston. They replace their old hammerlocks with the latest rifles and, like the Minutemen of New England, they march up the creeks to their tents and cabins with the grimness of soldiers in a revolution.

The next morning, alarm bells ring from the state capital to the national capital. The United States Senate calls attention to the revolutionary war that is building up just three hundred and fifty miles from Washington. The sleepy eye of the national government has just awakened and is finally focused on the remote coalfields of West Virginia.

A senatorial investigation is immediately ordered to inquire about the conditions that are eating out the heart of the coal industry and leading to the prospect of armed conflict in West Virginia.

Most importantly, the press becomes interested and Americans hear the plaintive cries of the oppressed, hungry and homeless souls who are the source of the country's prosperity, but trapped like animals in the coalfields of West Virginia.

I am pleased with the results, although I have always counseled against violence as a means of getting what we want. The threat of violence, however, certainly does have its effect when all else fails. For example, the man threatened by the banner that said he would be hung on a telegraph pole if he wasn't out of town by dark? He leaves town.

Nevertheless, my reason for telling the men to buy guns is not so they are to be used on offense. It is for defense. And it will soon be proven that they need them. My boys are ready to meet force with force.

Chapter Eight
Chicago ~ October 28, 1871

One Saturday afternoon, not long after the Great Fire, it is unseasonably warm. I decide to take a break from sewing and tending to the needs of people. I go for a walk along the Great Lake. Our new clothing factory isn't yet finished and we are supervising dressmakers in a nearby church where we are also living.

The lake is undamaged, of course. It is beautiful and the breeze off the water gives me respite from the burnt smells coming from behind me.

I also hear footsteps behind me. When I turn, a smallish but pleasant young man smiles and says, "Excuse me, ma'am, but I saw you come out of the church. I could have sworn you were a woman I used to know down in Memphis. Could it be?"

"Yes, sir. I was there for several years and left after the yellow fever epidemic."

"You were the wife of George Jones" says he. "You're Mary Jones if I'm not mistaken."

"Well, yes. How do you know this?"

"I worked with George at the foundry in Memphis and he got me interested in the Iron Molders Union. After I joined, George and I began working together to recruit members and to organize other foundries."

"Oh!" I am embarrassed. "Then George must have spoken to me about you. I've put so much of that out of my mind to help me forget my tragedy there. Please forgive me for not recognizing you."

"Yes, you lost your husband and your children to the disease. I am so sorry."

"Well, now," says I. "I've just lost my dressmaking shop here in Chicago. Bad news seems to follow me wherever I go."

"Again, I am so sorry, Mary."

"Well, I'm accustomed to starting over, and that's what I'm doing right now. I hope the fire didn't leave you in a bad way."

"My wife and I didn't have much to lose here. We were renters and had very little in the way of belongings. But I don't know how long I'll be out of work. Fortunately, I am a volunteer with a labor group here that is already pulling us back together and giving us hope.

"We're meeting every day in a burned-out building just about a mile from here. The roof and everything else about the building is gone but the brick walls still stand and it gives us a place where we can speak freely without worrying whether a spy or company boss sneaks in. I'm one of the men who stands at the door to separate the good guys from the bad."

"Really?" I marvel. "When I went to George's meetings with him I don't remember anyone having to hide from management. As I recall, the Iron Molders always welcomed the other side so management could hear what labor had to say."

"Well, the attitudes of management were more friendly in those days and in that place, Mary. Our organization can't be as open. We are a secret society."

"Secret society? I don't understand why it would be secret."

"Well, if the bosses here find out we have attended a labor meeting, they'll probably fire us. And if they find out we've joined a union, they'll not only fire us but blacklist us as well. That would fix it so other employers won't hire us either. We would have to leave Chicago to find work."

"Oh my," says I. "Does this secret society have a name?"

"The Noble and Holy Order of the Knights of Labor is what we're calling ourselves. It's the same name as a group that formed in Philadelphia a few years ago. A bunch of men who had fought on both sides during the Civil War got together.

"Northerners and Southerners had one thing in common. They understood the Civil War freed the black slaves. But the irony for both sides was that these mostly white men were now virtual slaves to their employers. Together they wondered who was going to fight for them? That's when they decided they would organize and fight for themselves."

"Very interesting," says I. "So the Knights of Labor is a national union?"

"Well, not actually a union. And not yet national. They're a society, not a union. They've been chartered to be a national organization, but so far there are no chapters outside of Philadelphia. The Philadelphia Knights know about us here in Chicago and there's talk of organizing chapters all over the country. They did give us a copy of their constitution and we adopted the same principles. If you're really interested, why don't you come to our meeting tonight? I'll see to it that you're admitted and you can learn more about the Knights."

"I'd like that," says I.

"If I'm not at the door, just ask for Liam. That's me."

—◆◆◆—

That night, I am following Liam's directions, but I still have to hunt quite a bit before I find the place. There is no sign. It is just a shell of a building. I suppose the original sign burned up if that's where they were meeting before the fire. Now there is no indication the building is even occupied.

Liam isn't at the door, but I mention his name. When he comes out he speaks to the others about me, and then of George in glowing terms, and we walk through the door together. The walls and floor are black from the fire. The roof is open to the sky. The room has been cleared of most of the debris and a platform has been built on the far end. There are no chairs for the people to sit on.

Liam leads me right up front because I am a little less than five feet tall and with everyone standing I will not be able to see the speakers. As I walk forward I notice a few women sprinkled about. There is plenty of room in the front because people all seem to want to hang back.

Everyone is so quiet. Those who speak to one another whisper behind their palms, as if to keep even a fellow workman from hearing.

When it is time, a man, still in his work clothes, ascends a set of temporary concrete block steps to the platform.

"Good evening. I'm John. I want to thank you for coming," the man says. "I know this is a sad time for most of you and it is a sacrifice for you to be here instead of with your families. I promise being here will be worth your while."

I muse. Another Irishmen. Are all workers in Chicago Irish? I wonder.

"I see many new faces and to you I say 'Welcome.' To the regulars, I ask that you seek out the first timers, not only to welcome them, but to hear their stories and answer their questions.

"The reason there are so many new faces tonight is because this is the night we set aside each week to introduce newcomers to the Knights of Labor. Before we get into what the Knights stands for, let's talk about why the Knights was formed."

He then introduces another man who says his name is Lars. He's dressed in clean street clothes. He is a big, burly man who gives the audience a big smile and then puts on a serious face that stays for the duration of his talk.

"They say the big fire made us victims," he begins. "But we were already victims of a force of another kind." Before we became victims of the fire, he says, we had already become victims of this thing they call the Industrial Revolution. During this revolution, big business became a plague that wiped out many small businesses and replaced working people with mechanization.

"Companies are no longer owned by families but by corporations. The sense of responsibility, which was once assured in a simpler world, is gone. It is replaced by robber barons who are driven by greed and who treat people like slaves even though we are supposed to be free.

"Capitalism, not democracy, rules this country now. People have no say in the workplace and sometimes not even in the home. The situation calls for big labor to offset the power of big business. And, the bigger labor becomes, the better we will be able to fight the power of both business and government, for they collaborate with one another against us working people.

"Now after the fire, we have an even more urgent reason to organize," the speaker says. "When a company comes up against hard times, what does it do? The very people who can help them get back up and running are let go. The workingman. To the company we just cost money; we don't contribute anything to making money. And we are expendable, interchangeable if we don't tow the company line.

"We are also the first to feel the brunt of an economic disaster whether it's a depression or a fire. The last to feel the pinch are the stockholders, the board members and the bosses. They continue to prosper at our expense.

"We cannot stand still for that. We need to speak now and with a unified voice. That is why we, the Knights of Labor, are working so hard to bring working people together, to build a large membership that can speak with one strong voice."

—◆◆—

The next man steps to the platform saying his name is Frederick. Ah then, this organization embraces all nationalities. First an Irishman, then a Norseman, now a German. I wonder when a woman will speak. I figure it will probably be me!

"Okay," Frederick begins. "John has given you an overview of why we face the problems we do. My job is to tell you what we need to do about our problems and how the Order of the Knights of Labor can help.

"Number one. We can organize a strong, unified voice both inside and outside the workplace. Unorganized grumbling among our fellow workers whether at work, in the barroom or at home, won't get us anywhere. Speaking to your boss or your employer on your own behalf won't do it either. Taking some of your fellow workers for an informal meeting with the boss won't do it. In fact, none of this asking with hat in hand will do it.

"Number two. Some of you may be skilled laborers who do have the power of collective bargaining through your union. That's great. You're lucky to be in a union, but since your union only represents skilled tradesmen, it only has the power of a fraction of the workers in your company. And, although new unions are rising up every day, many of you have skills but no union.

"Most of you, I'll wager, aren't skilled workers. There is no union for you. Your wages and working conditions are decided behind closed doors by your boss or his boss or his bosses' boss. The first you hear about it is when you get the bad news. You haven't had the chance to have your say about it, and you never will if you continue to stand alone.

"Big business necessitates big labor."

I want to shout "Amen, brother" like they do in those hellfire and damnation meetings that the traveling preachers run. But the audience behind me remains silent and I figure, I should hold my fire.

Frederick goes on: "Now, this organization was formed by six of us fellows who are just simple workers like you and me. You notice I was sitting out there with you before I came up here. The rest of the half dozen are sitting out there with you now. One of them might be right beside you.

"The point is the founders of this organization are just ordinary people. But they come to you with an idea that will make us more than just a bunch of separate individuals. This is an idea that will make life better for all of us and all of our families in the months and years to come.

"And, like you've been told, it's not just our idea. Four years ago another group of ordinary people formed an organization in Philadelphia called the Knights of Labor. Like us, they didn't form a union, but a fraternal order, an army of working people like us who would stand together and fight for their rights in the workplace. They were skilled laborers of every kind along with unskilled laborers of every kind, every race, every religion, men and women alike. Together they now fight for their rights in their workplaces and the rights of others wherever they work.

"Their motto is 'An injury to one is a concern for us all'."

"We have adopted that motto. To my way of thinking, an injury is the same as an injustice. The rest of my brothers feel the same way and we've pretty much adopted the standards and the bylaws of the Philadelphia Knights of Labor.

"Now please don't let the word 'fight' concern you. We are beginning to see wildcat strikes among unrepresented workers in and around Chicago. Strikes that too often have led to violence. The Knights of Labor, as an organization, does not expect to behave that way. For we believe that violence is not the answer. We are not looking for a fight. No, we just want to provide a voice — a stronger voice — for all working people."

—◆◆◆—

I raise my hand. He doesn't see it. So, I wave it around and jump up and down and speak at the same time.

"I like most of what you say, sir, but how do you get the big bosses to listen if you don't show force?"

"I'm sorry, ma'am," the speaker says. "What did you say your name was?"

"Oh," says I. "Please forgive my rudeness, sir. My name is Mary Jones."

"And, are you a worker, ma'am?"

"I was until I got burned out by the fire. My friend and I were dressmakers. Now I'm just a homeless person trying to help other folks find food and places to lay their heads. I don't work for no boss, but I have in the past. And my dear husband, may he rest in peace, was an organizer for the Iron Molders Union down in Memphis. I helped him recruit men into that union until they had enough to form a chapter of the Iron Molders."

"Well then, Mrs. Jones, I'm mighty glad to meet you. Now what was that question again?"

"How do you get the bosses' attentions without having a means of force?"

"That's a good question, Mrs. Jones. Our force will come from our numbers. Our means of force will be unity. When our membership is large enough, we will be able to represent the entire working class of that company. As their representatives, we will present the workers' needs to the company during the formal deliberations on matters like wages, hours and safety.

"We won't just be one person at the table; we will represent many, hopefully most of the workers in that company. Not just one or the other skilled class of worker, but all the classes. And, as representatives of workers in other companies, we will have the strength of workers throughout the entire region, the entire industry. You see what I mean?"

"I think so," says I. "You'll sit down with the big bosses and demand what's right for the working class."

The speaker clears his throat and flashes a sheepish smile. "Well, we won't *demand*, we'll negotiate. Ours will be the unified voice of reason. Before we have the meeting, we will have convinced the employer that we do represent most of their employees and we want to be there to cooperate in determining their futures. A better future for us and, together, we want to work for a better future for the company as well."

Says I, "I don't believe in violence either, sir, and I think your approach will work with some of the better employers. My husband worked for a damned good employer ..."

A gasp comes from the audience.

"Oh, please forgive me, everyone, I don't know what made me say it that way. I mean my husband had a wonderful employer who supported the Iron Molders Union all the way. But when Mr. Jones was trying to organize workers at other iron works, the bosses were pretty damned ... there I go again, pretty darned cranky. It was pretty frustrating and it made me angry enough to, to ... cuss!" Laughter.

"We of the Knights understand that, Mrs. Jones. But we've seen the harm that's caused when a union or even an unorganized bunch gets frustrated and out of control. The company digs in its heels and then it's even harder to make headway for the workers. It has been our experience, and it's why we are pretty adamant about non-violence."

"I see your point, sir. As you can see, I don't look like your violent type and I'm ready to join this here organization if what you say is true, that women can join. But is a woman a full-fledged member or are they like church auxiliary members?"

"No, ma'am. Women are workers. I admit it seems kinda funny for a woman to join an organization of Knights, but I guarantee, you won't be a 'Maid Marion.'" Laughter.

"No sir, I'll be no Maid Marion. I'll be volunteering right now as an organizer for the Knights of Labor. And I'll continue helping the families of out-of-work men and women who are trying to survive the aftermath of this terrible fire."

At first I divide my time between sewing for Jenny and recruiting new members for the Knights of Labor. The Knights give me a list of people to see and I visit workers and their families in their homes day and night. It reminds me of the days when George and I did the same thing. It feels good, feels like George is with me again, by my side now.

Most of these men are out of work because of the fire and so I organize many of them to join together as teams to help each other survive. I enlist Jenny in finding out where we can get money from charities and we use that to help unemployed Knights stay on their feet.

My conversations with the workers educate me much more about what the men do at work, their pride, their fears, their plights, their sense of duty and failure to their families. Every story is the same and yet, every story is different.

I am comfortable talking to these good people, but I keep my seat at the Knights of Labor meetings, stay quiet most of the time. In spite of my outburst during my first visit to the Knights, I am not sure I am ready to speak up in a large group like that.

Then one night a fellow by the name of Terence Powderly speaks to the Knights. I am surprised to hear my son's name spoken as an introduction to a grown man.

Mr. Powderly is a gentle man, tall and slender with a pince-nez perched on his nose and a huge mustache below it. He looks like an accountant but he says he is a machinist for a company in Scranton, Pennsylvania, that makes parts under contract to the railroad.

He tells us he is a member of the Machinists Union but he also is interested in the Knights of Labor because it is for all laborers and that the Knights has the potential of building greater strength for the cause of the entire working class.

He then goes on to lecture about the history of the working class.

"Seven centuries before the coming of Christ, men were divided into two classes, masters and serfs or lords and servants. These people of the upper class loathed men who worked for pay and treated them like slaves even though they were not. Those who were their slaves were no better off and had to be content with the meager food and clothing they were given.

"A master exercised complete dominance over their slaves," Powderly says. "It was even the right of the master to kill his slave without interference from any person or authority."

Mr. Powderly goes on to describe how, before the Christian era, men and women were forced to fight to the death for the gruesome entertainment of both nobility and commoners. The strongest of their slaves were sent to their deaths for sport, torn apart by wild beasts or by trained gladiators in an arena filled with cheering crowds.

"Slaves and freemen worked together in the fields and the mine," he says. "Often they worked naked, like animals."

"As the more intelligent among the commoners became incensed by their degradation, they exerted leadership and organized secret meetings during the dark of night. During these meetings they shared with one another their problems and talked about ways they might stand up for themselves. They looked for strength through togetherness."

This was one of the first attempts in history to organize labor.

"One of the first great strikes on record," he says, "took place in 413 B.C. in Athens, Greece, when twenty thousand workmen left their jobs and fled over the border to join Athens' enemy during the Peloponnesian War."

Mr. Powderly speaks admiringly of Spartacus, who was an escaped slave and gladiator seventy years before the coming of Christ. He too was forced to fight for sport before the kings and queens of his time.

After his escape, Spartacus organized other enslaved gladiators and, instead of fighting each other, they fought against the practice of compelling men to kill each other for the mere gratification of the lords and ladies in all their regal paraphernalia. With such a leader as Spartacus, laborers, both enslaved and free, waged courageous battles for centuries to crush the powers that had so ruthlessly trampled their rights and the rights of humanity.

Although the Spartacus story ended in his death and the crucifixion of some six thousand of his followers, the courage of Spartacus and his men left lessons in the minds of people for all time and inspired many of the oppressed to fight for their rights in centuries to come.

My breast swells with pride. To myself I pledge, I will be a modern day Spartacus in woman's clothes.

Mr. Powderly goes on to compare these labor movements of thousands of years ago to the efforts of the Knights of Labor today.

There is much more to his speech, but at the end he asks for questions. The room is silent. I, on the other hand, am bursting with words.

"Thank you, Mr. Powderly, for such an inspiring recitation of the history of labor and the disparity of the classes. I am but a small woman. However, from this day forward I aspire to be a modern day Spartacus."

He smiles and says, "Ma'am, then you inspire *me!*"

"You see, sir," I went on, "I have been associated with the labor movement since the last days of the Civil War and your comment about the lot of the freed slaves nearly eight thousand years ago rings true to me. When I was helping my husband George Jones in his efforts to organize the iron molders in Memphis, I heard many a discharged soldier from both the Union and Confederate camps lament that they fought over freeing the slaves and now they are slaves themselves."

"Excellent, ma'am! That is a point I meant to make but failed to say it outright. You have made my speech meaningful."

We go on talking to each other as if the rest of the audience has disappeared. Finally Mr. Powderly notices and apologizes to the crowd. "Ma'am," he says, "perhaps we should get together at the adjournment of this meeting. There is much left for us to say to one another."

After most depart the building, Mr. Powderly and I huddle in a corner and talk for hours. Someone brings a lantern over to us and asks that we bring it back to the next meeting. Then we are alone. And we are together as best friends for the remainder of our lives.

Chapter Nine
Pratt, West Virginia ~ March 6-7, 1913

"So it was love at first sight?" inquires Sarah.

"Oh, dear no!" says I. "Well, not love in the romantic sense. After all, he was married, devoted to his wife Emma. In fact, Emma and I also became very close and I stayed in their home over many years, sometimes for long periods of recuperation.

"But I did love Terence for what he was and as a dear friend. I've often thought, though, that our friendship was odd because although we were on the same side, we differed on so many issues. But we always respected the other's point of view and we were each a good sounding board for the other. In fact, we each gained balance from the other's point of view and often stepped across the line to think the same when it made sense. It takes true friends to do that."

—◆◆◆—

At that moment there came a gentle knock on the boards of the jailhouse door.

A female voice announces, "It's me, Mrs. Carney from the boarding house. The guard will let me in if you allow."

"Oh, do come in, Mrs. Carney!" says I. As the door swings open I meet her with open arms and hug her as I whisper in her ear, "Thank you so much for posting those letters the boy brought to you. I will pay you the cost of the stamps as soon as I can." I whisper so as not to incriminate Mrs. Carney in front of the other women in the room.

"No matter," says Mrs. Carney in a normal voice, "you owe me nothing. I've also brought you a few newspapers to read. I think you'll find them interesting."

Then she explains her presence. "I'm here to gather clothes from all you women to wash and iron. I'm told you will be taken to the Odd Fellows Hall tomorrow where the military court will sit. I want you to look as good as you can for your first hearing."

"How very kind of you," says I. "But this is the first we've learned of a hearing."

"Well, now you know," says Mrs. Carney. She has gathered twelve robes from women in the town and each of us is draped so as to strip privately underneath. When she receives Sarah's clothes she exclaims, "Oh, dear me, these will never do. I know you won't be going to this hearing, Sarah, but I will find you new clothes and have them back here this afternoon."

That afternoon Mrs. Carney returns, bringing the clean clothes. She has the boy with her, dragging a metal bathtub. The tub is blocked from view with a blanket hanging from the ceiling and the boy carries buckets of water to and from the tub until we have all bathed.

Many of the women, not just Sarah, are given new clothes and they look quite respectable now. They are fixing each other's hair with the combs Mrs. Carney has brought. The baths and new clothes put a fresh glow on each of their faces.

When Mrs. Carney has gone and we have settled down some, I begin reading the newspapers. I choose the Washington and New York papers first because I figure they will be somewhat fairer and have more impact on the public and political views of the country than the local press.

Besides, I figure the local newspapers are in the pockets of the banks and the coal operators and I expect their slant will be less than satisfactory to me. Their stories will probably paint me as a warmonger and the battle at Mucklow as an insurrection.

As I hope, the major newspapers have told the story pretty much as I had written it in my letters, but also they tell the story from the governor's and the military's point of view. I think that's fair, although the official story is wrong, wrong, wrong.

The official view is dominant in the *Charleston Gazette* and the *Daily Mail* and what I've had to say is merely inserted as hearsay. Of course, the reporters have not been allowed into the military zone and so they consider my account unsubstantiated.

But I'm still offended that they have prefaced my quotes with words that hint that my assertions are somehow suspect. "Mother Jones denied the governor's account and *claimed,* etc." Claimed hell. I know the truth, you fools!

I read the *Argus* last, knowing that the socialist point of view will be as warped in our direction as the *Gazette* and *Mail* articles are warped in the opposite direction. Of course, I like the exaggerations I find in the *Argus*. Exaggeration, after all, is one of my weapons. But I also know the socialist view will be dismissed by the general public as poppycock.

What really gets my goat is that the coverage of the battle at Mucklow is much bigger than the coverage two days before of the atrocious sneak attack on the sleeping families at Hollygrove.

The Hollygrove story reads more like rumor than fact and it is hidden among the advertisements on the inside pages. The Mucklow story is splashed all over the front pages. I realize the Hollygrove story is being suppressed and the newspapers have no way of knowing what really precipitated the battle at Mucklow. That makes me very angry.

I stew all night in the sleeping gown Mrs. Carney has left me, simmering over the poor press coverage and dreaming up ways to set the record straight from the dock the next morning. The same press will be there. Maybe what I say tomorrow and the appearance of these helpless, incarcerated women will open a few eyes.

—◆◆◆—

Our military guard escort arrives mid-morning the following day. I guess a military court likes to sleep late. Two soldiers stand at military present arms while I am shackled by two other soldiers.

Then one end of a long rope is tied around my waist. The rest of the rope is stretched out behind me and each of the other ten women is sharply ordered to grab hold of it and not to let loose unless she wishes to die. It is in this manner that we are marched to the Odd Fellows Hall, the soldiers marching two by two with their rifles over their shoulders.

I figure this is going to make some powerful pictures favorable to our side, but when we march into the main hall of the Odd Fellows building there are no flash powder explosions. Writers from the press are there, but no cameramen. I suppose photographers have been barred. I see no cartoonists with pens in hand, but perhaps they are there looking like reporters, ready to commit their images to memory for later.

Four men are seated at a table in front of the men who are in custody. Our guards point to the empty seats behind the male prisoners who are already seated. The fifty of us, the accused, have been assembled.

Being short, my view of the proceedings is mostly blocked by the men in front of me. But I remember seeing the men at the table, three of them together and another seated off to one side. The middle of the three men is a lieutenant colonel in a West Virginia National Guard uniform. I have learned military ranks during my previous experiences. The other two are also commissioned officers, captains as I recall. The fourth man is a lieutenant and he seems to be acting as secretary.

The lieutenant is also the first one to speak.

"This is a military court martial, not a civil trial. I am charged with explaining how a court martial works. There is no judge, but rather, a panel of officers who will hear evidence and report their recommendations to the commander in chief, who is also the Governor of the State of West Virginia.

"The governor will consider the recommendations of the panel and then pronounce sentences."

The military police officers on each side of this room are responsible to maintain order. Officers, who are also lawyers, will represent the prosecution and, similarly, officers, who are lawyers, will represent the defense. These officers are expected to conduct the hearing with a decorum fitting an officer and a gentleman. The accused and other guests of the court are to also behave accordingly.

"If any of the accused wishes to be defended by a civilian lawyer, rather than a military officer, the defendant may do so. If there are persons who cannot afford a civilian lawyer, then a military officer, who is a lawyer, will be appointed to defend them."

I see two men's heads bob up at the left front and one man says: "If it please the court, we are here at the will of the United Mine Workers, and we stand ready to represent all fifty of the defendants."

"Your names for the record, please."

"I am Howard M. Belcher," the one says, "and this is Harold W. Houston. We have proven our credentials during pre-trial motions."

The lieutenant looks over our delegation of accused criminals and asks, "Is there any one of you who objects to having Misters Belcher and Houston act as your defense?"

"Well I certainly do," says I.

"Who said that?" asks the lieutenant. He is a short fella himself and he can't see me behind all the miners in the first four rows, even though I am now standing.

"That would be me," I say, stretching to my full almost five foot height. "This drumhead court has no authority over me, a free United States citizen, a civilian who was arrested in Charleston by a civilian officer of the law and dragged here to a military zone where I was unlawfully rearrested and charged with a murder which was said to have been committed at a time when I was no where near.

"I need no defense, military or civilian, because the militia had no authority to arrest me and this court has no authority to try me."

The lieutenant doesn't miss a beat. "We disagree, there, Mrs. Jones. If you persist in your position we will appoint two military lawyers for your defense."

Four other defendants — John W. Brown, Charles H. Boswell, Charles Batley and George F. Parsons — also make statements similar to mine, denying the jurisdiction of the court. I know Boswell is editor of the *Argus* and the other three I think were deeply involved in planning the Mucklow invasion.

Two military lawyers are appointed to defend the five of us.

"Now if that's finished, I'll continue."

"I'm not finished," says I. Rising to my feet again, "Not only am I falsely and illegally accused, this here drumhead court is trying the wrong people for the wrong crime. Instead of trying us for what happened at Mucklow, you should be trying the bastards who attacked innocent men, women and children at Hollygrove two nights before. That, sir, is what precipitated this whole thing."

"Ma'am, this is not the time for you to make your case. You will have your chance when you take the stand."

"I told you before," says I. "I will not participate in any defense and I won't be taking the stand. For now, I've said all I'm gonna say to this drumhead court."

Then I turn to where the press is seated.

"If you reporters want the real story, get the hell out of here and go talk to the people about how the mine guards, National Guardsmen and the sheriff's men attacked sleeping families at the tent colony at Hollygrove two days before the battle of Mucklow."

"That will be enough, ma'am," the lieutenant barks, and I sit down. I've had my say anyway.

The lieutenant proceeds.

"Representing the prosecution for the State of West Virginia is Lieutenant Colonel George S. Wallace who is Judge Advocate for the West Virginia National Guard. Mr. Wallace, will you please stand so that you can be seen by the accused."

As Wallace stands, the lieutenant says, "Colonel Wallace has filed all charges against the fifty men and women including both the leaders and some of the followers arrested in the matter regarding the battle of Mucklow."

Wallace sits down.

"For formal purposes," the lieutenant continues, "those charges involve an attempt by the accused persons to steal a machine gun owned by the Baldwin-Felts security agency which was under contract to the National Guard of the State of West Virginia. In addition, the prosecution has filed charges of unlawful conspiracy and insurgency under the Red Man Act, the invasion by force a territory held under martial law, and the murder of sixteen men employed by the Baldwin-Felts security agency and in the service of the West Virginia National Guard."

Now there's an admission. If there were ever any doubt about the collusion of the mine operators, the sheriff's office and the state militia against the working man, there's your proof!

"Finally," says the lieutenant, "the prosecutor intends to show that Mrs. Mary Harris Jones, also known as Mother Jones, and ten other women conspired to aid and abet the commitment of said murders. Further, that Mrs. Mary Harris Jones was principal instigator of the entire event and is therefore charged by the prosecutor with second degree murder."

After a pause and a wary look in my direction, he says, "Now we reach the last piece of business for the day. The question is, how do you plead?

"Misters Belcher and Houston, how do your forty-five defendants plead?"

"Not guilty," says Belcher.

"And, Mrs. Jones," inquires the lieutenant, "how do you and Misters Brown, Boswell, Batley and Parsons, plead?"

I rise along with the other four and say, "We make no plea to this illegal court."

"Very well, then," says the lieutenant, and he turns to the officers who have been appointed to represent us. "Gentlemen, please state a plea for Mrs. Jones and Misters Brown, Boswell, Batley and Parsons."

"Not guilty, sir," says one.

The lieutenant turns sharply on his heels and salutes the panel. "I have done my duty, Sirs. Is there anything more?" There is no verbal response and he then drops his salute and turns just as sharply back to the room. "We are adjourned until tomorrow at ten hundred hours."

We women are escorted by our four military guards in the same fashion as we had arrived. The male prisoners remain seated while a whole troop of soldiers surrounds them. I think that's more to shield them from the reporters than it is to prevent their escape. Right away the reporters give up on interviewing the men and chase our column of women all the way from the Odd Fellows to our makeshift jail. I speak freely to a cluster of journalists walking backward in front of me. Our guards do not try to prevent me from talking to them, concentrating instead on keeping us in line and moving.

"How do you expect to beat this thing, Mother Jones?" asks one.

"Honestly, I don't know. As you can see, my hands and my feet are bound and ten unfortunate women are tied to my waist like draft animals. What you saw today is not justice. It is *in*justice. If you came up here on the railroad, then you just saw a railroad of another kind. We're *being* railroaded.

"Forget Mucklow and point your pens at Hollygrove where the real roots of this war began. That's where the first shots were fired and on innocent women and children as well as their sleeping men. Those shots were fired by the very company thugs and state militia that you see being glorified by this kangaroo court.

"They are some of the same ones that fired the first shots at Mucklow. Until then, ours was a peaceful demonstration."

"You sound very angry, Mother Jones," says another reporter. "Angry enough to kill?"

"No, but I'm angry enough to kick the shins out from under a bunch of dirty coal operators and their politicians. They've started this shooting war and I know from experience that this kind of violence never settles anything."

"That's not what they printed in the *Charleston Gazette*, Mother Jones," another says. "They quoted you telling the miners to 'get their guns and shoot the hell out of 'em.' Is that so?"

"Well, let me ask you," says I, "are you from the *Charleston Gazette*?"

"No, ma'am."

"Then you've got your answer," says I. "If you believe the *Charleston Gazette*, then you're working for the wrong newspaper."

All the reporters but the ones from the *Gazette* laughed at that one.

—◆◆◆—

The women are buzzing for a good hour after we get back to our jail. I am quiet until one asks, "What do you think of this day, Mother?"

"I think it has been a glorious day, my friend. The court will get a lot of bad press tomorrow just for looking silly all on its own. And I'm thrilled to have been given the chance to heap oil on the fire during our walk back here. This is where the real battlefield is, not Hollygrove and not Mucklow. We're in a battle for the hearts and minds of good citizens who will help us, in the long run, to overcome the injustices we face in our everyday lives."

"Oh, I don't know, Mother," says one. "The way they talked in there, they scared me. I could feel their power, Mother, and for myself I felt none."

"I know that feeling, my dear. But we must not bow to awful power. We must have courage, believe in ourselves and what we stand for."

Addie speaks up: "Well, there's no turning back now. We came to a crossroad and we made our choice. There is no place but forward."

"You've got that right, Addie," says I. "And I promise on my own name, Mother Jones, that you will look back on this some day and be proud of yourselves, for this will be one of the most important moments of your lives and the lives of many others. I promise."

Chapter Ten
The Carolinas ~August, 1874

My commitment as a volunteer with the Knights of Labor, my friendship with Terence Powderly and my own personal quarrel with the practice of child labor — these guide me through the next few years.

My work for the Knights is routine but satisfying. I recruit thousands of new Knights by visiting workingmen and women at their workplaces and in their homes. And I organize secret meetings of the Knights in industrial communities from California to Pennsylvania for the purpose of education, planning, encouragement and recruitment.

But, though I am seen everywhere, I stay in the background. I rarely appear on stage except to make announcements and such. I am simply an organizer, not a leader. My time for public speaking is yet to come.

Because of the depression which began in 1873, Terence Powderly loses his job when the railroads collapse and the company he works for loses its contract for making parts for steam locomotives. He becomes a free agent — like myself — for the labor movement. For quite awhile we correspond, me in Illinois and he in Pennsylvania. I often get a message from him by telegram asking for my help somewhere and I never turn him down unless I am already committed elsewhere.

Working at the behest of Terence, I find myself at railroad centers and construction sites in the middle of nowhere, factories in countless cities and towns and coal mines in Pennsylvania and across the country.

In some ways Terence and I are mismatched. We differ on how best to gain a position of power for the working class. He is opposed to strikes and remains so for his entire life, though he sometimes gives in when there is no choice. He is an idealist and believes that reason, negotiation and arbitration are the only acceptable tools. He likes to do things in a business-like manner.

On the other hand, I am practical. I am a born fighter. I do not believe in the deliberate use of violence but I do not shun it when confronted. If that's the game, then I play it. And without the *threat* of a strike — which doesn't necessarily need to involve violence — I cannot see how negotiation and arbitration can win. I have grown to believe that you have to meet power with power. I become more and more certain of this as my experience grows.

And so, when we are together, Terence and I spend hours arguing about these issues. Even so, we do it with a deep respect for each other's views and that moderates our thoughts and deeds over time.

—◆◆◆—

But the biggest influence on my thinking during this period comes from the textile mills of the Carolinas. I suppose it is the fact that my partner Jenny and I are on the retail end of the textile business and I share some of the guilt. I have heard that the material we use to make dresses for the upper class maids and maidens of Chicago comes from sweatshops that attract poor families from their farms and poor immigrants from Europe looking for a decent life — as did my father so many years ago.

These people are not finding that decent life in the textile mills of the South.

Please remember that the reason I accepted a three-way partnership with Jenny and the employees of our dress factory in Chicago was to use my share of the profits to fight for the rights of the American worker. What better way to do that, I'm thinking, than to fight for the wellbeing of mill workers and their children who are toiling ten hours or more a day amidst the unsafe machinery and fibrous air of the cotton mills of the Carolinas.

And what better mill than the one producing the cotton for fabric we use in our dress factory in Chicago.

Because I have lots of friends among the railroad workers of Chicago, I am able to catch a free ride. At night, a conductor sneaks me onto a train just before he picks up the step and signals the engineer that all are aboard. He tucks me into a sleeping berth and stows my luggage. The same thing happens in Baltimore and before I know it, I arrive rested and ready to catch a buggy ride to a nameless little mill town.

The village is a company town in the Piedmont Region. Several dozen houses, all alike, line one side of a dirt road facing cotton in bloom on the other side of the road. It is a beautiful white blanket as far as the eye can see. Like this village, mill towns are often located close to the cotton fields to avoid the cost of transportation.

Behind the houses is the mill.

I tell my driver to stop in front of the first house. I ask him to come back to get me in three days and begin walking with all my things wrapped in a shawl, a sack over my shoulder. Like a hobo. I wear my usual black dress with the white frills around the cuffs and collar and down the bodice. I also wear a black bonnet with an arrangement of flowers on it. My black shoes are practical with sturdy heels that raise me up to look a little taller than I am.

The houses look in good shape, but there aren't any people around them. No children. But a very old lady is sweeping dirt out her front door and I hail her.

"Hello there," says I. "Could I trouble you for a drink of water? I'm mighty thirsty."

"Well," says she, "I suppose so. I'll get it."

I expect her to step back inside to fetch the water, but instead she comes out on the road and starts walking away from me. Slowly.

"Where are you going?" I ask.

"To fetch the water," she says.

I follow her past a few houses and then she turns down between two of them. Now I can see the village well. She drops the bucket down the well, pulls it up, picks up a dipper, fills it and hands it to me.

I lay down my sack. "Thank you," says I, and I drink. "Tastes good."

She grunts. Then only silence.

"I'm looking for work," says I. "Are they hiring over there?"

"Don't know," says she. "Probably."

"Any place around here a single lady can get a room?"

"Don't know," shaking her head. "You might ask over at the mill."

—◆◆◆—

I thank her for the water and the advice and walk on down the road past some commercial buildings including a general store.

At the factory office I am told to take a seat. After a time, a fellow comes out and asks me a few questions, one being "Have you ever worked in a cotton mill?"

"No sir," says I, "but I was a dressmaker in Chicago before the fire."

"Well that's nice, but that doesn't mean you know anything about mill work," says the man who doesn't bother to introduce himself. "You'll have to go through training. That takes two weeks and you don't get paid for that. We will give you credit at the company store and you can start paying your store bill back when you get your first paycheck. Is that suitable?"

"It'll have to do," says I. "Any idea where I can find a sleeping room?"

"We have a family who has one room that isn't occupied by a mill worker," the man says. "The company houses have four rooms and we require at least one mill worker for each room. If a family doesn't supply four mill workers, then we require them to let us rent a room.

"I'll go tell them we are renting you a room and one of them will come out here to the office at the end of the shift. Your rent will also be deducted from your first pay. Now if there are no more questions, I'll see you here at six tomorrow morning."

As I turn to leave, he turns back toward me and says, "Oh," and checking his notes, he says, "Mrs. Jones, I strongly advise you to wear something a little more simple when you come to work tomorrow."

There it was. I'm undercover and I have my first piece of information. This company has a rule. In order for a family to live in a company house, there have to be four mill workers in the house. If the family consists of two parents and their children, then that means children are required to work in the mill. I'm sure age makes no difference.

—◆◆◆—

This nice friendly lady greets me in front of the office after her shift. She doesn't seem to be at all unhappy that she is being forced to accept a stranger into her family circle. "Come on, let's go to the company store and pick up something for supper," she says in a matter-of-fact way. She doesn't bother to ask me my name or give me hers. It's just like we already know each other.

We buy provisions for supper and enough canned goods for a few more days. She thanks me when I pay the bill. "That wasn't necessary," she says as we walk on down the road.

"It may not be necessary to you," says I, "but it is necessary to me. I'll take care of more than my share of expenses while I'm here. It's my way."

When we get to her house I realize it is the same one with the old woman who got me the water.

Inside we put our groceries on a rough hewn table in the middle of the first room. There is a fireplace on one side with a steel hook for cooking and a rocker in the corner. That's all there is to the furnishings. Along part of another wall there is a wooden countertop with a shelf underneath. I guess that's the kitchen. There are three doors leading from the kitchen, one for each additional room.

In this house there are two great-grandparents, two grandparents who work in the mill and a grandchild. Neither of the great-grandparents works at the mill. The two grandparents and the child are the three workers. I make number four.

My hostess points to one of the doors and says it will be my room. I peek in and I see a homemade rag doll in the middle of bed.

"Looks like this is the child's room," says I.

"Oh, never mind that," the woman says. "My granddaughter will remove her things when she gets home from school."

It turns out the granddaughter will be sleeping on a cot in her grandparents' room. Her grandfather will bring it home from the company supply room.

"So your granddaughter goes to school," says I.

"Yes, today she has a day off and so she's in school."

"Day off from what?" asks I, as if I don't know.

"From work. She works in the mill." That was the confirmation I was looking for.

"Oh?" says I. "How old is she?"

"Ten."

"And she works in the mill?" I wonder out loud. "What kind of work does she do?"

"You'll see tomorrow," says my hostess. "We work together." And that ended the conversation.

The grandfather arrives home on crutches. One leg missing. Another fellow is carrying the cot.

Grandfather, like the rest of the family, is pleasant enough but not much for talk. They eventually tell me their story. They left their rented farm when the grandfather was badly injured in an accident which resulted in the doctors amputating his leg, leaving him unable to do farm work any more. Some of their grown children came to help during the last harvest.

When everything was sold, the grandparents hitched up the one wagon they kept and headed for the Carolinas where they heard there was work in the cotton mills. They brought with them the great-grandparents and this young grandchild whose mother had died in childbirth. There is no known father.

Here, the crippled grandfather can sit on a bench and pick seeds and other debris from the raw cotton. The other jobs, pulling and carding, require too much mobility. The great-grandparents are of no use in the mill, but they are still loved by the grandfather. The young girl is able to work and she provides the additional income that keeps them all from starving.

—◆◆◆—

I am lying in bed at the break of day when I hear a low-pitched whistle outside the house. It rises to a high pitch as the boiler builds up steam. It's too shrill for a train whistle. Then it dawns on me it's coming from the mill. "Rise and shine," that whistle is saying to half the people in the village, the half that work the day shift. "It's five a.m." At five-thirty another whistle warns that workers need to be at their stations in twenty-five minutes, ready for work at six o'clock sharp. That whistle sounds throughout the day and night, maintaining the tempo of the mill and the village.

My first day is to be spent with my hostess who is now my tutor. She tends eight spinning machines, four on each side. I am allowed to touch nothing, just observe. And observe I do. I pay more attention to what the little children are doing than to what I am supposed to do. It seems to me there are as many children in the room as adults.

The whir of her machines and the clack and clatter of the looms in the next room create a steady din. My tutor has to shout her instructions to me. The noise is bad, but the worst part is inhaling the unseen fiber floating in the air. I pull out my hankie and cover my nose and mouth, but then I can't breath. The spinning room is huge, maybe a hundred machines whirling. All the windows are open but there is no air stirring and the humidity is unbearable.

I force myself to forget about my discomfort and think instead of those mill children.

Those who tend the machines are called spinners. Each machine contains many spindles, each with its own bobbin. It is the spinner's job to see that everything is running right. As a team, my tutor and her granddaughter are both spinners. The granddaughter is an especially good helper tending the bobbins when they sometimes develop strands or breaks that have to be repaired. Girls, I am told, are better at repairing threads at the bobbins because they are much more attentive than the boys.

Boys are called doffers; it is their job to remove spools filled with thread and replace them with empty spools. Many of these spools are located high in the machines and the boys have to climb up to switch spools, while other machines whir all around them. They are barefoot all day because it is easier to gain a good footing so they won't slip and fall into the next machine.

It is a frightening and unrelenting scene. By quitting time I am a nervous wreck.

But strange as it may seem, most of the workers and all the children are in high spirits when the day is done. When the children are at work, they work diligently, but in between calls to duty they play together and joke around. Their laughter seems so queer in this setting. I had figured these poor children would be sullen at work when in fact they seem like such happy little creatures!

—◆◆◆—

That night I speak openly of the shock I have experienced at the mill. I give my opinion that young children should never be forced to work like that, and certainly at such early ages. My hosts are dumbfounded.

"What do you mean children shouldn't have to work?" the husband barks. At least one member of this family has found his voice!

"We've raised twelve fine children and that's what children are for, to work. Every one of our children worked on our farm. We sent most of them to grammar school when there was time but when they were old enough to work full time we kept them on the farm. Ain't nuthin wrong with that."

"I think there's a time for work and a time for learning," says I, "and these young children have a whole lifetime ahead of them for work. For them, life should be for being children, not laborers. To deny them that opportunity is, is … a crime!"

"Ma'am," says the father with chin quivering, "if you was a man I'd knock your head off, but seein' as you're a woman .... " Words fail him and he heads off to bed.

He leaves silence in the room. Finally, his wife speaks.

"Ma'am," says the woman in a low angry voice somewhat like mine when I'm mad, "I'll never forgive you for that. You just don't know how it is. We have never harmed one of our children and we taught them way more than they could ever learn in school.

"As for now, we are grateful to have our jobs in the mill so as to have food on the table and a life to live. We don't need no outsiders to come here and tell us *how* to live.

"I'll be askin' my supervisor in the morning to find somebody else to train you. I'll have to put up with your presence in this house because the company says I must. But I would appreciate it if you would find yourself another place as soon as you can."

She gets up and follows her husband into their bedroom. I have never felt lower in my life.

The next morning I stay behind while the others are off to work. I have bundled my belongings and I am ready to hit the road. On the table I leave all the money I have with me. I write a note thanking them for everything and leave without anyone ever knowing who I am or what I am about. My buggy isn't due to return until the next day, so I set out on foot, hoping to catch a ride.

As I walk off, I look back. I can see this village isn't ready for Mary Harris Jones.

Chapter Eleven
Pratt, West Virginia ~ February 15, 1913

"Those people were stupid," Addie Thompson says.

I have just finished telling Addie the Carolina story. Addie was my first lieutenant during our women's march on Mucklow and now she wants to be my protégé.

Today she is visiting my newly appointed prison quarters following the conclusion of the trial. I have been convicted of second degree murder by military court martial but not yet sentenced by the commanding officer of the militia, the governor of the state of West Virginia. The court has decided I was the instigator of the battle of Mucklow and therefore guilty of murder.

Addie has been convicted and pardoned along with all the other women who were arrested for the part they played in the women's march on Mucklow. Never mind that their purpose was to prevent the shooting.

Now Addie and I are chatting like two sisters in a nice cozy room at Mrs. Carney's boarding house where I will still be kept illegally for several more weeks. The "jail" is a far sight better than the shack Addie and I had shared with the other women for weeks before the trial. But there are still military guards around the house to prevent me from leaving.

To get back to the discussion about the Carolinas, I explain to Addie, "They weren't stupid, Addie, and they weren't bad grandparents. They were just in a different time. They were people of the Agricultural Age newly transported to the Industrial Age and they didn't understand the difference between working for themselves and working for a heartless employer.

"On the farm the children did work hard, but they were surrounded by their mothers and fathers and grandparents who loved them and had their best interests in their hearts.

Somehow, that kind of child labor seems okay, even to me. But in the Industrial Age, child labor is no longer a family affair and it is not okay. It is the unconscionable exploitation of children."

In the Piedmont Region of the Carolinas, these people didn't know that. They still believed all people were naturally good, driven by the golden rule. They were naïve in a changing world, full of blind trust. They were easily exploited but they didn't *feel* exploited and they couldn't see that their granddaughter was being exploited too, being robbed of her childhood."

"But you said you felt low," Addie recalled.

"Low as a skunk," says I, "but righteous as a circuit riding preacher. What I learned in the Carolinas was that I need to be smarter about when and where to pick my fights. You can't fight on the side of people who don't feel like fighting. From that day forward I've never gone someplace to start a fight — just to prevent it or finish it.

"And, I've never forgotten the plight of those unfortunate children who were the unsuspecting victims of child labor in an unforgiving time. Not the children of the mill or the children of the streets, or the children of the shops, or the children of the mines. You'll see."

Chapter Twelve
Chicago ~ July, 1877

Across America in 1877, people do feel like fighting.

I am working out of Chicago when I first learn that the railroad brakemen and firemen of the Baltimore & Ohio Railroad in Martinsburg, West Virginia, have walked off their jobs, bringing all trains to a halt in that part of the country. Many people fear this strike will spread westward, probably as far as Chicago, possibly becoming the country's first nationwide strike.

Business and labor are bracing for the worst and I figure I'll be in the thick of it in Illinois.

In Pittsburgh it appears certain that something big is about to happen. I receive an urgent telegram from Terence Powderly asking me to come help him reason with the various railroad trade unions there and negotiate with the railroad bosses for a settlement to avoid a violent event before the situation gets out of control as it did in Martinsburg. He is there representing the Knights of Labor which, as I'm sure you recall, is a non-violent fraternal organization, not really a union.

Terence Powderly, always the optimist.

Of course I will go help him, but from what I am reading in the newspapers, this is not a limited strike; it is what they are calling the "Great Upheaval," a spontaneous uprising of the people.

While the strike has been initiated by the members of brakemen and firemen's unions in Martinsburg, they are quickly supported by the members of other trade unions, many of them not even associated with railroad work.

The newspapers have been reporting that even some of the business community is sympathetic to the workers because they believe the railroads are the main cause of the banking panic of 1873 and the desperate depression that still plagues both business and labor. People of all descriptions simply see this as an opportunity to strike back at the blamed railroads.

They are right about the railroads.

After the Civil War, the federal government — forgetting the war debt — went on a wild spending spree aimed at unifying the country by rapidly expanding its network of railroads.

Bankers and railroad barons benefited extravagantly from government loans and land grants. More money poured into their pockets from speculative investments by the moneyed class, buying into anything remotely related to railroads.

On the one hand, railroads and other industries were overbuilding. On the other hand, the government's paper money was shrinking in value, causing prices on most everything to rise.

While the upper class was throwing its money around, the lower class worked for slave wages, paid in paper money worth less and less. Now, with the depression, the worker was getting less and less of the devalued money.

So, the economy crashed. And the workers rebelled.

As always, when the economy falls, the first thing employers do is lay off workers and reduce wages, as in Martinsburg.

The blame for all of this was obvious to everyone, rich or poor.

The Jay Cooke banking firm, which handled most of the government loans, both those during the Civil War and the railroad loans and grants of the years following, closed its doors. The panic was on. A total of eighty-nine of the country's three hundred and sixty-four railroads went bankrupt. A total of eighteen thousand other businesses failed. Not only railroads. Factories closed, costing workers their jobs.

The public, the business community and railroad employees all blamed the railroads for the resulting economic conditions, especially among poor families who lived in cellars and drank impure water. Children were dying by the thousands each week from illness and starvation.

The business community saw an opportunity to retaliate against the railroads by joining hands with the working class.

The railroad industry had been imposing monopolistic charges for the transportation of freight to and from their business establishments. Businessmen resented it more because they felt the railroad tycoons were lining their greedy pockets with the generous government subsidies that were now responsible for a failed economy.

In July, 1877, in Martinsburg, railway workers received word that they would be receiving yet a second ten percent cut in wages. This came on top of layoffs that were forcing them to run "double headers," the dangerous practice of using two engines to pull twice as many cars, to reduce the size of the workforce.

Practically speaking, this resulted in half the number of workers to run the risk of smashing fingers, hands and feet between twice as many moving cars. The second engine required no engineer because it was controlled in tandem by the engineer in the first engine.

The reaction of the workers in Martinsburg was explosive.

Workers uncouple their engines, run them into the roundhouse and announce no more trains will leave Martinsburg until the ten percent cut is cancelled. A crowd of supporters gathers around the workers in the train yard. The West Virginia governor sends in the state militia. A train tries to get through under the protection of state troops, and a striker is shot trying to derail the train.

This incident angers the crowd, causing many of the militiamen — some railroad workers themselves — to refuse to interfere further. President Rutherford B. Hayes realizes the state militia is unreliable and decides to send in federal troops.

But he has a problem. Much of the Army has been busy fighting Indian wars out west, depleting the funding, and now Congress has not appropriated more monies to provide for additional federal troops. So in steps J.P. Morgan and other bankers who agree to pay the officers (but not the enlisted men) to maintain order.

By then, some five hundred trains are stacked up in Martinsburg and on mainlines and sidings. When the federal troops arrive, the trains begin to move. But slowly. The railroad system is beginning to break down beyond Martinsburg, keeping the trains from going anywhere.

A more violent story is playing out in Baltimore and railroad towns across Maryland. The strike is spreading north to New

Jersey and New York and east toward Pennsylvania and Ohio. It looks like a full-scale rebellion, a replay of the Civil War. Indiana and Illinois wait in dreadful suspense.

—◆◆◆—

I feel like I should stay in Chicago, but Terence is asking me to be with him in Pittsburgh. As always, I can't refuse.

When I carry my bag into the train station in Chicago, the depot is jammed with people on all sides of the tracks. I suppose some of them are outbound passengers like me, but I can tell by the numbers and the shouts of angry voices that the mood is ugly. A protest of some kind is in the offing.

I am very familiar with the station, having visited with rail workers there many times. I make my way through a side door to the ticket office and run into one of the agents I know.

"Busy day," says I. "Yep," says he.

"Are the trains running?"

"Westbound is okay, but we're just now ready to send the last train east."

"Are the tracks blocked?" I asked.

"Not yet. There would be no point in blocking them here, really. With the situation getting worse east of here we're afraid if we dispatch any more trains, they'll just get tied up down the line."

"Oh, that's bad news," says I. "I need to get to Pittsburgh. I've been asked to go there to help with the strike."

"Well, I wish you would," says he. "I'd like to see this thing stopped before it reaches Chicago."

"Then can you help me get there?"

"Yes, ma'am. I don't know if you can find a seat, but I'll get you aboard this last train. If you're lucky, it should get you to Pittsburgh."

I thank him as he takes me to the train and lifts me aboard. As the train lurches forward, my bundle is tossed in after me.

I am able to get a seat during a stop at the first station east of Chicago when a few passengers get off and before others get on. All the passengers are unusually quiet, many with worried looks on their faces. We are, after all, heading for trouble.

Chapter Thirteen
Pittsburgh, Pennsylvania ~ July, 1877

I have been in Pittsburgh many times before. A dirty, smoky city.

My train approaches Pittsburgh on a track that runs through one of the worst smoke producers anywhere. Coke ovens. It is the wee hours of the morning, nothing but blackness out my window. I can tell by the movement of the car that the train is slowing to a crawl and it repeatedly lurches to a stop, then jerks forward again. I presume the engine is running into traffic.

Suddenly my window brightens from the open firelight of a brick beehive coke oven. There is another track running parallel to ours, several feet higher than ours, a narrow gauge track where small hopper cars are being used to deliver fresh coal to the ovens. I can see outlines of workers scurrying about.

The train lurches forward again and I watch a string of coke ovens pass by, a beautiful sight in the cover of night, all flaming arches and silhouettes. It is like a mile-long stage production. But it is coke production and I know from my experience in Memphis that the sight is not pretty by day.

The coking process accomplishes two things. Foremost, it transforms the coal into hard coke that burns hotter than coal. The other is a side benefit. When the coke is burned in industrial furnaces, it is less smoky. Smokeless coal it is not. During the coking process, some of the smoke goes up the flues to be blown by the wind in whichever direction it's going. Most often from this valley it's going to Pittsburgh.

Unlike Memphis, these ovens are close to town — to Pittsburgh, known as the Iron City. Both iron and steel production require the intense heat of coke. And the best anthracite coalfields in the world are located just outside of town. Best for quality and best for accessibility.

You see, at this time coal is so plentiful in Allegheny and Fayette counties, it can be seen exposed in outcroppings right on top of the ground. Free for the picking. Independent workers and their children can pick ten ton of coal in a day and get two dollars and fifty cents for it at the coke ovens. The coke ovens can turn the raw coal into ten dollars worth of coke. Being close to Pittsburgh, transportation to the nearby mills is cheap.

So now I'm thinking, that's why coal mines are at such a competitive disadvantage outside of Pittsburgh. Still, I don't think it's fair for the miners to be worked like slaves in order for coal companies to compete with the easy coal production and transportation.

—◆◆◆—

The train slowly pulls into the Pittsburgh station, the cowcatcher pushing through thousands of people at the front end. Ordinarily the crowd would not be making trouble for a passenger train, but this one has a bunch of freight cars coupled to the end of the passenger cars. The practice of doubling up engines is also being practiced in Chicago and Pittsburgh and freight trains coupled to passenger cars are now targets for protesters.

How in heaven's name, I wonder, am I ever going to find Terence Powderly in this crowd?

I pull my bundle of personal things down from the shelf above and when I turn around, there he is. Terence Powderly! He gives me a big brotherly hug.

"Mary," he says, "I am so glad to see you, but I fear it's almost too late to avoid a riot."

"That was my thought when I left Chicago," says I, "but we have to do what we can."

"I think what we should do now is run for the hills," Terence says.

"No," says I, "what we have to do is go where we're needed. Where are our boys now?"

"The main action is down in the yards," he says.

"Okay, let's go."

"Not easy to do," he says. "The crowds are thick all the way from here to the yards."

"Well, let's just stay on this train," says I.

"This train will never make it there," Terence says. "The yardmen will disconnect the engines, leave the cars here on the track and take the engines to the roundhouse."

"Well then, let's hitch a ride on one of the engines," says I.

And that's what we do. We go up to one of the two engines, announce ourselves and our intentions, and Terence lifts me up in his arms like a baby. One of the engineers pulls me up onto a platform and guides me into the engine. Terence follows.

We inch forward out of the station with the steam whistle shrieking. I sit on a steel stool behind the engineer while the fireman stokes the fire behind me. The noise of the engine drowns out any sound from the outside and, of course, I can't see what's happening out there. Only the engineer can see through his side window.

Abruptly the engineer shouts and the brakeman locks the wheels. The engine slides to a stop on the track.

"What happened?" I shout, panicked.

"A switchman was throwing the switch for us to head for the roundhouse and the troops opened fire," the engineer says. "It's pandemonium out there. A regular war."

The troops he speaks of are not the local militiamen. The local militiamen have been sympathetic to the strikers and so the authorities have brought in troops from Philadelphia, the archrival of Pittsburgh, even in good times.

These Philadelphia troops have been inspired by the words of Andrew Carnegie's mentor, Thomas Scott of the Pennsylvania Railroad. It has been reported that Scott has urged the militia to give the strikers "a rifle diet for a few days and see how they like that kind of bread."

The people of Pittsburgh are even stronger in favor of the strikers than those in Martinsburg. While I have been steaming toward the roundhouse, the troops from Philadelphia have been facing an angry crowd and a shower of stones.

Back at the station I just left, the troops empty their rifles into the crowd killing twenty men, women and children and wounding twenty-nine others.

When the news reaches the nearby mills and manufacturing shops, workers leave their workstations in droves and head for the train yard where the Philadelphia troops now continue to wreak havoc. Meanwhile, the protesters have broken into a gun factory and grabbed five hundred rifles and enough ammunition to start a small civil war.

Miners and steel workers have come pouring in from inside and outside the city. Many of those coming from their homes carry their own weapons. The crowds have swelled to the tens of thousands.

And that's the way it is there in the yard when that switchman throws the switch for our trek to the roundhouse. As quickly as that poor man goes down, strikers open fire on the Philadelphia troops who then run to the roundhouse for protection. I insist on going to the aid of the downed switchman and, over Terence's protests, the train crew helps me down to the ground.

I run to the front of the engine and kneel down over the man, just a boy, really. I soothe him as best I can. He is still alive, his eyes fluttering open and shut.

"I am so proud of you, young man," says I. "Don't worry. Everything's gonna be all right."

"Mother," he says. "Oh, Mother." He thinks I'm his mother. I don't mind. And then he is dead.

For the first and last time in my life, I faint. Fall across his body. I don't know how long I am out, but when I awake, another man is shaking me and asking, "What is your name?" I can't think, can't remember my own name. Finally I say, "Jones. My name is Jones."

Still in a daze, I look into the eyes of Terence Powderly who pulls me off the fallen boy and leads me away from the crowd and to the top of a hill overlooking the rail yards.

From there I watch the rest of the tragedy play out below me. In the twilight I see the strikers chase the Philadelphia troops into the roundhouse. See the angry crowd torching the railroad station back up the tracks where Terence and I had boarded the engine. See them torch other railroad buildings and scores of railroad cars. See men shove a blazing oil car into the roundhouse to burn the troops out.

They say those troops, trapped inside the roundhouse, stripped out of their uniforms and tried to sneak out to hide in the crowd. They were half naked, but somehow they blended into the frenzy and escaped.

By midnight, some twenty thousand surround the roundhouse, five thousand of them are later said to have been armed. We listen, Terence and I, as workers and soldiers exchange gunfire throughout the night. We huddle together and somehow sleep.

In the morning, we awake to a scene of awful devastation. A pall of black smoke from the rail properties hangs over the valley aided by the thousands of smoke stacks and chimneys that are Pittsburgh's bane, the smokiest city in America. The train station and train yards are destroyed but still packed with people milling about.

We make our way into the city and find a hotel almost empty of occupied rooms. Most of their clientele have either escaped during the night or never arrived the previous day. We take adjoining rooms and share toiletries from my bundle which Terence, ever the gentleman, has toted through the night.

A young woman brings us several newspapers. I read the local papers first, anxious to learn more. The reports are that the riot is not really over. The crowd is still in control of the railroad and all its rolling stock. President Hayes has issued a proclamation warning strikers and sympathizers to go home or else. The governor of Pennsylvania has ordered every regiment in the state to report for duty. Clashes between troops and strikers in Reading, Pennsylvania, are adding to the death toll.

While the people are clearly on the side of the striking railroaders, some of the newspapers, the pawns of the powerful capitalists, are blaming it all on the working class. One article, however, sympathizes with the strikers and tells of the switchman who died before my eyes. The reporter says I collapsed on his body after he had called me "Mother." Then the reporter also calls me Mother, because I have only given him my last name.

He calls me Mother Jones.

Chapter Fourteen
Pratt, West Virginia ~ April, 1913

"Well, he got that right," Addie says, referring to the first reporter to ever call me Mother Jones. "Somewhere along the way, you ceased being Mary Harris Jones. You became mother to all your boys, the working men. Women and children too. You were truly Mother Jones before anyone called you that."

Addie, my faithful protégé, sits in front of me, wide-eyed at the telling of my first-hand story of the Pittsburgh railroad riot. Ever since the court martial ended, she has been visiting me here in my new jail, that is, Mrs. Carney's boarding house.

I have been illegally convicted of second degree murder by the military tribunal but the governor of the state of West Virginia, who is also commander in chief of the state militia, hasn't the guts to sentence me.

He also doesn't have a women's prison. His only choices are to leave me here at Mrs. Carney's boarding house or turn me over to the federal government to serve time at the new federal penitentiary at Alderson, West Virginia.

He has to know that my rights as an American citizen have been trampled. And if he sentences me to jail, well, there would be hell to pay, a hellish public outcry. A lot of the press has become sympathetic to me and, more importantly, to my cause. The public has come my way and the U.S. Congress is preparing for hearings on the conditions in the coalfields of West Virginia. I'm expected to testify.

Mrs. Carney's boarding house is a perfect headquarters for my public relations campaign. I constantly publicize the truth about what really happened at Mucklow and at Hollygrove, which had provoked the whole Mucklow mess. I lay it all on the behavior of the bastards who turned a peaceful strike into a shooting war. And I make hay while the sun shines, publicizing all that is wrong with the economic and social slavery in the mines and the culpability of wrong-headed politicians and corrupt law enforcement.

Mrs. Carney, bless her soul, remains my ally and courier, running mail to the post office in the next town where my letters won't be intercepted.

The newspapers particularly like my articles about my favorite cell mate, poor Sarah, whose life story is a perfect example of the cruelty faced by innocent souls in the isolated backwoods coalfields of West Virginia. Governor Hatfield has pardoned Sarah and seen to it that her baby boy is delivered back into her arms. He has gotten her a good job away from the coal mines, and approved a grant to pay for a full-time nanny for the baby.

A boarding house has become an effective headquarters for a little old lady, a hellraiser now known as Mother Jones, who has never forgotten the bitter lessons learned in the Pittsburgh riot so long ago.

Chapter Fifteen
Scranton, Pennsylvania ~ August, 1877

The results of the Great Upheaval are as distressing as the conflict itself. After the riots, railroad workers gain nothing and people of the working class become extremely militant in their attitudes toward work. They survive, but in defeat they toil like dead men.

In one newspaper article a worker says he used to be proud to be a mechanic, considering himself above the average working man. But with the arrival of machinery and the subdivision of work on the assembly line, he has sunk from skilled worker to laborer. He is no longer prized for his abilities. He is as interchangeable as the machines he tends.

It reminds me of a story Terence Powderly often tells. "A man who used to call himself a shoemaker now works in a shoe factory but he only makes one part of the shoes, the sole. He is no longer craftsmen nor tradesmen; he is a mere laborer. There is no pride to be found in that."

—◆◆◆—

There was a time, not long ago, when work was a big piece of what a person was — a farmer, a carpenter, seamstress, an ironworker, a cook. Now, these are no longer a person's life's work; they are just jobs.

A mere laborer is unappreciated. A man indentured without recognized value. The work is mechanized, homogenized, so routine that even an untrained, unskilled common laborer can do it. Many do.

Dammit, I think to myself, the public should know what these strikes are really all about. Not just gripes about pay, hours and working conditions. They go much deeper than that. The Industrial Revolution has taken away the workman's pride, his joy, his way of life.

Capitalism has taken the worker's self-respect and handed it to the capitalists. Additionally, government — through loans and grants — allows capitalists to line their pockets, furthering the schism between workers and employers. The greed of the capitalists has wrecked the American economy time and time again, the latest occasion being the collapse in 1873 that brought grievous times to poor Americans.

This is why the workingmen's anger explodes during the Great Upheaval. Worse now, workers are quietly seething, silent but still dangerous. Fearful but fuming. Hungry in their souls as well as in their bellies. Now, after these riots, they are left with an even more desperate feeling of helplessness.

The riot may be over, but the storm will rise again. And again.

How ironic then that newspapers are reporting rage among the capitalists. Until now, capitalists have not given the lower class worker much thought other than to hire and fire at will. But now they've noticed those workers. That's for sure.

They are looking at them now with angry eyes, accepting no culpability for themselves. No concern for the role they have played in creating the divide between business and labor that blew wide open along the tracks of American commerce.

Instead of making any effort to ameliorate issues, like raising wages, shortening hours or improving conditions, the business owners hire private security forces like the Pinkerton Agency and prepare for future battles.

All they see is lawlessness and their solution is to take measures to protect themselves from a repeat of lawlessness by the "loathsome lower class."

That strategy alone begs for more violence.

Factory owners string barbed wire around their plants and the railroads hire thugs and badge them as police to patrol the rails and what is left of the rolling stock and buildings, including the prized and opulent train stations before they were burned.

Government, governors, politicians, even the president beef up military forces and station them in strategic locations. They build fortified armories ready for any siege the American people might stage against their own government.

The stage is set for major class conflicts through the rest of the 1800s and into the next millennium.

—◆◆◆—

In Scranton, Pennsylvania, Terence is lecturing me again.

"Violence. Even the threat of violence is not the solution. You see how unsatisfactory the results of these riots have been."

"I agree, Terence, but we cannot be meek in the face of forces like we saw in Pittsburgh."

We are arguing as we have breakfast at his home in Scranton. I have followed him there from Pittsburgh to recover and to plot strategy for ourselves and the Knights of Labor following the railroad strikes. We are both members of the Knights, but we are independent volunteers under whatever flag flies on behalf of the workers.

"Well, regardless of philosophy, we can't afford any more outbreaks like that.," Terence says, "and we mustn't be the instigators."

"Again, I agree," says I. "But we must meet aggressive force with defensive force. We may not like the game, but how the game is played is out of our hands. The capitalists are playing rough. They've got the government on their side. They're blaming the riots on the unions while we know the strikers were overrun by others who were not part of the strike but upset with the conditions of life in general. The capitalists have won a big battle and now they'll expect to win the war. You know it, Terence."

He bows his head.

"I know, Mary."

"Well, here's something we can agree on," says I. "We need to recruit like crazy over the next year or so and build the Knights of Labor into a unified force capable of standing up to the capitalists and the government.

"Right now there is only big business. There isn't big labor, an organization broadly representing the working class. The working class is fragmented with several hundred small, specialized unions. We need to unify them. Sometimes they work together. But there's no guarantee. When it comes down to it, every trade union is out for itself.

"Without unified support across all the unions involving all workers in a company or an industry, there is little hope we can avoid the kind of fiasco we saw in Pittsburgh."

"Unity is the force I've always stressed," Terence says. "That's what the bylaws of the Knights calls for."

"All right then, now is our best chance. We need to organize our forces and take advantage of the mood of workers right now. The other side is already beefing up."

He bows his head again.

"I know, Mary." With a sigh, "Let's get it done."

We agree I will begin recruiting key leaders in railroad towns in Pennsylvania, concentrating first on Pittsburgh and then fanning out to the rest of Western Pennsylvania. I'll find key regional leaders and, in turn, they will recruit local leaders in a pyramid fashion.

At the same time Terence will ride the rails east to recruit key leaders in railroad towns from Pittsburgh to Martinsburg, West Virginia, where it all started, and then north through Maryland, New Jersey and New York, again concentrating on railroad towns where the Great Upheaval has spread.

Terence agrees with me that we should talk tough, but I have my doubts he can do it. He is a man of reason, not bravado. He knows a soft line will not recruit many leaders and members from the ranks of disgruntled workers, but he cannot abide the risk of violence.

"They're mad," says I, "and they have to see that we're mad if we are going to convince them that we're serious and capable of a better fight."

As soon as I finish launching the organizing effort in Pittsburgh, I will board trains heading west and repeat the same efforts in every train yard between Pittsburgh and Chicago. Terence works his way eastward.

Chapter Sixteen
Pittsburgh, Pennsylvania ~ September, 1877

"Sir," I say to the first key leader I meet, "we can't let this go. We may have lost our battle, but this fight is only just beginning. I am so proud of you, my brother, for the courage and leadership you showed during the riot here in Pittsburgh."

"Lost, hell!" he exclaims. "We showed them bastards. Look at the damage we did to the buildings and rolling stock. Even tore up the railroad tracks. We sure as hell got their attention!"

"Yes, you did," says I. "And you have a right to be proud of that."

I'm not so sure it is a thing to be proud of, but I humor him.

"But now we need to regroup and get ready for the next battle and the battle after that. Next time we will be better organized and we'll be able to use our strength to get those bastards to give us what we want."

"How we gonna do that?" he asks.

"This time we demonstrated our strength," says I, "but we were unable to use our strength to negotiate a settlement. That's because we weren't organized. We just wanted to show our anger. In a way, we were like little children, throwing a temper tantrum but with no clear plan to get our way."

"I don't know. I don't see it that way. We had a purpose."

"Of course you did, but not a plan. When things got out of hand, you never had a chance to achieve your purpose. Now those capitalist bastards are grinning from ear to ear and ready to put it to you again. We can't let that happen."

"Now that makes sense," he says. "I'm ready for another fight and this time we'll do it right. Tell me what I need to do."

The rest of my task is easy. I explain the value of having everyone employed by a company work together for the good of all. "For instance," I explain, "we need to organize not just engineers and firemen but all tradesmen and laborers of the same company, skilled and unskilled."

Making it clear that joining the Knights of Labor doesn't mean turning his back on his trade union, I tell him it would be best to get trade unions to encourage their members to affiliate by joining the Knights too. It means being part of a larger, broader organization with greater power to help both tradesmen and laborers fight for their common goals ... together.

"If we can just harness the energy we saw during the riot," says I. "If we can just get the movement on the right track, we can get the results we need. That's my aim. That's the intention of the Knights of Labor."

I finish by suggesting he join and then contact key leaders wherever he has connections in other companies. Get them started recruiting their own.

"Right now I'm very busy having these same conversations with others like yourself. When I finish in Pittsburgh, I'll do the same along the tracks from here to Chicago. Others like me are doing the same thing from here to Martinsburg and up the East Coast."

I conclude, "If at any time you think you need someone to appear at a meeting for your recruits and your prospects, I'll be there or have good speakers from the Knights to help you out."

Not all my recruiting talks go so well. Most of the people I approach like what I have to say but they lack faith in their ability to get it done, lack faith anyone can get it done under the present circumstances. When that happens, I end our conversation and move on.

At the end of each day I have stated my case to a dozen or more men and women and can count only one or two dependable organizers. Sometimes none.

I feel like I am wasting too much time and I think I will never be able to recruit enough organizers from here to Chicago.

Then I remember the epiphany I had in the Carolinas. I remind myself of the lesson from my failure there at that cotton mill down on the Piedmont: never try to help people who aren't ready to help themselves.

What I need to do is go where I stand the best chance of success. Instead of trying to *create* supporters, I need to tap into the energy of those who are natural borne leaders. But, the task and the territory, they are so vast. How can I reach those motivated people?

At the same time, I worry about the bad press labor is getting. Labor unions are accused in the papers of causing the riots by instigating strikes. Worse yet, the capitalists are getting the good press, portraying themselves as the victims, not the reason for the strikes.

Yellow journalism raised its ugly head during the Golden Age following the end of the Civil War. Yellow journalists are still around and linked up with big business, reckless with the truth while whoring for the capitalists.

In my way of thinking, freedom of the press means the newspapers are free for the taking — free for purchase, that is, by the moneyed class with their hoards of gold.

Then it comes to me. What if it is greed for sensationalism that drives the press, rather than capitalist money? Maybe I can turn the newspapers around. Maybe they aren't in the pockets of the upper class as much as I think. Maybe they're just in competition with each other and capitalists just know how to exploit the press.

Many of the newspapers in Pittsburgh and across the country are themselves big businesses and they're always looking for a good story they can exploit just to sell papers. They're in tune with their big business brothers yes, but why can't I get them singing my tune? I've got some good stories!

I am betting the press will think my bold talk will help them sell papers, even if my messages aren't in the best interest of big business. I've never done anything like this before, but maybe they'll like my rough talk. They might laugh up their sleeves at me, might make light of what I have to say. But I bet they'll print it.

And when they do, the positive side of the labor movement will be heard and the eager leaders I'm seeking will want to get involved. They'll be coming to me then, and I won't be wasting time with reluctant recruits.

And so, my new personal strategy is to stop thinking of the Fourth Estate as the enemy and instead, take my fight to the press. Become an actor — Mother Jones on the stage of social conflict. Speak for the people, the worker, the families whose voices are muted or unheard. Speak loud and be heard often by the public, business and labor leaders. Strike fear in the hearts of the industrialists. Recruit the support of the American people. Plant courage in the hearts of the workers. Attract, rather than recruit, leaders and organizers.

Now I have a new strategy as well as a new name. Mother Jones, hellraiser on the scene and in the press.

I choose for my debut — my first press interview — that fellow who asked me my name as I held that poor switchman in my arms, the reporter who first called me Mother Jones. I have kept a clipping of his story, which has his byline. I send him a telegram and tell him to meet me on top of that same hill where Terence Powderly and I watched the riot just a week or so before. I tell him the place and time for us to meet. I sign the telegram "Mother Jones."

—◆◆◆—

"Hello," says I. "Have a seat on this here log. I'll introduce myself as Mother Jones. You gave me that name and I thank you for it."

He smiles and says, "You're welcome, ma'am."

"You got one thing wrong, though," says I. "You said I am a social worker. I'm no social worker; I'm a hellraiser!"

He laughs.

"I thought you were a union organizer."

"I'm a volunteer with the Knights of Labor which is a society, not a labor union."

He makes a note.

I look down the hill at the scene in front of us where the railroad riot took place and where the smoke still lingers. Not just from smoldering freight cars and railroad property. From the smokestacks of mills and factories. From thousands of chimneys atop commercial buildings and tenements. From fires in steel barrels heating cold homeless hands on street corners. From houses and shacks as far as the eye can see. Smoke rolling in from the coke ovens, all adding to the grime of the city.

"What do you see out there?" I ask.

"Pittsburgh," he replies.

Now I laugh.

"No, young man. What you see is hell with the lid taken off."

He chuckles and his pencil begins to fly over the pages of his notebook as I go on to say pretty much what I've just said to you. I don't give him much time to ask questions. He is too busy writing.

As I get up to leave I say, "Now I've watched you take lots of notes, young man, and so I know you've got plenty to write about without making it up. I will tell you this; when you write your story, if you so much as put one false word in my mouth, it will be the last interview I ever give you. There are plenty of reporters in this town and I'm sure they will want the chance you're getting to have a scoop from Mother Jones. And I'm going to be in the thick of things for a long, long time, so think hard before you cross me up."

With that, I get up and walk away.

I read his article the next day and he does put a few words in my mouth, but I like them! Wherever I had mentioned the robber barons of Pittsburgh, he inserted "Andrew Carnegie," "Henry Clay Frick" and "Andrew Mellon," the very czars of the hell I had shown that reporter. I made a mental note to be more specific in future interviews.

Chapter Seventeen
Pratt, West Virginia ~ May, 1913

I am alone in my room at the boarding house when a gentle rap comes at my door.

"Who is it?" asks I.

"My name is Brown, ma'am. I was sent by a friend of yours, Upton Sinclair."

"Oh my!" says I. "Please come in!"

I look up into kind, inquisitive eyes. Eyes of brown, same as his name. Tall. I'm guessing in his mid-thirties. He reaches down to shake my hand.

"Welcome, Mr. Brown," says I. "How is my friend Upton?"

"Well, ma'am, he was too busy to come visit you and sent me instead. I'm a reporter for the *Washington Star.*"

"How in the world did you get into my jail?" I ask.

"I checked in as a guest of the boarding house, ma'am. Paid for room and board for three days.

"The *Star* is an afternoon newspaper in the capital, the leading newspaper in Washington," he adds. "We do a lot of in-depth features and my editor agrees we need to do a special edition to follow up on the Battle of Mucklow and your long incarceration, which I might add, seems to be waiting for a resolution."

"I'll say! I've been illegally held in jail for pert near five months. Don't let this nice boarding house fool you, though. This is my jail now, but you ought to go down to that shack of a jail I occupied with my ten sisters for the first few weeks. Thank goodness the rest of the girls were let loose after that drumhead trial was over. But then I was put here with a militiaman downstairs to stand guard like I am a dangerous criminal."

"Well, I understand you were convicted of murder," says Mr. Brown. "That could mean a very severe punishment."

"I didn't murder anybody, but I don't care if the governor hangs me," says I. "It's wrong. They say that military tribunal convicted me and recommended a sentence to the governor, but the governor knows it's wrong. He knows I did not cause those deaths at Mucklow and he knows where the true fault lies. And he's afraid to sentence me. He's afraid of the outcry it would bring from a public that knows what the truth is. And he knows the sentence won't stick because the trial was a sham."

"Well, that's the story I'm here to write," the reporter says, "how Mother Jones is still trapped here, the victim of injustice but unafraid of the governor."

"I think you're after the wrong story," says I. "My being trapped here is old news. Your newspaper colleagues have been telling that story every day for five months and I thank them for it. They've helped me tell the story, but if you write that same account, it will just be another update — the latest on poor Mother Jones.

"But you're a living legend, Mother Jones. You're always a big story."

"Maybe," says I. "Always glad to have the boys of the press pumping up my image. It gives me the opportunity to speak up for the working class. However, the real story isn't here in Pratt. It was never here, never was about Mother Jones or this ridiculous trial. The real story has always been up there in those hills — it's the poor wretches up there who have been trapped for years, facing life imprisonment worse than anything the governor or the mine owners can dream up."

"All right, then," the man from the *Washington Star* says. "Tell me the story of what's going on up there in the hills."

"No good," says I. "Dozens of reporters have already written what they've been told second hand, quoting a convicted murderer like me and the biased mine owners who have plenty to cover up." I smile. Smiling seems to be working so far.

"The most powerful story will be written by the reporter who goes up there and sees first hand what's causing all this trouble."

"You don't mean me, do you?"

"I'm assuming Upton Sinclair didn't send you here because you're afraid to go after the real story," says I. "If you've got the guts, you'll get the best story. You'll beat every reporter before or after."

He stiffens, a little offended maybe, but proud to believe that the great Upton Sinclair believes in him.

"I've got the guts, ma'am, but honestly, my gut tells me I'll be arrested before I get halfway up there."

"Pshaw," says I. "You're a free man. I'm the prisoner. I've been up there to the hills twice since I was arrested and I'm a jailbird. Don't tell me you can't get up there if you've got the guts to do it."

"You've been up to the mines since you've been in jail?" He looks shocked.

"Indeed I have."

"Why?"

"To let those boys know Mother Jones is still alive and kickin'. To give them the courage to keep fighting."

"But me," he pondered. "I don't know about me."

"Well I guess I don't know about you either if you're afraid to go," says I. "But I don't think Upton would send anyone less than a good reporter. Upton sent you here and he's the best damn journalist there ever was and he believes in you.

"But there you stand, looking opportunity in the face, and doubting yourself, afraid to take the risk for the biggest story of your career. Are you sure my friend Upton sent you?"

His face is beet red as he stands there, silent. Then his complexion returns to normal and he smiles.

"You sure are a tough one, Mother Jones. All right, I'll do it. But you'll have to tell me how."

"I'll do better than that, Mr. Brown. I'll show you how! I'll be your escort."

Chapter Eighteen
Paint Creek, West Virginia ~ Next Day, 1913

Mrs. Carney takes in laundry for several unmarried miners, not just people staying in the boarding house. I ask her if she would please get me a couple of sets of miner's clothes, one for me and one for Mr. Brown. Dirty clothes.

"You're gonna do it again," she says with a big smile. I may stand convicted of conspiring to commit murder, but there is no one who enjoys conspiracy with a hellraiser more than Mrs. Carney. She has outfitted me twice before and covered for me when the guards check to see if I'm in my room.

—◆◆◆—

The railroad track through Pratt is used to haul coal down to the main line and lumber back up to the mine for roof supports and such. The few miners who hop a ride on the flatcars are returning from rare time off or they are scabs on their way to displace striking miners.

Since many of the riders are former African slaves and European immigrants who don't speak English, there is very little conversation on the ride. Others who speak English don't have much to say, keeping their thoughts to themselves. They are all strangers to us — and to each other.

And so, Mr. Brown and I are just two unknown day shift miners on the way to work. With my hair stuffed up inside my soft miner's cap and my face obscured, I can easily be mistaken as Mr. Brown's small son.

The train rolls right through numerous mine guards posted between Pratt and the Paint Creek mine. The guards see nothing unusual about our presence on the flatcar. They're looking instead for unauthorized persons on the dirt road or in the creek, both running parallel to the railroad tracks. They have caught me in the water and on the road a number of times before, but today I am invisible.

We pass by the tent colony at Hollygrove which is now abandoned. This is the same campground that took gunfire from an armored train a few months back. The UMW is in negotiations with the miner owners and the men and their families have temporarily moved back to the mine.

Mr. Brown and I are already blackened by the smoke from the engine, unprotected on the open flatcar.

"Let's go," says I when we get to the Paint Creek mine, beckoning Mr. Brown to jump from the slow-moving train. By the time we reach the mining operation Mr. Brown has slipped out of character, swiveling his head from side to side, taking in the sights like an outsider would.

"Not now, Mr. Brown. Remember you're playing the role of a coal miner. You're not here to gawk. Keep your eyes on the ground and when there's a need for talk, let me do it."

"Oh, I didn't realize …."

I cut him off with another warning about talking now and he follows me to the lamp house. Since we are running late, all the men have picked up their lamps or candles. The lamp man recognizes me right away but shows no alarm when he sees the tall man with me.

"Ezra," says I. "This is my friend, Mr. Brown. He's interested in knowing how the mine operates and I'm taking him on a tour. Of course, we don't have the official blessing of the big bosses, but we'll be sure we're not found out. If one of the company men questions us, we'll say we are mine inspectors from Washington and they better leave us be."

"No problem, Mother. I suppose you'll want a couple of these newfangled oil lamps." He hands us each a brass disk with a number on it, which he has plucked from pegs on the wall bearing the same number. He writes something into his log book. We pin the disks to our shirts to be returned at the end of our shift. That way, our return will be accounted for.

We strap the lanterns onto our hats but we won't light them until we enter the mine. As we walk toward the mouth of the mine, I give Mr. Brown permission to look around. It is quite a sight up and down that mountain valley.

The first big building at the head of the valley is the company store.

The track we have ridden in on continues past the tipple, which is a tall building where raw coal is sorted, sized and dropped through metal chutes into coal cars on a train like we just rode. Coal dust, steam and a constant racket emanate from the tipple. I will take Mr. Brown for a closer look when we return from the mine.

Further up the valley, perched on the side of the hill opposite the mine, there are several dozen miner's shacks. We will visit at least one family there later on.

Over on the mine side of the valley we can see metal chutes carrying coal down the mountainside to the tipple. Alongside the chutes are slag piles where pickers throw slate, shale and rock picked from the coal. A steam shovel at the bottom of the slag pile is busy making way for more tumbling slag. A closer look will have to wait for our return.

At the mouth of the mine we wait to catch a ride underground. This is what they call a drift mine because the shaft is punched straight into the side of the mountain where the coal seam is first exposed by digging on the surface. From there, the coal seam is not quite level; it drifts down a slight slope for a distance of several hundred yards into the mine.

A hopper car is pulled out of the mine to a place where it is tipped sideways and the contents spill into a stationary hopper that feeds the coal into the chutes we have seen from below. Then the pulley operator slackens the cable, stopping the car at the mouth long enough for Mr. Brown and me to climb into the emptied car. A couple of other miners also catch the same ride to work.

I strike a match and light Mr. Brown's lantern. I ask him to do the same for me. Once the hopper begins moving, it will be impossible to hold still enough to light our lanterns.

This is one of several mine mouths situated along the side of the mountain where the same sequence is taking place: hoppers of coal are pulled out of the mouth, dumping coal into a chute to tumble down the mountain; pickers remove slate from the coal, miners climb into the empty hoppers for the return trip into the mountain, lurching down a narrow gauge rail.

Reflected light from the mouth becomes dimmer as we go. Within less than a minute we are in pitch black darkness unlike anything anyone has ever known, except underground. Our eyes widen uselessly until ahead we see the faint light thrown by lanterns in the main cavern.

It is there that our hopper is disconnected from the cable and hitched to a mule for further transport to the surfaces where coal is being mined.

There is too much noise for talk, but I can imagine what is going through Mr. Brown's mind. I remember my first time underground. It was frightening. Now that I know more, I'm even more frightened. I appreciate that fearless image the newspaperman gives me, but anyone who isn't frightened beneath millions of tons of earth is a fool.

I reach over and pull Mr. Brown down until he is almost lying on his back. The roof will soon be too low for us to sit up in the hopper.

We arrive at a central cavern where side tunnels veer off in all directions. I choose a tunnel and we walk to the face. So far, no one has even noticed us.

At the face several miners are dragging the last of a pile of coal from the wall. I signal to Mr. Brown to help them and I too go to work. There is no heavy equipment here and it is relatively quiet.

The roof is even lower here. No higher than the coal seam except where there has been a slate fall.

"Ouch," Mr. Brown complains. Without realizing, he is walking a little more erect where there had been a roof fall, and then he runs into a low hanging ceiling. His soft hat offers little protection.

"Hurt yourself, did ya?," says I.

"It's nothing," Mr. Brown says with male bravado.

"I agree," says I. "Just a little bump. Nothing like what the miners felt when they were killed in that roof fall when that ceiling gave way."

"A miner was killed?"

"Two of them. Yesterday," I says. I had chosen this tunnel because I knew of the two deaths during the evening shift the day before.

—◆◆◆—

"What are you doing down here, Mother?" The voice of one of the miners is friendly and familiar.

"I'm fighting for you, brother. This fella here is a reporter from Washington, D.C. He's learning what it's like to be a coal miner and he's going to tell the world about it."

"Well," he says, turning to Mr. Brown. "The outside world needs to hear about it, that's for sure."

"Then tell me about it," Mr. Brown says.

"You keep loadin' that coal and I'll load your brain with the straight of it," the miner says. "Those two little helpers there, they're my sons. They don't work for the company; they work for me. The company pays me by the ton. The pay my sons get is a roof over their heads and food in their bellies. If they don't work for me, I can't earn enough to support my family. That's the straight of it."

"How old are your sons?"

"Can't rightly recollect," the miner says.

I am sure he knows exactly how old the children are, but won't say.

"Any how, it don't matter. They don't work for the company and so the company doesn't care, long as my diggings fill up them hoppers."

Counting this family group there are five of us with oil lamps on our heads providing a flickering faint light all around us. Enough to barely see each other.

One of the boys takes a whistle from his pocket and blows.

"That hopper's loaded," his father explains.

A hopper holds about two ton of material. Once all the debris has been picked from it, the company weigh-man will claim it's two thousand pounds, less any debris he estimates.

While the mule pulls the hopper away the dad says, "Now we have to drill more holes in the face and put sticks of dynamite in 'em."

"The company gives you dynamite to blast down here?" Mr. Brown asks, incredulously.

"No. Company don't give me nothin'. I have to buy it from the company with part of my wages. They dock me for it. Have to buy everything — dynamite, fuses, shovels, picks, hammers for me and my boys. Everything."

"But what if there's mine gas? Won't we be blown up?"

"I've got a pretty good nose for gas," says the dad. "If there's gas, my nose knows."

With that, the interview's over and dad and sons are drilling holes using round, hand-held chisels and sledge hammers. One son swings a hammer while the other rotates the chisel in his hands to form a round hole. Father does his own holding and swinging.

Mr. Brown offers to help the father, but he refuses, explaining that whoever holds the chisel runs the risk of getting his hand smashed if the hammer ricochets off the head of the chisel.

Father slides fuses into four small sticks of dynamite, each fuse a little longer than the other. He stuffs them in the holes with the longest fuse on the nearest end, shortest on the other.

"Get back now," he says and commences to light the four fuses, shortest one last. The boys have already moved back. Then the dad scurries back to where we are all crouching, our backs to the blast area, hunkered over. Four thumps, four bursts of percussion to our bodies. No flying rocks this time. Back to work.

Mr. Brown and I move in close enough to see the results of the little blasts. After picking up a few lumps of coal, we thank father and sons and make our way back to the central cavern to catch a mantrip, a shuttle built to transport miners back out of the mine.

Our shift isn't over, but we're finished here.

"How long is a shift?" Mr. Brown asks.

"This mine is in operation twenty-four hours a day," says I. "They run two twelve hour shifts. That means the miners, their helpers and everyone else (including the children) spend about thirteen hours down there every day, six days a week. The clock doesn't start until each shift reaches the face.

"The mine shuts down on Sundays so the bosses can get all spiffed up and go to church to pray for their sins. Actually, there are lots of workers here on Sunday repairing equipment and doing other chores while the operation is idle."

"How old do you think those boys are?" Mr. Brown asks.

"I would guess they're less than fourteen years old. That's why their father wouldn't tell you exactly. But even if they were over fourteen, there's no doubt in my mind they started when they were nine or ten years old."

"All these child miners are minors, then?" Mr. Brown is being clever now. I smile. I like his style.

"No, but of the family we just worked with, only the father is a certified miner. His sons are minor miners or they would have earned their certificates and would be drawing a wage. The children will probably get their certificates when they reach the age of fourteen and then those kids will hire other youngins' to work for them. If they keep it in the family, they may actually earn enough to buy their way out of debt at the company store."

"My God," says Mr. Brown, "I'm thinking there are more children than men in that mine."

"More than you think. There are lots of other jobs down there for children. Some of the most dangerous jobs are done by children who hook and unhook hoppers from mules and cables.

The easiest but most boring job for a child is what they call trappers. They sit all day listening for a whistle to blow, signaling them to open and close tarpaulins that form air traps between sections of the mine. That regulates the amount of air flowing to various parts of the mine from fans outside the mine which are powered by steam engines.

"Miner's helpers are in danger of physical damage, of course. Trappers are subject to mental damage. Imagine sitting somewhere in a mine, with only a candle for light, nothing to do most of the time, no one to talk to, nothing to learn. A trapper usually grows up without social skills and that will mark him for life.

"Come on," says I. "Let's go visit some more children."

—◆◆◆—

We follow the routes along which children pick slate and shale from moving coal. We pick with them so Mr. Brown can see that it is not only hard labor but dangerous. Debris is being pitched helter-skelter as fast and as far as those little boys can throw.

Near the tipple where children pick the last of the foreign material before the coal hits the processing machinery, we work with children who have missing fingers, bruises, festering cuts. We can see how easy it would be for a child to fall into the conveyor and be swept away into the tipple machinery to be tossed and torn, reduced to bits and pieces and thrown into coal cars ready to power the Industrial Revolution.

I interrupt Mr. Brown's thoughts.

"It's a common fact, Mr. Brown. Children are routinely and often fatally injured at every stage of the process. Those trapper boys you saw in the mine? They probably graduated to that job after losing a hand or an arm from picking slate outside. And if we had time, we might have seen a trapper who was a grown man, one who was badly injured at the coal face and demoted to a job he can perform with only one arm or leg."

"The lifecycle of a coal miner," Mr. Brown muses. "From slate picker to trapper to miner's helper to certified miner and back to trapper again."

"And forever in debt to the company," says I. "This, my friend, is economic slavery involving work that is far worse than what most black people endured before the Civil War. And, then as now, without civil liberty."

—◆◆◆—

"We're running out of time," says I. "The sun will go behind those hills in just a few minutes. Let's go talk to a family before the man of the house starts the night shift."

We walk up the steps to a front porch big enough for just one straight back chair. Knock, knock. Door opens and there's my dear friend, Sandy Rankin.

"Yes?" She doesn't recognize me because of my outfit and the fact that my face is coal black.

"Sandy, it's me, Mother Jones."

"Oh for gosh sakes, Mother, you are a sight for sore eyes. And who's this?"

I introduce her to Mr. Brown and we are invited inside. It's a typical miner's shack with a main room and one sleeping room. Families of a half dozen or more occupy shacks this size, but the Rankin family consists of only four people — husband, wife and two girls.

There are two straight-backed chairs and a bentwood rocker in the front room. Mr. Brown sits on a straight chair and I sit in the rocker.

"Caleb," Sandy calls out. "Mother Jones is here."

"Be there in a minute," Cal answers.

By now the joy in seeing me fades from Sandy's face and she resumes a sad look. She is the mother of two dead boys, the only boys she ever had. If it weren't for her two daughters, Sandy would have no reason to live.

"What'cha doin' here, Mother Jones? Cause'n trouble I suppose."

"I sure hope so," says I.

Cal enters the room.

"If it isn't Mother Jones again. That jail doesn't hold you down."

"Ain't no jail ever gonna stifle Mother Jones," says I. "This here's Mr. Brown from the *Washington Star*. That's a big newspaper in the nation's capital. The president and members of Congress read it every afternoon to see what they oughta do the next day. Mr. Brown is up here to see for himself why the miners and their families are so angry.

"In Washington there's talk of a federal investigation of mining conditions in West Virginia and Mr. Brown's story just might turn all that talk into a little action. That's my hope anyways."

I introduce Cal as one of the men arrested after the battle ended at Mucklow. One of forty men convicted and then pardoned by the military court, he and his family are among those allowed back to a miners' shack, not the one they were evicted from.

Mr. Brown starts his questions and Cal is full of answers.

"Mining is a very dangerous business, Mr. Brown. You can't get around the danger and I don't blame the company for that. What I blame the company for is its total disregard for the miners and their families. To them, we are animals. They have no respect for the miner and no concern for the danger miners are in every day, every night."

"I thought the issue was about money," says Mr. Brown.

"Yes, the root of all the issues is about money. Right now I'm getting paid thirty-eight cents per ton of coal I blast, pick and load. I'm not employed by the mine. I'm what they call an independent contractor. My equipment, my productivity, my safety, that's my own problem according to them."

Mr. Brown mentions what he has learned from the miner he worked with at the coalface. Then he says, "You sound very angry, Mr. Rankin."

"You're damned right I'm mad. At my wages I was forced to take my two little boys into the mines with me to work, to increase my productivity and my family's income. Now both boys are dead. One was killed instantly by a slate fall."

"I heard about those roof falls," Mr. Brown interrupts. "Isn't there any way to protect against that happening?"

"Sure there is. The company is supposed to have timbers placed across the roof every several feet, but to save money they only brace the ceiling where they think it might be weak. You can't really tell where the roof might give way. But the company would rather sacrifice people than sacrifice the time and money lost bracing the roof."

Cal continues.

"My other son had an arm mangled when he fell onto the conveyor belt picking slate at the tipple. The company doctor wouldn't send him to the hospital in Charleston because he thought it would heal on its own. It didn't. Gangrene set in and he died."

"Company doctor?" Mr. Brown puzzles.

"Yes, the only doctor here works for the company like all the rest of us. Everything, everyone belongs to the company," Cal says. "The store. This shack. My livelihood. My life. My family. Even transportation in and out of here belongs to the company. And they owned the lives of my two boys when they were alive. If you was me, wouldn't you be angry?"

Mr. Brown reckons how he would.

"I was counting on my youngest son to join me as a helper in the mine when he finished working his time picking slate outside. I was looking forward to him replacing his dead brother as my helper at the coalface.

"But no. Both my sons were killed and now I have to pay my young helpers part of my wages to keep my production up. Meanwhile, my debt at the company store keeps going up and we get tired of having soup beans and cornbread for supper. Angry? I'm more than angry, Mr. Brown. I'm desperate."

—◆◆◆—

We catch a ride on the train back to Pratt. When we get to the boarding house, we clean up, eat, and I fill Mr. Brown in on what he didn't learn first hand.

Demand for West Virginia coal is soaring I tell him. But wages here are the lowest of any coal-producing state in the Union.

The companies say it's because it's harder to get the coal from these remote hollows to the market. They also blame the pressure of competition with coal producers outside the state — Pennsylvania, Ohio, Indiana, Illinois, and even in the northern part of West Virginia. But the real issue is the competitive greed that goes on between coal companies right here in these very hills.

In the case of Paint Creek, the mine is located just a few miles from Cabin Creek and the two companies fight like hell to beat the other on price and even the availability of coal cars to transport the coal to market.

"I was able to organize the miners on Paint Creek because the treatment of the miners there is so terrible," I tell Mr. Brown.

"At Cabin Creek, the mine owner is paternalistic. He provides a lot of free services to the families like a recreation hall, a church. He distributes gifts on holidays. Makes folks over there feel appreciated. And if not content, then passive.

"But all that's no substitute for a living wage or a safe workplace. They are still economic slaves," says I, "and they are still sacrificed in the name of competition.

"Nevertheless, the folks over there are kinda like the ones down in Carolina and I have been unable to unionize Cabin Creek."

"Then I guess," says Mr. Brown, "Cabin Creek was the winner when Paint Creek went on strike."

"Yep," I admit. "The coal operators in Cabin Creek were. But that's only temporary in my opinion. Sooner or later those folks at Cabin Creek will see their lot is really no better than Paint Creek miners and they'll join the cause. By God, I'll shame them into it. All miners, regardless of where they work, have to stand together for the good of the cause, for the common good of each other."

"You really *are* militant, like they say," Mr. Brown says.

"I guess that depends on what you call militant," says I. "I've seen violence far worse than anything I've witnessed in these hills. And I know that violence doesn't work. It's not worth the cost to either side. But don't take the Bible's advice, Mr. Brown, because if you do turn the other cheek, you will get a capitalist's boot up your butt!"

Chapter Nineteen
Chicago ~ May, 1886

Two incidents, one in Chicago and another in Arnot, Pennsylvania, deepen my belief that peaceful demonstration can be productive and that violence is almost always counterproductive.

Leading up to the first incident, Terence Powderly and I keep our pledge to each other after the Pittsburgh riot and work many years toward building power through organization, not violence. I take the low road, organizing and hellraising among the working class. Terence takes the high road, raising the power of his voice by getting into politics.

He is elected mayor of Scranton in 1878 and serves six years. At the same time he is rising steadily in the Knights of Labor, becoming corresponding secretary for the District Assembly in Scranton in 1877 and assuming the national leadership as grand master workman in 1879.

Working separately, but in concert, we are responsible for the Knights' rapid growth in the eighties, peaking in national membership in 1886 to nearly seven hundred thousand members.

People greet Terence with cheers wherever he travels. They write songs and poetry about him. Mothers and fathers name their children after him. But the grand eloquence and idealism of Terence Powderly's leadership is fraught with dissatisfaction among the membership. Many do not agree with Terence's idealistic rhetoric, his instinctive caution and his desire to avoid open conflict.

He does not support strikes as a way to resolve problems, but workers are wound to a high pitch, ready for violent action in industrial centers across the nation. They are rough and tumble mill workers and factory workers, used to settling matters with their fists. They want more than talk.

At one point in Chicago, I go back to work in my partner's dress factory but spend much of my time supporting striking workers all over the city. They listen to my moderate preaching but it is clear they are not content with unsuccessful strikes.

Disagreement grows between the national leadership of the Knights and local assemblies which are free to take whatever course the local membership votes. Although the Knights is a national organization, it is a loosely organized federation controlled by the will of the assemblies, not by the grand master.

At the same time, other organizations are forming, taking advantage of the weakness of the Knights and playing to the fears, frustrations and anger of working men and women everywhere. They are not afraid to embrace violence. Among these organizations are the anarchists, also loosely organized, but galvanized by a common fury.

The anarchists are plowing fertile ground. In the 1880s, enormous immigration from Europe crowds the slums, further depressing wages and dropping the standard of living even lower than it had been during the depression of the seventies. There is appalling unemployment, long lines at the soup kitchens and hundreds of children dying of starvation every week. Those who are working for a slave wage are among those in the soup lines.

I attend several meetings of the anarchists in Chicago, but slip in and out without being noticed. I'm not interested in joining their movement, because the gist of their argument is to "throw the bastards out" and "take over the country." In frustration, I have often felt that way, but even though I lean toward unionism and am becoming a radical, I think the anarchists go overboard. I fear their approach will lead to violence and I have already seen the carnage and uselessness of that.

However, the Chicago Assembly of the Knights of Labor thinks differently and votes with great emotion to endorse the anarchists who are planning a citywide strike.

—◆◆◆—

On May 4, 1886, the mood at an outdoor meeting of the anarchists is ugly. The anarchists are holding a meeting in a poor section of town called Haymarket Square. It is in a shabby, dirty district within sight of the McCormick Harvester Works that is currently being run by scabs who have crossed picket lines. Around the factory are dozens of tenements where the workers live and beer joints where they drown their sorrows.

My height being what it is, I am always able to keep a low profile and I do not expect to be noticed on this day. But a gentleman recognizes me and shouts out in the crowd.

"Hey, everybody," he yells. "Here's Mother Jones!"

That creates a small commotion around us and soon they are chanting, "Mother Jones, Mother Jones, Mother Jones!"

I try to sneak away but the chant spreads across a crowd of what must be a thousand men, women and even children. I have no place to turn.

A man comes down off the wall where an orator is shouting through a bullhorn. He makes his way to me.

"Mother Jones," he yells above the blare of the bullhorn, "you must join us on the wall."

"No sir," says I, "you wouldn't want me to address this crowd. These people here are as hot as firecrackers and this is not the time for me to be stirring them up. If I were to go up there I'd do everything I could to calm this crowd down. I don't think you'd like that and the crowd probably wouldn't either. But that's what I think you ought to do. Calm this crowd down before all hell breaks loose."

He frowns and walks away without a word.

Word does go out through the crowd, however, that I have refused to join the oratory and the chant dies down. I think I am free of interlopers when a tap comes on my shoulder. The words of a popular poem runs through my head as I turn and think, "and what to my wondering eyes should appear?" It's not even Christmas but here's Carter Harrison, the mayor of Chicago. He's got the power to avert a disaster.

"Hello, Mother," he says, smiling. "Rumor has it you won't speak to this group."

"I did refuse, Mr. Mayor, but what on earth are you doing here?"

"I'm taking the temperature of this crowd," he says.

"Well, then you know it's hot," says I. "They don't need another hellraiser up there."

Mayor Harrison and I have a long history together. We go back to before he became mayor to the days following the Great Chicago Fire when we worked side-by-side to help the people pick themselves up out of the ashes.

"Well, we don't need any more hellraisers, that's for sure!" says he. "The anarchists are doing way more harm than they are good, Mother."

"That's a fact," says I. "I've been attending their meetings but this is the first time I've gotten caught. I'm just here to find out what they're up to so I can advise the Knights of Labor."

"Well," says he, looking down at his feet, "I see by the newspapers that the Knights have become an anarchist organization."

"Not so," says I. "The local Knights voted to support the strike plans of the anarchists, just like all the trade unions have. But the vote was only to support the strikers. They did not adopt the plans of the anarchists to overthrow the government and take possession of the mills and factories."

"I'm mighty glad to hear that, Mother."

"Well, let me tell you, Mr. Mayor, that I have organized about a hundred members of the Knights of Labor to do the right thing here, to help me calm the crowd by circulating through it and talking common sense. From what they're reporting to me, I think we will be able to see this crowd finish the rally and disperse peacefully."

"That's also good to hear, Mother. I came here today hoping for that very word. I'll go over to the Desplaines Street Police

Station and tell Chief Bonfield to disperse his men, spread them all back over the city where they belong."

"That's a very good idea, Mayor. I've seen it too many times, a crowd all fired up but doing no harm, then the police or a militia comes in and all hell breaks loose. I saw that very thing in Pittsburgh during the railroad riot."

"I know, Mother. I know."

"But you might want to keep a reasonable force here to protect this crowd from the Pinkertons," says I.

I told him about the meetings that had been going on over at George Pullman's Prairie Avenue mansion and the mansion of Wirt Dexter, a corporation lawyer. A group of industrialists has been discussing the strikes taking place across the city and devising methods for killing the eight-hour movement, which is the chief demand of this citywide strike that's backed by the anarchists.

The method they've chosen, I've been told, is to hire a veritable Pinkerton army to wipe out the opposition.

"That's very important to know," the mayor says as he walks swiftly away from the crowd.

—◆◆◆—

Mayor Harrison and I must be the only clearheaded people in all of Chicago.

The people are surely jaded in their views of what has been going on between labor and management. Capitalists are quaking in their boots. Employers are openly defiant in their expressions of fears and hatreds. Their views are widely publicized while the plight of the workingman is suppressed.

Since the industrialists are in control of the Chicago newspapers, the press is full of stories and photographs uncomplimentary to the strikers. Workingmen are shown attacking, not defending.

The *Chicago Tribune*, one of the organs of capitalism, has suggested that farmers of Illinois feed strychnine — as they do to other pests — to those who flee from the city to the country asking for farm work.

All who favor the eight-hour day are labeled anarchists, whether they are or not. They are portrayed as foreigners and un-American. The people of Chicago seem incapable of discussing the purely economic issues surrounding the struggle of the workingman without getting excited about anarchism.

Adding to the distortion is the antagonistic bluster of Police Chief John Bonfield who is heralded for his suppression of meetings where men peacefully assemble to discuss wages and hours. Because of him, our non-violent organization is being portrayed as the "black Knights." He is being touted as the "white knight."

Well, I am glad Mayor Harrison is headed over to the police station to tell that "white knight" to unsaddle his horse.

John Bonfield doesn't unsaddle his horse.

I am standing just where Mayor Harrison left me when Bonfield and his men charge into the crowd with his mounted police. A bomb, seemingly from nowhere, is dropped from a window overlooking the square, killing a number of policemen. The battle is on before I think to seek shelter.

Gunfire erupts everywhere and I learn later that seven policemen and four civilians are killed. Countless others are wounded. I am told all the injuries and fatalities among the policemen were inflicted by the police themselves while wildly and randomly shooting into the crowd.

No one ever finds out who dropped the bomb, but in a rush to judgment, eight anarchists are tried and convicted of conspiracy. Seven are sentenced to death, one to 15 years in jail. Two of the death sentences are later commuted by Governor Richard Oglesby. A third hangs himself in jail rather than face the gallows. Four are hanged in 1887. In 1893, a new governor of Illinois, John Peter Altgeld, commits political suicide and pardons the remaining three defendants while criticizing the trial that convicted them.

Saddest of all, we have lost a good friend in Mayor Harrison. He is so traumatized by the Haymarket tragedy that he has imposed martial law on the city, closed down Chicago's leading labor newspaper, banned public meetings and severely restricted union activity — all in the arbitrary style of the tsar prior to the Russian revolution.

The miserable lives of laborers in the city resume, unresolved.

I'll say it again. Violence is rarely the answer.

Chapter Twenty
Arnot, Pennsylvania ~ 1899-1900

My second lesson during this period comes in Arnot, Pennsylvania.

For the remainder of the 1880s and through the 1890s my attention turns from the hellholes of America's industrial cities to the dark holes of the mining industry in remote areas from Virginia, West Virginia and Pennsylvania in the East to Illinois and Indiana in the Midwest to Colorado, Utah and even up to the Pacific Northwest.

It is now long after the Haymarket Square disaster. I'm at a little mining town called Arnot, where unlike Haymarket, I am about to see the opposite effect of a non-violent and unhampered strike and its benefit for both management and labor.

For the first time I am now a paid organizer for a union, the fledgling United Mine Workers. The Knights declined rapidly after Haymarket and most of the Knights who worked in the industrial cities shifted their union membership to the new American Federation of Labor.

The United Mine Workers was established in 1890 and the miners who were left in the Knights of Labor began transferring their allegiance to the UMW. My friend Terence Powderly was voted out as grand master workman of the Knights in 1893 and soon after what was left of the Knights merged with the UMW. That's when I joined the Mine Workers.

—◆◆◆—

Now, the UMW is focused on organizing the coalfields of Pennsylvania which has never been organized by labor. I have been sent here.

Because of the flood of immigrants to this country from Europe and China, labor is cheap in the Northeast and mine owners and operators take cruel advantage of immigrants in a foreign country where they don't even know the language. Blacks from the American South, still not far removed from the slave experience, are likewise easily manipulated.

Men here work fourteen-hour days, never seeing the light of day except on Sunday, trudging underground before sun up and coming back to the surface well after sundown. They live in poverty with their families in shacks owned by the company. Their children are dying by the hundreds from starvation. The shacks are not fit for pigs to live in and sewage from outhouses overflows on top of the ground.

Just recently I have moved into the temporary home of a striker family whose daughter is found dead the day after I've become their guest. I am giving them everything they need to survive, but all I can do for their daughter is pay for a proper burial.

At the funeral I am shocked to learn that her mother is actually relieved that her child is gone, that her awful life is finally over. Her daughter worked with her in a nearby mill. Textile mills are often located near coal mines to take advantage of the availability of the wives and daughters of desperate coal mining families.

I know all about this and so I should not be so shocked. I know it is common for a mother to prefer death for a child rather than to see that child suffer a life in virtual servitude. But I can't help thinking of the loss of my own children and cannot imagine how anyone could celebrate the death of a child. I do thank my God that my own children were never forced into slavery.

—◆◆◆—

The UMW has organized most of the coal mines in the district but the Arnot mine has refused to recognize the union. The president of the district, Mr. William B. Wilson, is a close friend and ally of the new national president of the UMW, Mr. John Mitchell.

Mr. Wilson is a good man. He has talked the mineworkers at Arnot into going out on strike in order to obtain union recognition and then to make the usual list of demands around safety and compensation. The strike has been long and hard on the miners and their families who are all evicted from their shacks when they join the strike.

The Wilson family, three generations of them living on their own land, has somehow managed to keep its farm, rather than sell out to one of the big farming corporations or worse, the coal mining industry. Mr. Wilson and a couple of his kin are working at the mine in order to supplement the farm income.

When things grow tough for many of the strikers, Mr. Wilson organizes other independent farmers in the region and collects food and clothing for the miners and their families. He gets merchants to pitch in. When some families have no place to live he moves them into his barn and when it is full, he gets his neighbors to do the same.

That is the situation when I arrive here and I am now doing my part to raise funds for the striking miners. There is no need for a hellraiser at this point. The strikers are strong and I simply give them some good rowdy speeches to keep their spirits up. The spirit of these people is splendid.

—◆◆◆—

Presently I move into the Wilson home and I am visiting in the living room one night when a knock comes at the door. Mr. Wilson answers it himself and finds two well-dressed men standing there, suits and ties, one short and businesslike, the other large and stocky. The latter looks like a mine guard to me, dressed up in Sunday-go-to-meetin' clothes.

"May we come in, Mr. Wilson?" the shorter man — who does all the talking — asks. "We have a business proposition to make."

"Any man is welcome in my home," says Mr. Wilson. "Come in and have a seat."

The men sit down on the empty couch and look cautiously my way. Mr. Wilson introduces me as Mother Jones. I am ignored.

"Mr. Wilson," says the visitor, "this is rather private business. Do you suppose we could be alone for a moment?"

"I am not in the habit of conducting my business privately," says Mr. Wilson. "Mrs. Jones is my guest. If you have something to say, then say it."

"All right, Mr. Wilson. Our employer is very much wishing to end this strike."

Mr. Wilson interrupts, "Wonderful! Let's hear it!"

"The owner of the mine, you may know, is president of the bank board that owns the mortgage on your home and farm."

"Yes," says Mr. Wilson. "I believe he ... that is the company ... owns the bank."

"That is correct, Mr. Wilson. What the owner has in mind is to forgive the loan if you will just let the strike die."

Mr. Jones leaps to his feet, his face red as a beet.

"Gentlemen," he bellows, "if you come to visit my family, the hospitality of the whole house is yours. But if you come to bribe me with your dirty money, trying to induce me to betray my fellow mineworkers, you are not welcome here! Begone with you. Begone!"

He shows them the door and slams it behind them.

The strike continues and I can see I am not really needed in Arnot as much as I am at other mines in nearby districts. The union leadership is strong, the men and their families are well cared for, and their spirits are high.

Much to the embarrassment of Mr. Wilson, I often tell the story far and wide of the attempted bribery and it has the effect of strengthening the cause even further.

I leave Arnot, assuring Mr. Wilson I will come back at a moment's notice.

A month or so later, on a Saturday morning, I am working over in Barnsboro, Pennsylvania, when I receive a phone call at the boarding house where I'm staying. It's Mr. Wilson.

"Mother," he says. "Mother." His voice is so low I can hardly hear him on the party line.

"You people get the hell off here so I can hear this man," says I.

"Mr. Wilson, what are you trying to tell me?"

"They voted, Mother. They voted to go back to work on Monday morning."

"What?" I nearly drop the phone receiver.

"Voted to go back, Mother. Come quick! The boys are tired of the strike and they're desperate. They don't believe the strike can be won."

I hurry back to Arnot as fast as I can. My mind is awhirl. Those idiots! Those fools! Those cowards! What could have possibly turned them around? The strike was about won when I left. That bribe was surely the company's last-ditch effort.

I can't get there until late tonight. Everyone will be in church on Sunday morning. On the phone I have instructed Mr. Wilson to call for a meeting Sunday afternoon, after church. I have never been angrier. Do I dare say what's on my mind? Damn right I do.

At the train station at Roaring Branch, it is several hours before the next train will arrive. What can I do? I pace. Then I hear this soft voice. Young William Bouncer, secretary of the Arnot union.

We drive with horse and buggy over sixteen miles of rough mountain roads, a bitter cold night, to arrive in Arnot. Bouncer takes me to the company's hotel, the only hotel, but before I can get into my night clothes, there is a knock on the door.

It's Bouncer. He's been downstairs taking care of my registration.

"Mother, I was not able to get this room for you after all. A company man came in and said this room is already engaged and they won't rent us another. I'm afraid you'll have to stay at my house tonight."

"Not a problem, Mr. Bouncer," says I. "I wouldn't be able to sleep tonight anyway and the more discomfort I store up tonight, the more anger I'll have to heap on those stupid miners tomorrow afternoon. Lead the way, my boy!"

My bonnet nearly blows off my head in the wind as he leads me up a mountain where he insists I sleep with his wife in the only bed.

"So they put you out, Mother Jones," says she. "They'll roast in hell some day."

Mr. Bouncer sleeps at the kitchen table with his head cradled in his arms. Their three children sleep as they always do, on the floor.

—◆◆◆—

Mrs. Bouncer lets me sleep late the next morning but presently a light knock comes to the bedroom door and I hear her crying.

"Mother, are you awake?"

"Yes," says I. Truth is the knock did wake me.

"I am so sorry, Mother, but you will have to get up. The sheriff is here and he's putting us out. This house belongs to the company and they have told the sheriff to put you out and us with you."

The family gathers up all their earthly belongings — clothes, their pots and pans, the holy pictures — and puts them in a small hand-drawn wagon. We start for the meeting, but stop along the way to eat some cold gruel and drink cold coffee from an old pot they brought.

At noon Bouncer leads me around the mountain to a large hunter's cabin which men use when they come out here from the nearest cities for their recreational killing. I am hoping they'll have a few guns in a rack hanging around there so as I can use one to raise the roof.

As we approach that hunting cabin, the sight of the father and mother pulling that wagon with the children and me tailing behind raises an angry cry from the men mulling around outside. Once inside, the rumble of their angry voices causes me to wonder if I should not revise my speech.

I don't.

Mr. Wilson is there and I give him a nod before I take my place in front of the group.

"I hear your angry voices," says I. "But who the hell are *you* mad at? The company didn't cause us to be put out in the cold last night," I railed. "*You* sonsabitches made that happen! You lily-livered sonsabitches went and voted yesterday to go back to work when you just about had the strike won.

"Now look who's back in control. The damned company bastards! You gave them the freedom to kick us out in the cold. And now you act like you're upset because they've treated us this way?

"Humph! They been treatin' you and your women and children this way for years. These poor Bouncers. They're suffering the same injustice you've been suffering and now you're ready to go back in them mines and take some more abuse from the coal lords.

"What the hell's the matter with you men? Are you cowards as well as stupid? You're going back to work like beaten mules with not one damn thing to show for all that you've put your wives and children through these past many months.

"If you go back tomorrow, what about your brothers in other mines in this district? Will you be doing the same thing to them? Encouraging the mine operators, giving them free reign in their mining operations? You'll be giving them the go-ahead to kick all your bothers and sisters and their sons and daughters out whenever they like.

"In a strike, it's all for one and one for all. You give in here, you break the strike there. And there. And there."

Silence. I stew in the silence, looking for one man who has the guts to look me in the eye. Only one — Mr. Wilson.

In my low, angry voice, I say to them, "You boys make me sick." I say "sick" like I'm spitting it out. "I'm done with you. You hear me? I'm done with you. I want you to go back to your places now and stay with your children until I say you're needed."

Silence.

"Got that?"

Mumble.

"I asked you if you understand me."

Louder mumble.

"Now, when you get back to your places I want you to send me your women and older children," says I. "I want them to come here directly. Do you hear me?"

Stronger mumble.

"Tell your wives and your older children to bring with them dish pans and cooking pots. Tell them to bring their stirring spoons and ladles. Tell them to carry a mop over their shoulders. We're goin' to march on that mine and we're going to stand guard to see that no scabs are allowed in. Do you hear me?"

I don't hear an answer.

"Say 'Yes Mother'."

"Yes, Mother" comes in chorus.

"Then begone with ye," says I. "Begone." I liked that word when Mr. Wilson used it the night of the bribery. First chance I had to use it and what a good time to do it. "Begone!"

—◆◆◆—

The first of my women's army shows up in five minutes. They are fully assembled in a half hour.

One of the ladies was apparently sleeping very late when she was rousted. A gnarly Irish woman like myself, red hair all askew. She has grabbed a red petticoat and slipped a cotton nightgown over that. Has an old miner's jacket around her shoulders. I notice she wears two different colored stockings, one white and one black. Her eyes are red and her face is frightening mad. I'm not sure who she's mad at. Maybe me.

"Perfect," says I aloud to her. "You look the perfect part to make a rumpus. I appoint you the leader of this here army. I see you brought a hammer. I want you to take that tin pan of yours and go out that door banging it with your hammer. Head for the mine."

She salutes.

"The rest of you ladies follow doing the same thing, and take your older children with you. They'll get a big charge out of this!"

As they turn I continue my instructions.

"Every step you take I want you hollering and yelling like banshees. When you get up there, I want you to mill around together right on the edge of the mine property. Keep up your racket and don't stop. You may be there for a long time, so spell each other so as you can go to the toilet or just take a rest. But keep it up for as long as it takes. Don't let the noise stop. Got that?"

Deafening shouts! Out of the hunting cabin they go. I wish the men could see it. That's the spirit!

I join the women at the mine and begin walking back and forth, shouting at the scabs I see. Many of the scabs turn back from the mine right away, but there are the mule drivers who are rousting the animals into the mine.

"Don't frighten these mules," one says to me. Before I can say a word, the women throw up a racket louder than before. The mules start rearing up, kicking. Presently all of them are loose and scattering in the woods.

"Those mules won't be scabbing today," shouts I, and we all have a good laugh. The drivers go off in another direction, not looking to catch the mules. I'm guessing they're gonna follow the example of the mules and go on strike.

These heroic women keep constant watch and commotion all the rest of the day and several successive days. The mine is completely shut down while the miners stay home with their babies and the scabs keep away.

—◆◆◆—

Meanwhile, I go out in the surrounding area to do battle with company men who are out there asking farmers not to help the miners with food or money. I use a wagon pulled by a union mule, that is one of them that has gone out on strike. I hold meetings with farmers and get them solidly on our side.

There is a place near Arnot called Sweedy Town because a bunch of Swedes live there and I hear the company is planning to go over there to get them to come to the mine to scab for them. I get a bunch of farmers to go over there to Sweedy and stand guard to make sure no Swede leaves town.

I take my rest at Mr. Wilson's where I often return after midnight, having been in the bitter cold. These nights are miserable. It is often below zero and the wind blows sleet and snow in my face until I look like a snowman when I come through the Wilson's front door. I leave a whole cadre of snow women behind at the mines.

After months of terrible hardships, the strike is finally won.

I go back to Arnot the following summer to attend a special celebration in honor of those who sacrificed so much during the strike. It is being held in the large company hall. Actually, the company is sponsoring the event and paying for the refreshments. But what surprises me most is that among the celebrants are dozens of company men who seem to be as happy as the workers with the state of affairs.

"Mrs. Jones," a voice says behind me. I turn.

"They call me Mother Jones," says I.

"Well," says he, "they call me a lot of things, but I prefer to be called Boss."

He smiles. I hold my tongue, but the hellraiser in me wants to say not my boss.

"Mother Jones it is then," says the boss. "I want to say thank you for what you've done for our men, their families and this company."

I am tongue-tied.

"I did not understand what a benefit it would be to this company to have men who are satisfied, happy and loyal, men who feel as much the owners of this company and its accomplishments as any of those who own the stock. Our production is twice what it ever was before we settled with the union and that makes paying higher wages and doing things in the right way a bargain for us."

"Well," I says, "I'm surprised to hear you admit it, but not surprised that it's so. You see, in a way, I am also an entrepreneur. I'm part owner of a dress factory in Chicago and we share our profits equally with our employees. Our profits — those of the owners and the employees — are far greater than any of our competitors. Actually, we *are* the competition. No one can better our prices, our styles or our quality. What I'm telling you, Mr. Boss, is that management and labor cannot only get along, they can prosper when they play on the same team."

Chapter Twenty-One

Pratt, West Virginia ~ July, 1913

Living in that chilly, damp shack prior to the court martial gives me a bad cold that is still hanging on when I take that reporter on the tour of the Paint Creek mine. It gets a lot worse after the reporter ends his visit.

Mrs. Carney does everything she can to cure me, but nothing works. She steeps the minty-flavored fuzzy leaves of the horehound plant in water to make a tea and adds some honey.

When that doesn't seem to help, she makes another kind of tea from wild raspberries and wild cherry tree bark. Even tries an onion poultice on my chest. The Vicks VapoRub seems to help most of all, but I still am feeling poorly. I keep telling her a little whiskey will do the trick and she does finally bring me some.

Still, the cold gets worse. "A cold just doesn't last this long," frets Mrs. Carney. "I'm afraid you've got pneumonia."

"It could be so," says I. "I'm prone to it."

That afternoon, Mrs. Carney knocks on my bedroom door. "Mother? Are you awake?"

"I am," says I. "Please come in." She sticks her head through the door.

"Mother, I have taken the liberty of calling a doctor for you. He's here now and wants to come to your room."

"All right," says I.

Presently the doctor opens the door and talks his way into the room.

"Hello, Mother Jones. I am Doctor Hatfield."

He sets his black bag down on the foot of my bed and places his hat beside it. Raises his pince-nez reading glasses from his vest where they hang on a silver chain.

"How are you feeling, Mother?"

"I don't feel so good. But before we get into that, who the hell are you really? I've got this funny feeling I know you from somewhere."

"Well, Mother, we've never formally met, but I suppose you might know me as Governor Henry D. Hatfield. I believe you call me 'that son of a bitch who keeps you wrongly held in the prisons of Pratt'."

Governor Hatfield replaced the former governor, William E. Glasscock, just after Glasscock had me arrested and jailed. I have not yet met Hatfield, but I've seen his pictures in the newspapers.

"If that doesn't beat all," says I. "You've caused me the death of a cold and now I suppose you're here to finish the job. What kind of a quack doctor are you anyway?"

He laughs.

"Well, I've been a pretty damned good doctor for a hell of a lot longer than I've been a governor, and I've come because I've heard you may have a case of pneumonia."

"I guess I'm supposed to be impressed, you coming all the way up here from Charleston just to doctor me," says I.

"No," he says, "I didn't come up here just to doctor you. I've been coming up here every day since my inauguration, doctoring sick miners and their families. Just like I've done in southern West Virginia since the day I received my medical degree."

"Oh, you're a company doctor then. In my experience that makes you a quack."

He laughs again.

"No, ma'am. I'm neither a company doctor nor a quack. I did have a contract with the railroad to look after their men, but I've never worked for a coal company. My regular practice has been down in Logan County where I've taken care of sick working men, women, and their children for several years."

The governor tells me he used his political influence when he was in the state House of Delegates to get funds to build the first ever miners' hospital at the town of Welch where he then served as chief of staff.

"So if you're not company," says I, "then you must be union."

He interrupts me by extending a tongue depressor toward my mouth.

"I can't believe I'm saying this to Mother Jones, but open your mouth."

We laugh together.

"I don't know if you can call me a union man because I've never belonged. But I am very concerned about the conditions under which coal miners work and their families live," he says. "For many years now I've visited them in their shacks and their tents just as you have. I've gone into the mines to help pick slate off miners' bodies. I've carried them out on my back when I've found them still alive.

"I don't belong to any union, Mother, but I do belong to human kind. And, my life before has been devoted to helping the poor, the working class."

I am stunned, even speechless. I've never thought of a governor as a human being.

From what I have read about this man in the newspapers, though, I like his pedigree. He is the son of a Civil War soldier from Mingo County. He grew up in a mining community in nearby Logan County and returned there with his medical degree.

I am most impressed that he is a Hatfield, a name with a different kind of reputation. Surely you know the name of Hatfield of the Hatfields and McCoys fame. His kin was the famous Devil Anse Hatfield, leader of one of the warring clans.

"Devil Anse was a hellraiser, that one was," says I. "A hellraiser like me!"

"Yes, but make no mistake, Mother Jones. Not all Hatfields are hellraisers and I'm no hellraiser either. I may have the family name, but we never took sides in the feud. Our branch of the family tree got along fine with both the Hatfields and McCoys.

"We were peacemakers," the governor continues. "We tried to stop the killings and I'm here now to stop these killings in the southern coalfields of West Virginia. I abhor war as much as I abhor injustice."

"Then you recognize there is injustice."

"I do, Mother. I agree with the case you make in your crusade to set things right in the coal industry. And in all industries that so callously exploit the working class."

"All right then," says I, "why do you keep me locked up here in Pratt now that you're the governor?"

"I inherited you, Mother Jones. I inherited a problem. I inherited this insane civil war. You've been convicted and I'm supposed to punish you. I'm in a real bind, Mother. I just don't know what to do with you."

"Now you're soundin' like your predecessor, that gutless Governor Glasscock. He was such a Nervous Nellie he couldn't make up his mind which wagon to hook up to. First he would do something to support the union cause and then when things went bad, he would back the coal companies."

"I agree, Mother. He was and is a good man, but he just wasn't cut out to be governor. Not in these times. His election was a surprise even to him and all he could think about was getting back to Morgantown and his law practice. In the meantime, he was afraid. Afraid he would sully his name. Afraid of making enemies that would affect his law practice when he got back home"

He paused.

"I'm not afraid, Mother Jones. I am intent on stopping these coal wars and improving the lives of the men and families who dig up the riches of this state and bring them out of the ground. I'm every bit like you, Mother Jones. I'm opposed to exploitation of grown men and women and I'm opposed to child labor. And I'm committed to doing something about it."

"But you're not a hellraiser?" I ask.

"No, Mother, that's your job. You put the problems before the citizens of this state and country. My job is to do something about the problems."

"I could not agree more, your Excellency." I called him that with respect. "Now I don't mean to insult you, but how the hell are you going to do it?"

"For the next four years I'm going to use the power of the governor's office," he says. "You were imprisoned here and so you weren't there on the banks of the Kanawha River when I gave my inaugural address and spoke to the press.

"On that day of pomp and ceremony I was the first governor of West Virginia to ride in an automobile in the parade to the capitol.

"It was a glorious celebration but it did not hide the fact that the state faces a grave crisis in the coalfields. Here in Paint Creek and over in Cabin Creek, less than twenty miles from the site of my inauguration, martial law has been imposed and you, Mother Jones, sit in jail.

"Thousands of desperate miners and their families, driven from their company-owned houses, have fought a mine war for nearly a year and it isn't the first mine war fought in West Virginia.

"In my speech I referred to the situation as a bitter contest between labor and management affecting thirty thousand miners statewide, costing the state over two million dollars and an untold number of lives.

"I promised on that day I would go into the Paint and Cabin Creek areas to investigate conditions for myself, and here I am. I'm doing even better than I promised, Mother Jones. I'm personally involved, bringing medicine to the sick and wounded, seeing the devastation first hand."

"You are taking great risks by being here," says I, giving credit where it is due.

"As are you, Mother Jones. As are you."

He pauses.

"Do you know, Mother Jones, that you are just one of thousands of people in these coalfields suffering from pneumonia and other diseases affecting the heart and lungs? Victims of the dark, damp depths of underground mining, of the dust in the air outside. I listen to them coughing and wheezing, struggling for a breath of air.

"So you see, Mother Jones, you and I see things very much alike. Some people say we are risking our very lives to be personally involved in these wars, and I suppose that's true. But where you and I differ is not in what we see or in our goals. We differ in our methods. You raise hell and you raise public awareness. I stand between business and labor seeking solution and compromise. But I cannot be successful unless I have the support of the public. In that way we are alike, Mother Jones. We are a team.

"But make no mistake about it, I am neither inconsistent like Governor Glasscock nor reckless and flamboyant like Mother Jones. I am methodical in my doctoring and diplomatic in my negotiations between business and labor. I am committed to finding a cure for this conflict between the mines and the miners.

"I've always liked to say that there are three sides to every story — one side, the other side, and the in-between. I'm on that third side, the in-between, on the side of the Great State of West Virginia and its people. For they are the ultimate winners and losers."

A little time goes by while he catches his breath and I catch up on my thinking. Finally, I speak.

"That's quite a speech, Governor, and I know you mean every word of it. But I can't help but wonder. If we're on the same side, me raising the hell and you seeking the solutions, then why have you left me locked up here in Pratt?"

"Because," says he, "you are so good at raising hell from jail. Do you know how I know? Because I've heard it from you! You've told too many people too many times that you get more attention when you are in jail."

"It's true," says I.

"And besides, it keeps you out of mischief."

We both laugh at that one.

"Do you know how you got away with taking the Washington reporter on a tour of the Paint Creek mine?" he asks.

"Don't tell me you knew what I was up to."

"Deed I did," says the governor. "I encouraged him to come up here and sent word to my troops to look the other way if he approached the mines."

—◆◆◆—

"To change the subject, Mother, I believe your pneumonia is life-threatening, especially at your age. Your health is especially bad because you are too old to be traipsing up and down these mountains.

"You, Mother Jones, are going to be the first hellraiser to ride in the governor's official car. I am going to take you back to Charleston and put you in a hospital bed there where I can treat you every day until you are well. I have two more visits to make before I head back to the capitol. I'm going to have Mrs. Carney pack up your belongings and have you ready to ride with me tonight."

I do as I'm told. I have two new dresses I've sewn for myself while staying at the boarding house and a new bonnet. I tell Mrs. Carney to give my old dresses to a deserving poor woman. I wear one of my new dresses and Mrs. Carney wraps the other with the rest of my personal belongings in the shawl I always use as my knapsack, my bundle of personal things.

The governor comes to call again in about two hours and escorts me to his car, an International Harvester Autocar. It is a monster in black. I have seen one before and know that it is a truck outfitted with three bench seats instead of a cargo space. It has a cloth top and looks like an overgrown automobile.

It has great big iron wheels like they used out West on the great Conestoga wagons of pioneer days. I'm guessing the governor has chosen this high-wheeled machine so as to rise out of the ruts in the roads between patients' homes.

He lifts me up onto the seat, which is far above my head when I'm standing on the ground.

Mrs. Carney brings blankets and pillows from the house and wraps me so I can recline on the seat behind the governor. She bids farewell and the governor starts the engine of his contraption. At the last moment I remember Addie, so I raise up and yell to Mrs. Carney. "Be sure to let Addie know where I've gone."

We have hardly moved forward before I am grabbing for handholds to keep myself from being tossed off the seat. In the midst of the car's clamor, the governor has no idea of the dilemma behind him. Finally, I sit up for the remainder of the ride to Charleston. I am deposited at the brand new Saint Francis Hospital where the governor visits me every day until I am well.

—◆◆◆—

"Mrs. Jones," says the nurse one day, "Doctor Hatfield has signed your discharge papers. You are free to leave whenever you like."

"Discharge papers?" says I.

"Yes, ma'am. He has discharged you from this hospital. You are well. You are free to go."

"But what about the guard?" I ask.

"What guard?" asks the nurse.

"The guard that I presume has been standing outside my door all this time."

"There has been no guard, Mrs. Jones. You have been our patient, not our prisoner."

Chapter Twenty-Two
Looking Back from the Future ~ 1880s-1890s

My head is bursting with foul language for Governor Hatfield, but I have a smile on my face in spite of myself as I leave the hospital. I am a free woman, not cleared. Charged and convicted, but not sentenced, and not caring as long as my reputation is intact and I can continue my cause.

But first, let me return to the story of how I got here in the first place.

The final years of the nineteenth century were as traumatic for me as many others due to the turmoil among my fellow comrades with the conflicts between management and labor.

Many organizations were competing with each other to represent the interests of the underclass. The weakness of the trade unions was that each was relatively small compared to the total working force and they were focused entirely on their own specific wants and needs, not those of labor as a whole. None was powerful enough to successfully negotiate with their employers.

For example, the railroad engineers represented engineers across the lines of many railroads, but their numbers were small compared to the total working force of the railroad industry.

That's why the growth of the Knights of Labor was so important in the eighties and nineties. As I've mentioned before, the Knights accepted all working men and women, skilled and unskilled. Together, the members had a unified voice and the potential of building solidarity.

Unfortunately, the members of the Knights came to feel that though loud, the voice of the Knights was not effective enough. Although I will love my dear friend Terence Powderly forever, I have to admit that his deliberate, lawful and gentlemanly style of leadership did not fit the times or the troubles.

Compounding that problem was the fact that the Knights were loosely organized. Although it was a national organization, it was not centrally controlled. Terence carried the title of grand master workman and there was a central council and staff, but they did not have absolute power over the assemblies. The central office of the Knights of Labor had to rely on guidance and persuasion to keep a local assembly in line with the overall policies and objectives of the Knights.

The organization was a pure democracy and Terence liked that, regardless of the difficulty he had in keeping order.

His beloved democracy turned on him.

Assemblies, as evidenced by the one that endorsed the anarchists in Chicago, often made decisions for themselves that were contrary to the national policy. Then, after the endorsement of the anarchists in the Haymarket debacle, members left in droves and those who remained removed Terence from leadership and eventually banished him from membership altogether.

I have always been an independent agent, no matter what organization I am with. The demise of the Knights and Terence's own new directions, nevertheless, left me without a "home place."

Terence, of course, got into politics by successfully running for mayor of Scranton while he was still serving as grand master workman of the Knights of Labor. He never wavered in his devotion to the Knights while serving as mayor, but his attention was divided. And it was divided again when he decided to study for a law degree. And divided again when he became career oriented.

We drifted apart.

Politics had always been an interest of his, but his attitudes were initially anti-establishment. His political campaigns were always aimed at breaking up the establishment, always running against the status quo in government. Always aimed at working for the people from the inside.

In the 1875 U.S. presidential election, he supported the Greenback ticket, which was formed in opposition to the government's currency policies following the economic depression of 1873. Following the several railroad strikes of 1877, a Labor Party was organized which partnered with the Greenbacks to get Terence elected mayor of Scranton.

Terence never betrayed his devotion to the underclass, but he was becoming part of the establishment and that would continue for the remainder of his career. He advanced his ambitions in 1896 by campaigning for William McKinley who appointed him Commissioner General of Immigration in the U.S. Treasury Department.

After McKinley was assassinated, the new president, Theodore Roosevelt, fired Terence based on lies that had been told by former employees at Ellis Island. They were vindictive lies against Terence who had fired them when he had discovered corruption at the Ellis Island facility.

Later, Roosevelt realized the accusations against Terence were false and reinstated him as a special immigration inspector. Eventually, Terence would become an important figure in the new Department of Labor.

And so, Terence had taken his fight for the rights of the American people inside the establishment. I trusted him, but it was a departure from my own path. And, I missed his partnership deeply, especially at a time when the class struggle on the ground was becoming even more fractured.

I was largely ambivalent as to which organization might best represent labor in the class struggle. I did show my support to several of the competing organizations, which included both labor unions and socialists. I lent a hand in the establishment of some of these organizations and participated in the work of others.

My guiding principle was always to support any organization that supported the working class, regardless of any other of their principles and philosophies. The exception was the anarchists which I considered wrong headed and much more radical than me.

My motivation was simple. I could not do my hellraising alone. One woman, I thought, no matter how strong, cannot fight against the horrors of capitalism all by herself. From time to time, I would need these organizations and these organizations would need me.

—◆◆◆—

If there were ever one man who could replace Terence Powderly as my guiding light, it was Eugene V. Debs. More than my guiding light, he was a contemporary who in many ways was a mirror image of me — Mother Jones wearing men's clothing. He was of the underclass, tough, direct and using the same kind of rough language and strong messages as I. Fearless. Bold. He thought like me and was always there in the middle of a fight.

But he was a "dreaded" socialist.

Eugene Debs had to quit school when he was fourteen years old and became a fireman on the railroad. Later he took night classes at a local business college in his spare time and then took a job as a billing clerk in a wholesale grocery.

In 1875 he founded the local chapter of the Brotherhood of Locomotive Firemen, BLF, while he was still working at the grocery. He used part of his salary from the grocery to help the fledgling union get started but it then followed the model of so many trade unions, that is, mostly selling cheap life insurance to its members.

Though he rose to the editorship of the national BLF publication, he eventually became disillusioned with the very organization he had founded, realizing it was of very little value to the members as a tool for fighting for the rights of workers. It was mostly a capitalistic scheme to sell insurance. A business, not a cause.

In 1893 he became president of the American Railway Union, the first effective, broad-based industrial union in the United States.

The ARU made its mark in 1894 with a successful strike against the Great Northern Railway. Then on May 11 of that year the Pullman boycott and strike began in Chicago.

I was not with him in Chicago then. Instead, I was in Birmingham, Alabama, working with 8,000 miners in a strike there. But I supported "Debs' Rebellion," as I liked to call it, convincing my miners in Birmingham to extend their own strike to support the one hundred and fifty thousand railroad workers striking against Pullman.

Fifteen railroads shut down. Without trains, the country ground to a halt and the mines in the Birmingham area could not get transportation for the coal being produced by scabs. President Grover Cleveland called in federal troops. Birmingham became an armed camp and I was forbidden to leave town.

On July 23, Eugene Debs and other leaders of the ARU were jailed for defying a federal injunction to return to work. In May, 1895, they were again jailed, this time for contempt of court in connection with the Pullman strike.

While in jail, Debs concluded the plight of the worker was more accurately viewed as a class struggle. He became active as a socialist and in 1898 I assisted him in the founding of the Socialist Democratic Party.

I fully shared his view of the ills of capitalism. His writing was eloquent.

In an article in a socialist newspaper of the time, *The Appeal to Reason*, he wrote:

> When machinery was applied to industry and the mill and factory took the place of the country blacksmith shop; when the workers were divorced from their tools and recruited in the mills; when they were obliged to compete against each other for employment; when they found themselves in the labor market with but a low bid or none at all upon their labor power; when they began to realize that as tool-less workingmen they were at the mercy of the tool-owning masters, the necessity for union among them took root, and as industry developed, the trade union movement followed in its wake and became a factor in the struggle of the workers against the aggressions of their employers.

I have seen no better description of the bitter roots of capitalism and the need for an opposing organization to fight against its human consequences. The disease lies in the private ownership of my bread, with one class of men saying how much I shall eat and how much my children shall eat.

The machinery of capitalism is rotten to the core. Capitalism is owned lock, stock and barrel by the ruling class. The upper class owns the wealth while the masses are impoverished. It is reason enough for a socialist, not a capitalist, society. But it is folly to believe that socialism can ever become an acceptable alternative in America.

I realize that socialism scares most Americans. Socialism is forever stained by our tainted picture of it as practiced by the despots of medieval Europe. In this country too many people see socialism as anti-American. But, rather, it is *capitalism* that is anti-American. Capitalism works against every ideal of American democracy – freedom, individualism, equal opportunity, equal rights for all, not just the ruling class.

Eugene Debs saw this as he studied socialism in jail, and from that point on he devoted his life to the cause of working people and the socialist ideal.

I never fully embraced the ideals of socialism, but I did agree with some of its philosophies when it came to the rights of working men and women.

And so, I became a strong supporter of Eugene Debs wherever he fought for the American worker. You will see that later in my story when I stand on the platform with Eugene Debs in 1905 at the founding convention of the Industrial Workers of the World. Though Eugene Debs often drew the disfavor of the American public with his extreme and open views, I will support him for the remainder of our parallel careers. You'll see.

Meanwhile, because my work at this time is concentrated heavily on helping coal miners, it seems to me that my best opportunity to borrow strength is from the young United Mine Workers.

So here I sit on a train bound for West Virginia in the grips of coal mine capitalists.

In its first ten years the UMW has successfully organized miners in Pennsylvania, Ohio, Indiana and Illinois. Attempts to organize West Virginia, however, failed in 1892, 1894, 1895 and 1897.

I am told at this time that there are an estimated twenty-three thousand miners in West Virginia and only a few more than two hundred are union members. What's more, I'm told the rest are afraid to join.

How could this be so when West Virginia mine owners pay the lowest wages in the country, forty-three cents per ton, an average of two hundred and seventy five dollars per year. In

Indiana miners are paid more than twice that at eighty-eight cents per ton.

From each paycheck, the companies deduct two ton of coal for house rent, two ton for the company doctor, two ton for water and several ton for credits owed the company store. Often times, miners go home on payday without any pay in their pockets.

Do these men have no self-respect? Will I really gain strength by representing a big organization like the UMW? I'm about to find out. The job of organizing West Virginia belongs to me.

Chapter Twenty-Three
Southern West Virginia ~ October, 1901

I have been sent to West Virginia to spread the union's message in the coalfields of the southern part of the state. The mines there are scattered up and down every hill and hollow of the rugged Appalachian mountain chain. The only way into a mining camp is on foot and most often, the land, the road and the railroad right-of-way are owned by the mine and guarded by company gunmen.

You wouldn't believe some of the things I experience.

At one point I decide that the streams flowing through those lands are public property and so I wade up them to reach the camps and spread the messages of the UMW.

During many of my treks I am threatened at gunpoint, carried bodily down the mountain and thrown in jail just for talking to those miners and their families.

One time, when a guard aims a Gatling gun at me, I climb up out of the creek and stick my finger in one of the barrels, the one lined up to fire first. There are six barrels on a Gatling gun that rotate as they fire. It's not exactly a machine gun. It's like six guns firing one after the other in rapid succession.

I am not intimidated.

"I have five hundred men up in those woods behind me," I say, "and if you shoot me with that thing, they'll shoot you full of holes before you can turn tail." There are no men up there, but the gunman doesn't know that. He twists the wheels that carry that gun clean around and hightails it out of there.

I don't need to repeat to you the working conditions I find in those isolated mountain camps, except to say that the miners and their families are totally cut off from civilization.

Many of the young boys in those camps are brought into the world by the company doctor, attend the company school, pick slate from coal as mere children, enter manhood through the mouth of a company mine and too often end up buried by the company undertaker before they are old enough to shave. Many of them die from a mining accident or of consumption without ever seeing the outside world.

—◆◆◆—

Now I'm working with a brave union organizer by the name of John Walker who, like myself, is from Illinois and a stranger in these parts. We have formed a close personal relationship that will carry us through untold dangers throughout the coalfields of West Virginia.

At night, during our early days, John and I often sneak up near a coal mine to hold an informational meeting after dark. The scene is usually only lighted by an oil lantern we bring. Sometimes the moon and stars above help, but not in the deep woods where even the sun doesn't shine.

People come from all over to hear me. Those meetings often last for several hours. Afterward, John and I pick our way back down the mountain in the middle of the night, using our oil lantern to light the way.

In 1902, John and I work our way up and down both sides of the New River. We hold meetings and organize men into union chapters in Smithersfield, Long Acre, Anilton and Boomer.

It is neither easy nor safe. During our travels along the river, men who join the union are blacklisted by coal mine operators. Their families are thrown out of their company shacks. Men are beaten and shot. Many disappear without a trace. They need courage or a sense of desperation to join our cause.

—◆◆◆—

After a meeting we hold at Mount Hope, John and I go back to our boarding house, late as usual. We aren't there long when there comes a tap at our door.

"Come in," says I.

A tall, lean miner enters the room, bent over and coughing between his words, trying to clear the black coal dust from his lungs.

"Mother," says he. "There are twelve of us out in front of this boarding house. We liked your speech tonight but the bigwigs at the national UMW office already told us we should only go about educating our men, not organizing yet. We have been told that would come later.

"But we don't want to wait, Mother. We want to organize now. We're reckoning we might be dead from coal mining before 'later' comes and we want to organize now, before we die."

"Well," says I, "there are twelve of you. That's the same number of disciples Jesus had and it was enough for him. It surely is enough for you. And it's enough for me. I just hope there isn't a Judas among you."

"I guess, like Jesus, that's the chance we'll have to take, ma'am, but I believe we have twelve good men and we're ready to recruit an army."

I have him bring the other men into the room, get the paperwork out of my union kit and sign those boys up. As they have no money for their charter or dues I say, "I'll take care of that. Don't you worry.

"Now boys," says I, "you go back up there to the camp and you preach the gospel of better food, better homes and decent compensation for the wealth you produce. Your Maker will bless you for it."

Three weeks later I receive a letter from one of the group. It says the leader is dead of miner's consumption. But before he died the letter says, he and his men recruited eight hundred more. Stuffed in the envelope is money to pay back what I had contributed for their charter. I guess the dues from the eight hundred men will have to wait.

—◆◆◆—

Once, when I visit a camp on Caperton Mountain, I'm told a story about seven union organizers who were sent up Laurel Creek. All came back shot at, beaten up and run out of town.

"Mother," says the man who saw it, "you mustn't go up there. They've got gunmen patrolling the roads."

"If they've got gunmen patrolling the roads," says I, "then the miners are prisoners and they need me."

A week later, on a Saturday night, I hike up to Thayer with a group of children and trapper boys who work inside the mines. We camp there, about six miles from Laurel Creek, for the night and on Sunday, I climb on up behind the camp to look down on its scattering of dirty shacks.

I sit down on a rock above that camp and tell the trapper boys, "Now I want six of you children to go down to the camp and tell every miner you see that Mother Jones is up here and she wants to see them. Tell them I am going to speak at two o'clock. And tell the mine boss that Mother Jones extends a cordial invitation for him to come along."

As cruel as mine operators are to the working man, Sunday is still observed as a day of rest, the only day of respite for these miners. The only chance many of them have to see the sun. I expect I will have a good-sized crowd around my rock by afternoon.

Meanwhile I send two other boys down to a nearby log cabin to get me a cup of tea. I see them enter the cabin and moments later a man steps outside and beckons me to come down to the cabin.

As I step through the door, my eyes fall on a straw mattress on which rests a beautiful young girl. She has the gentlest eyes I have ever seen. But they are sad eyes. I see in them a desperate illness.

"What is wrong with this girl?" I ask the man.

"I don't know," says he. "Too much work I reckon. I couldn't earn enough in the mines and so my daughter went to work in the boarding house. They worked her so hard she took sick."

Around a fireplace with a small fire in it sits a group of dirty children, ragged and neglected-looking. I learn from the man that his wife is dead and so he fixes my tea and pulls a few cookies from a tin.

That afternoon a great crowd comes up the mountain. The mine boss doesn't come but he sends a lackey instead. The miners tell me that this black man was sent to spy and I say to the man, "See here, young man. Don't you know that the immortal Abraham Lincoln — a white man — gave you freedom from slavery? Why do you now betray your white brothers who fought for you then and who are fighting for you now to free you from industrial slavery?"

"I have to stay here for the meetin'," the man says, "but I understand what you're sayin' to me. Let's just say my hearing and my eyesight ain't very good today. Don't you be worrin' 'bout me. I ain't gonna have much to report."

That afternoon we organize a strong group of newly joined union men.

The next day the man who had served me the tea in his cabin is stopped at the mine and told to go to the office to get his last pay and settle up what he owes the company. The boss tells him no man can work for him who entertains agitators in his home or joins a union.

When he returns to his shack to pack up, his daughter guesses the problem. "Father," she sobs, "you have lost your job." Her sobs bring on a coughing fit from which she falls back on the pillow. Dead.

I am able to get this man a job with the United Mine Workers and he makes one of the most faithful organizers I have ever known. The rest of the new union miners are also fired but it doesn't matter because they've already walked off the job and they go on to hold one of the finest strikes seen anywhere in these mountains.

—◆◆◆—

I have hundreds of heartbreaking stories I could tell you from my early days in West Virginia. But by February of 1902, I can see a few rays of sunshine beginning to break through in southern West Virginia. Two new chapters of the UMW have formed in the Kanawha River Valley.

In Thurmond, a crowd of three hundred miners meets my train; they clasp my hands and ask me to stay with them while they fight for the rights of the coal miners of that region. They have their UMW buttons on and they're not afraid or ashamed to wear them. Their enthusiasm is a harbinger of things to come.

Chapter Twenty-Four
Northern West Virginia ~ October, 1902

Things are not going so well in the coalfields of Northern West Virginia and UMW President John Mitchell sends for me to help up there. I take my faithful friend and cohort, John Walker, with me.

The Fairmont Coal Company controls all the mines for fifteen miles along the West Fork River near Fairmont and the Clarksburg Fuel Company controls the mines in the hills near Clarksburg. It seems like they employ more gunmen than they do coal miners.

One of our first meetings takes place in a little mining town in the Fairmont District. When we arrive there I ask the local organizer where I am to speak and he points to a frame building that turns out to be a church.

It is a Sunday afternoon and it appears services concluded not too long before. There are lighted candles on the altar and fresh flowers all around. The miners are all sitting quietly in the pews.

I notice the preacher at a small table off in one corner, counting money.

"What's going on here?" I demand of the organizer.

"Well," says he, "we're going to hold a meeting."

"What for?" I demand.

"For the union, Mother. We rented the church for a union meeting. You are our speaker."

I walk over to that preacher and say, "Preacher, what are you doing there?"

"I'm counting the money your union man gave me for the rent of this church," says he.

I grab the money from his hand and say, "Preacher man, you ought to be ashamed of yourself for turning this house of God into a commercial enterprise! There will be no union meeting here today or any other day as long as I have something to say about it."

I go back to the union man and say, "Sir, this is a house of God, not a proper place for a union meeting. I have some things to say today that God would not want to hear in His own house.

I turn to the miners in the pews.

"Boys, I want you to get up, every one of you, and go across the road. I want you to sit down on the hillside over there and wait for me to speak to you. Do it now!"

Beside us on that hillside is a schoolhouse and I point to it and say, "Your ancestors fought for you to have a share in that schoolhouse. It belongs to you. It's yours and it's there as a place of education, not of worship. A union is an educational organization, not a religious organization. From now on I want you to arrange for your meetings in that schoolhouse.

"You get the school board to have that schoolhouse open for your meetings every Friday night and you have your wives clean it up every Saturday so as the children can enter a clean schoolhouse on Monday.

"On Sunday mornings you can go to that praying institution over there. But on Friday nights you are attending meetings of a fighting institution and the proper place for a fighting institution is in a schoolhouse where you can learn what you are fighting for."

I end my tirade with a version of my favorite saying, "Pray for the dead over there and fight like hell for the living over here."

—◆◆◆—

Small but deadly private wars are going on all over the state. So many I cannot possibly get to them all. But in spite of the fighting, I realize these isolated battles are never going to accomplish our goals. What West Virginia needs is an all-out campaign.

I correspond with UMW President John Mitchell along those lines and on June 7, 1902 he calls a statewide strike for better pay and shorter hours. I am elated. But, Mitchell's declaration turns out to be just words. The union sends no more help to wage such a war — no people, no money.

The day after the strike is declared I take part in a rambling march from Flemington to Grafton in the heart of the Fairmont Coal Company holdings. Several people are listening to me speak at a school near a strikers' camp when the sheriff comes by, arrests the strike leader and places a ban on meetings in Taylor County. I take over in the leader's stead and keep right on meeting. The sheriff doesn't have the guts to arrest an old woman.

Later that week I travel to Parkersburg at the southern end of the Clarksburg field. The mine owners in that area have already gotten a judge to ban meetings there, but of course, that doesn't stop me.

On June 20, ironically the state's birthday, I am condemning the actions of Judge John Jay Jackson using my strongest God-fearing words when a federal marshal comes to the platform and says I am under arrest for defying the judge's order.

"I'll be right with you," says I, "but you've got to wait until I run down." I keep right on speaking with roars of approval from the men ringing in my ears. I conclude: "Goodbye, boys. I'm under arrest. I may have to go to jail. I may not see you for a long time. You keep up this fight and pay no attention to that scab judge."

The marshal arrests me and eleven other organizers. They put the others in jail but they attempt to take me to a hotel instead. I refuse to go.

"I'm not going to no hotel when my brothers are in jail," says I. But they have no place in the jail for a woman and so the jailer takes me to his residence beside the jail. He and his wife treat me like family until the trial.

At the trial the prosecutor calls me "the most dangerous woman in the country today." I want to thank him, but Judge Jackson, feeling the heat from what the newspapers have printed that morning about the arrest of an old woman, rebukes the prosecutor and says he might release me if I will agree to abandon my strike activities and leave the state.

"All the devils in hell could not cause me to give up the fight," I says.

He releases me anyway. Free without bail until my trial can be continued, I get the feeling there'll be no more trial in Judge Jackson's court.

—◆◆◆—

Free as birds, John and I decide to go immediately to Indiana where the UMW is holding its national convention. I want to argue for better funding for the West Virginia statewide strike.

I get up on the stage there and describe life as a coal miner in West Virginia. I tell them about the gallant battles going on there. And I tell them they must approve more money and send more union organizers to bring the statewide strike to a successful conclusion.

Others, however, argue for more concentration on the coalfields of Ohio and Pennsylvania. In the end, the UMW votes to put their resources there.

I am furious with the UMW. Even though those poor excuses for union leaders have agreed to a statewide strike in West Virginia they have failed to provide the support we need to carry it out. My loyalty to the UMW is slipping.

Still, my boys in West Virginia need me and I am not afraid to go to jail for them. I returned to Parkersburg and insist I want to stand trial.

Judge Jackson makes no bones about his sympathy for the mine operators but he doesn't send me to jail because he doesn't want me to use jail as a means of working up sympathy for myself, and my cause. He apparently has become familiar with my methods.

"I am warning you not to take part in any more strike activities," says the judge. "If you are going to stay in West Virginia, I suggest you consider charity work."

"I already do charity work," says I. "My charity is the union miner and my work is to get him a decent wage and a better working condition. But I have a forgiving heart, Judge Jackson. We are both old and don't have long to live. I pray we die good friends and that we meet again in Heaven."

"I doubt, Mother Jones, that you and I will meet in the afterlife," he says with a grin. "I doubt we will both be in the same place."

The crowd laughs heartily at that and I figure everyone is wondering which of the places Judge Jackson and Mother Jones will be in.

I return to the coalfields, encouraging strikers in the New River and Kanawha River valleys of Southern West Virginia. I comfort the widows and children of seven miners who have been brutally murdered at a coal camp near Stanaford Mountain. I fight alongside the miners in the Kanawha Valley until seven thousand miners in that region win improvement in working conditions as well as a shorter workday, nine hours instead of twelve to fourteen.

It is the only success in the statewide strike that comes to an end in 1903 with the rest of the miners, living and dead, having nothing to show for it. Wages remain unconscionably low, the workday for them remains long and the cost of living higher than anywhere else due to the prices charged by the mine operator's predatory company stores.

I blame the union for the loss, the men in their pinstriped suits and their partying at the convention in Indiana.

Chapter Twenty-Five
Philadelphia, Pennsylvania ~ Spring, 1903

With the coal war senselessly lost in West Virginia, my anger at the failure of the United Mine Workers to back the courageous men and women in that state has made me positively ill. I am sick of the UMW and I am sick of the coal wars. I'm thinking about taking a rest.

But then I hear about a strike in the Kensington area on the outskirts of Philadelphia involving between seventy-five thousand and one hundred twenty-five thousand textile workers. One report estimates ten to fifteen thousand of them are children.

The Textile Workers Union is striking for more pay and less hours, while six hundred mill owners are proposing less pay and more hours. One story says the workers have proposed a compromise, agreeing to less pay if they also work less hours. The mills don't like that idea very much.

What worries me most, however, is that nothing I read seems to include concern for the child labor issue. I'm wondering if that is an oversight by the press? Or does the textile union not care about child labor? Given my experience in mines and mills, I fear the children of the mills aren't getting much representation in this fight.

And so, my brothers on the railroad give me a ride to Philadelphia.

—◆◆◆—

Technically I am still an employee of the United Mine Workers, but I have notified President Mitchell that I am taking a leave of absence from the coalfields and he does not need to be sending me a paycheck for awhile.

"You're mad, aren't you, Mother Jones."

"You're damned right I'm mad, John. You led those miners in West Virginia to the slaughter house and then you just left 'em high and dry. If you weren't going to back them, you shouldn't have declared the statewide strike.

"You'll play hell ever organizing the UMW in West Virginia again."

"And so you're quitting the union?"

"No. Not yet. But right now my sights are fixed on the textile mills of Kensington and my mind is back on the business of child labor. When I'm finished up there in Philadelphia I'll let you know and we'll see if there's still a future for me with the UMW."

"Fair enough, Mother Jones. If anyone asks, can I say that you're still with us then?"

"Yes, just tell them I'm on a leave of absence to fight this battle in Philadelphia. It's the truth."

I sleep all night on the train and seek out the Textile Workers Union headquarters the minute I step onto the railroad platform in Philadelphia the next morning.

"Who's the boss?" I ask as I walk through the door.

The young woman says the boss' name.

"Is he here?"

"Yes."

"Well tell him Mother Jones is here too."

"You're his mother?"

"You don't know me, do you? Well, I'm everyone's mother. Now tell him I'm here and I'm in a big hurry."

She frowns but then walks down a hall behind her desk. It doesn't seem like it's been a minute before a man appears from where she disappears.

"Mother Jones? Is it really you? What an honor! Welcome. Welcome." He blubbers some more and I ask if there's somewhere we can talk. He takes me to his office.

"What brings you here, Mother?"

"I might be here to help you," says I. "It all depends on the answers I get to my questions."

"What questions?"

"I have lots of questions, but I'll ask my most important one first. What are your strike demands with respect to child workers?"

"Well," and he thinks a minute. "There isn't anything specific in our strike demands with reference to children. If they're working in our mills, then they stand to gain as much from a settlement as anyone else."

Now I think a minute.

I find my voice. "I have read that children make up as much as fifteen to twenty percent of the workforce here in the textile mills of Pennsylvania. Children. Not young adults. Underage kids. Is that so?"

"It's a fact, Mother."

"And does your union support the wanton abuse of little children? Do you think it's right?"

"Well, we've never really discussed it, so I'm not sure I have an answer for you there, Mother."

"Are you telling me that little children don't come into your union headquarters every day, bleeding with cuts, missing fingers and hands? Stooped little things with their shoulders round and their bodies skinny?"

"Well," he thinks again. "Yes, and we do our best for them. We have a union doctor here who looks after them and it doesn't cost them a cent."

"But there's no talk about stopping the harm that's coming to these little children in the name of profit for the moneyed class? Is there?"

My head is about to explode. I lower my voice. I always lower my voice when I am angry.

"I want you to call a meeting for tomorrow night. I want you to send personal invitations to all of your officials and anyone else you might think should listen in. Just tell them they are going to meet Mother Jones who has some things to say before she decides whether she stays here to help you with your strike."

He frets awhile. "I don't know as how I can do that, Mother."

"All right then," says I. "Call them day *after* tomorrow and explain that Mother Jones was here, but she left because you couldn't get a meeting together fast enough."

Silence. I get up.

"I'll see you tomorrow night," says I. "I'll be here at nine o'clock."

—◆◆◆—

At the appointed hour the next night a sizeable gathering awaits me. I come in wearing my usual black dress with white frills and my sometimes best grandmotherly smile. My demeanor is considerably improved from yesterday. I'm sorry I was so mean yesterday and I realize I was taking my frustrations with John Mitchell and the UMW out on the leader of another union.

More importantly, I reasoned overnight that I would not get what I wanted from this group by bullying and bludgeoning them. Persuasion. That's the ticket. I've been told persuasion gets the best results. I'll try it.

"Good evening, Mother Jones," says a nice middle-aged man still in his work clothes. "I am president of this chapter of the Textile Worker's Union. We all know of the wonderful work you are doing for the working men across this country and we are honored to have you visit us at this time."

"Thank you," says I, "and I thank your leader over there for organizing this meeting on such short notice. Thank you, young man."

The man I abused yesterday looks stunned.

I go on to explain the purpose of my visit, which is to find out if I can help in their great fight against the greed of textile capitalists in this city and its surrounds.

They aren't as concerned about the mill children as I am, but they like my arguments. I tell them I will use the mill children to gain public support for their general cause, which, in turn, will raise lots of money to support the strikers. I'm sure the workers are already hurting for money or they would not be considering compromising with the mill owners so soon.

As a result of my persuasive reasoning, they vote to add the child labor issue to their list.

After the meeting, the chapter president pulls me aside and in a low voice says, "Mother, I have to tell you that this child labor thing will be a bit touchy for our members."

"How so?" says I. Already I suspect the answer.

"It's like this, Mother. Most of those child laborers are sons and daughters of mill workers, coal miners and their wives. These parents are unhappy and ashamed but they also have desperate reasons for why they allow their children to be used as cheap laborers in the mills.

It's bad enough when a miner or a mill worker can't earn enough to support his family, but it's even worse when the father dies and the mother becomes the sole support of her children."

"So you're saying if laws are passed to regulate child labor, it will hurt your members."

"It is a fact of life, Mother Jones."

It is clear to me then that from the start I have two foes. One, the mill owners. Two, the facts of life.

It is not a surprise to me. I have seen these facts of life at work in every mining camp I have visited, and as you know, it was made abundantly clear to me when I snuck out of that Carolina mill town with my tail between my legs several years ago.

But these facts of life don't make things right. The right answer is to remove these young children from the mills and pay wages to adult workers that are sufficient enough to support a family. Sufficient enough to keep the children in school learning, preparing themselves for a *better* life, not the *facts* of life.

Immediately I propose a March of the Mill Children from Kensington, Philadelphia, to Madison Square Garden in New York City. They will hike one hundred twenty-five miles through some of the region's largest industrial areas to protest the enslavement of young children by an economic system that prevents a working man from earning a salary that provide sufficient monies to support a family and keep his kids in school where they belong.

I conscript recruiters from the rank and file and send them out to find men, women and children — especially children — who are on strike and willing to follow me on this great adventure.

Surprisingly, many mothers and fathers whose children are child laborers, come and volunteer to join me on the march. These parents are indeed ashamed, but courageous enough to do what it takes to fight their way back to respectability.

One of the unfortunate victims of child labor who volunteers is young Gus Rangnow who works six days a week, eleven hours a day, packing stockings in a Kensington hosiery factory. Gus is a mere boy who works too long and sleeps too little. His tired face makes him look like an old man.

"I'm not sure I can walk that far," he says, "but I'll sure give it a go."

James Ashworth, who is only ten years old, is another consequence of capitalistic greed. He is stooped over like an old man from carrying bundles of yarn that weigh seventy-five pounds apiece. His pay is three dollars a week and his sister, who is fourteen, works for six dollars a week. They are children of the lower class who are wasting away in a carpet factory ten hours a day so the children of the upper class can get an education.

In the 1900 U.S. Census, twenty-six percent of male children and ten percent of female children between the ages of ten and fifteen are gainfully employed for a total of about one and three-quarter million child laborers in the workplace. A *New York Times* article claims that due to the keeping of family secrets, the count is underestimated and that the figure is somewhere between two and three million.

In Pennsylvania, there are over one million children of school age but more than three hundred thousand of them are unaccounted for.

I can account for them. They are in the workplace. Children of the wealthy class are receiving more and more education, delaying their careers until they are in their mid-twenties, while children of the working class are increasingly missing an education altogether, starting their careers in sweatshops before they reach puberty.

People need to see these pathetic children, I'm thinking. Our march will shock the citizens along the way, and the newspapers will spread our stories across the country — and the world.

Chapter Twenty-Six
Philadelphia City Hall ~ July 7, 1903

In the morning, I arrive at our meeting place where my army of about one hundred adults and two hundred mill children have assembled on the steps of city hall, just as I have instructed them. On the street, a few hundred interested citizens and curious bystanders look on.

Some of the school children carry signs that read: "We want to go to schools, not hospitals" and "All we want for Christmas is justice."

There is a cluster of newspaper reporters in front of the gathering crowd and it is to them I go first.

"I'm glad to see you here, boys," says I. "It's about time you write something about these poor children and their imprisonment in the mills and factories here in Philadelphia and all across this nation. Why haven't you done it before?"

"We want to," says one, "but those capitalists you speak of own most of the stock in the newspapers and the editors won't print stories like that."

"Well," says I in my most civil voice, "my stock is in these mill children and I intend to create such a spectacle in the next few days that the press won't be able to ignore it. You'll get your stories printed because too many people between here and New York will have first-hand knowledge about our march and what it stands for. They'll be looking for your stories in the newspapers and your censors won't dare try to keep the plight of these children a secret any longer.

"The people will know the truth about the children and if they don't see your stories in the newspapers, they'll see the bias in the press and that won't sell newspapers. The people will know

which newspapers aid and abet the terrible treatment of these
mill children and their parents by the way they are hiding the
behavior of the profit-mongers of industrial America."

Then I walk up through the first few rows of my assembled
army of marchers, taking with me a few of the worst-case mill
children. When I reach a point where I can be seen, surrounded
by children even shorter than me, I begin raising their arms,
one by one, showing the onlookers their mangled and missing
fingers and hands. I call attention to their bent bodies and their
aged faces.

"The barons and baronesses in Philadelphia's mansions wear
fancy clothes and walk on plush carpets manufactured at the
expense of these children's broken bones and quivering hearts,"
I begin.

"That's right, you photographers, move in real close and get
pictures of these broken children for they are the evidence of an
economic system gone mad."

I go on to explain why these young children are forced into
economic servitude.

"You see before you broken adults as well as children. These
good people are the mothers and fathers of these children and
they represent thousands upon thousands of families and
children like them.

"They are sorely ashamed of the facts of their lives, that they
themselves are paid such poor wages by the mills and factories
of this community, that they cannot keep decent food upon their
tables, or keep themselves decently clothed.

"They can't even afford to send their children to school to
better themselves, to build a foundation upon which to make a
better future for the next generation.

"They are forced to cut the childhoods of these youngsters
short, to take their precious children with them to the sweatshops,

because they can't leave them home alone and they need the extra money their children can raise in the factory in order for the family to survive."

"You ask why they've gone on strike? Because they're mad as hell! This is not the land of promise and plenty they were expecting when their forefathers fought against the tyrants of Europe and the enslavers of America. The Civil War may have been a victory for freedom, but capitalism has turned freedom for blacks and whites into economic slavery.

"But you make no mistake about it. They may be broken but they are not beaten! They will be heard and they will arise from the depths of servitude to claim their rightful places as self-respecting Americans."

The next day the Philadelphia press is full of stories about what I said directly to the press and then to the crowd. After our meeting yesterday, reporters descended on our army of parents and mill children, got their stories first-hand, and printed them in the morning papers.

Today we assemble again, this time in Independence Park across from city hall to be greeted by a much larger crowd. Again I raise the arms of crippled children. I say their lives are being snuffed out by the pursuit of the almighty dollar. I accuse officials standing over there in the windows of city hall of wearing some of the blame for the puny arms of the mill children because neither city nor state officials have lifted a finger to stop the abuse. I see people shrinking back from the office windows.

I call upon the millionaire manufacturers to cease their immoral maiming and murdering. I turn and cry up to the city officials who are now hiding in the shadows: "Some day the workers will take possession of your city hall. And when they do, no child will be sacrificed on the altar of profit."

By the time we reach the city limits I am losing some of the parents and their children because of shame and poor health. Some of the parents are uncomfortable with what I am saying about them in public, with them right there. We are all becoming aware that some of these children are just too sickly to make the trip, which is just getting started.

I understand all that, but I also understand that the attention we are getting in the press is worth the pain. Most of my adult and child soldiers think so too and we still have a decent-sized army when we leave the city on the first leg of our journey.

The Textile Workers Union owns an automobile and they lend it and a driver to me so I can speed ahead of the march each day to alert people of those coming and make arrangements for meeting and camping places, food, water and better lodging for the frail among us. The car looks just like a buggy but it requires no horse and it makes good speed.

Even though the horseless carriage is a necessity, it is also a source of discontent among some of the marchers. Their days are spent walking in one hundred degree heat and breathing the dust and dirt of traffic and surrounding factories. In the midst of all of that, they see me holding onto my bonnet while I bounce off in an automobile.

I'm sure they are wondering why I'm not marching along with the rest of them. I join the march when I can and explain what I'm doing and why I'm doing it. Most of them understand.

I want to be with them on the march. I surely do. Some of my most satisfying times have been spent hiking through the woods of West Virginia, sometimes camping overnight. Staying with striking families in tents and lean-tos. I'd much rather be walking with them than bouncing back and forth in my borrowed contraption.

But my duty is to go ahead of the marchers. Solicit food supplies, water and other necessities. Talk with police and local

officials in every town. Secure meeting places and resting places.
Get the word out about the meetings. Get local union organizers
to promote attendance. Stir the interests of the press.

We're fairly well-equipped for this march. The children carry
knapsacks on their backs, each with a knife, fork, tin cup and
plate inside. Also other personal necessities. They have bedrolls
strapped on top of their knapsacks. They look like human mules.
We do have a mule to pull a wagon containing a boiler in which
to cook food on the road.

One little fellow has a drum and another has a fife. They are
our marching band.

Unlike the adults, the children are having the time of their
lives. Until now, their only travel has been between their homes
and workplaces. They have never camped out like this, never
gazed at the stars at night or the birds and bees by day. They've
never swum in a stream.

A few of them, however, are in such poor health that they
sometimes have to be carried and I secure lodging for them in
boarding houses, hotels or private homes along the way.

Some of the children have to drop out of the march because
their parents think the march is just too hard on them. I
understand. Some accuse me of exploiting the children just like
the employers we're protesting. I wince at those arrows when
they strike my heart but I don't accept the accusation.

Nevertheless, I arrange transportation back to Philadelphia
for the dropouts. These laggards are a burden, not a help. In some
cases I even encourage the malcontents to go home.

After the first couple of days, the number of marchers isn't as
important as the number of people who turn out for our rallies.
Crowds are growing larger every day. We are generating very
positive publicity.

A reporter with the *Philadelphia North American* is actually marching with our army and he stays with us the entire way. He files his first story on July 7 and includes pictures of our children's army carrying mannequins, effigies of "Mr. Capital" and "Mrs. Mill Owner."

His reports are getting picked up by other newspapers and that prompts still other papers to send their own reporters, including pundits from the big New York City press. The Philadelphia papers are already on the newsstands in the city of New York, forcing that city's papers to compete for more exclusive stories.

I arrive in advance to placate authorities in every community as the children's army approaches. On July 9, our traveling newspaper reporter describes our march into Bristol, Pennsylvania, with its five mills and twenty-five hundred workers.

At first, I have trouble with the Bristol authorities, who are in the pockets of the mill owners. But when our troops arrive, they are led by the town's marching band. More than two thousand people hear me speak and we collect a generous amount in donations. The money rejuvenates the marching parents.

On the same day I give a speech to the Plumbers' Union in Morrisville, Pennsylvania.

During my advance visit to Trenton, New Jersey, where I've crossed the Delaware River, the mayor refuses entry for the marchers. But he finally agrees to permit a meeting in Monument Park. By the time the marchers arrive, their numbers are down to around one hundred, but the crowd is estimated at five thousand people. Trenton is a union town.

The following day we go to Princeton, the home of a great learning institution and I address the students by explaining how the other half lives. We go to the residence of former U.S. President Grover Cleveland, who is away. But the caretaker of the residence is a gracious host and provides us shelter for the night.

On July 14, our army reaches New Brunswick, New Jersey, after a dusty week on the road. Men bunk in an empty meeting hall while a handful of women stay with me in the City Hotel. The last two of our young girls have returned home.

In Rahway, New Jersey, on the following day, we receive an enthusiastic welcome. To keep advance publicity going, I announce that our destination has been extended to go beyond Madison Square Garden. From that great hall we will go with the children to see President Roosevelt, who is vacationing at his summer home at Oyster Bay, Long Island.

I say I plan to have some of the children in tow when I urge the president to ask Congress to pass a law prohibiting the exploitation of childhood. I say I'm expecting Mr. Roosevelt might compare these children, when he sees them, to his own children on the playgrounds of Oyster Bay.

The suspense this creates intensifies the coverage we're getting in the newspapers, which helps union organizers who are now working with me ahead of our route to get the crowds out.

On July 17, I have time to be with the marchers. A news photographer gets a shot of me cooking pork and beans in our steam pot for my army which is now camped in Elizabeth, New Jersey.

On July 23, our little army reaches one of the bridges to Manhattan Island. There are only about fifty of us now with only a few boys from the mills. We are met at the bridge by a sizeable police force and we are informed that New York City Mayor Seth Low has ordered the police to prevent us from crossing into the city.

"Does that order refer to our group or does it prevent me as a single person to walk over that bridge?"

"The order is against your group," the police spokesman says.

"All right then," says I. "My followers will stay on this side while I go over there and talk to the mayor."

"Well, ma'am, we will allow you to cross the bridge, but I can't imagine the mayor will see you."

"Well," says I, "you don't have the imagination I've got."

My imagination turns out to be better than the policeman's. My arrival at city hall is expected and I am ushered right in to Mayor Low's office. We exchange pleasantries.

"Mr. Mayor," says I, "they say you have forbidden my children's army to cross the bridge into Manhattan. I am very disturbed about that, but I am also surprised.

"I thought you were elected on an anti-Tammany Hall platform. I thought you are the mayor who is cleaning up graft in city government. I thought you are the mayor who just announced a new civil service system that will hire municipal employees on the basis of merit, not political patronage. That sounds like the work of a union man to me."

"Thank you, Mother Jones. I *am* a union man. I am very concerned about labor issues. I support collective bargaining but I favor arbitration over strikes."

"Well, then," says I, "why on earth have you blocked the march of the mill children from entering your city?"

"I didn't do that directly, Mother. I simply told the police commissioner that I was fearful of the political unrest you bring to this city when the fight you are fighting is not here but in Philadelphia. You and your followers are not citizens of New York and your quarrel does not belong here."

"I am a citizen of this country," I declare, "and Mr. Mayor, tonight I will be a citizen of this city when I put my shoes under my bed. The courageous men, women and children who are with me are also citizens of this country and will be sleeping near their shoes too. I want them with me tonight, here, in the city of New York. We are all American citizens."

With a bit more banter during which we both agree on the futility of violence, the mayor, who is also the president of

Columbia University, shows his wisdom as a thinking man and orders the police commissioner to convert his roadblock into an honor guard to escort our marchers into town.

The mayor cannot, however, get me the use of Madison Square Garden as it is already booked for another event. Instead, he has the police cordon off a large area of Madison Avenue where the newspapers report that fifteen hundred people attend my speech about child labor and sweat shops.

Afterward, I deliver the same speech to another thousand people at Coney Island where there is a special exhibit of lions and tigers. I have three of our most pitiful children, those who are stooped over from hard labor, placed in an empty cage to pose for pictures. Those photographs are plastered all over the front pages of dozens of news sheets, displayed on the wooden news stands of every corner of New York City.

We complete our day's work early and the children and the parents are given free run of the amusement park by the managers. They sleep right there with the carnies.

—◆◆◆—

The next day it is on to Oyster Bay.

I enter the president's vacation mansion with just three of my marchers, three of my most pathetic and graphic examples of the human exploitation of child labor.

"The president does not meet with people who do not have an appointment," a secretary tells me.

"I made my appointment in the newspapers," says I. "Surely he got the message I was coming."

"The proper way to get an appointment with the president," says the secretary, "is to write a letter."

So, I write a letter, right there and then.

The next day I'm informed in a formal letter from Mr. Roosevelt's appointment secretary that he will not see me or the mill children. There is a note attached from the president saying that neither he nor the Congress has the power to act on behalf of the mill children or the mill workers. These, he claims, are matters which are in the purview of each of the states.

I'm not surprised. It is clear to me, based on my experiences back in West Virginia, that the federal government is still struggling with the issues of federalism versus states' rights.

Americans and their state governments still remember the oppression of colonialism. The Civil War was the country's first major fight over the rights of states and the power of the federal government. Federalism won that war, but, after all these years, governments — national, state and local — are still nervous about maintaining a balance of power.

In my final note, I respond strongly to President Roosevelt: "It is a very sad commentary on the President of our Nation that the plea of suffering little children, who have walked one hundred twenty-five miles to see you, should be turned down."

I point out in my letter that it is ironic that on the same day these children attempt to see him, he is frolicking in Oyster Bay with his sons and nephews, enjoying the kind of leisure time the mill children are pleading for.

Immediately afterward people are saying our march is a failure. I disagree.

We may have failed to get the president and Congress to pass national legislation right away. But, for the first time we have raised the American consciousness, not only to the plight of these mill children, but to that of workers from the underclass in the mills and factories and coal mines all over this country. No message has ever been stronger, before or since. It has taken the story of the mill children to finally get the attention of a here-to-for apathetic nation.

In the following year, the voices of great Americans such as former President Grover Cleveland, Harvard President Charles Eliot, South Carolina Senator Benjamin Tillman, Columbia professor Felix Adler and Jane Addams, Hull House founder, join the newly formed National Child Labor Committee to campaign for reform.

It will take another ten years for Pennsylvania and a few other states to enact child labor laws setting the minimum age at fourteen and another year for the first federal child labor law to be enacted.

The fight for the underclass is not just about battles. It is about hundreds of battles, won and lost, that add up to the conclusion of a war. And this war, if it is ever to be won, will take many more battles.

Chapter Twenty-Seven
Colorado ~ Fall, 1903; Illinois ~ 1902-1904

After the Children's Crusade, I'm not quite ready to return to the mine wars of West Virginia, and so I return to Illinois instead. I suppose I'm thinking I'll take a rest, but I use the home of my friend and dress factory partner Jenny Flynn as my base and respond to as many invitations as I can to assist miners on strike or to give speeches at socialist rallies around the state.

I'm not a card-carrying socialist, but the socialists think of me as one of them because we share similar views regarding the underclass. I do support them because they champion the causes of organized labor and because, as I've said, I have a strong personal relationship with their spiritual leader, Eugene Debs, who is now a socialist candidate for president of the United States.

I am receiving requests from all over the country, but I figure I can accomplish the most by keeping to a circle around Chicago and depending on the Chicago press to generate stories that will be picked up nationwide. Even the radio station in Chicago has a huge broadcast area that reaches beyond the Midwest.

I am still getting a lot of attention from the press and I take advantage of it by using my experiences from the March of the Mill Children to call attention to the wide geography of industrial slavery. Even though, in my local travels I may be speaking in Midwestern towns to Midwesterners, I'm talking about issues that go far beyond these backyards.

Child labor, I say, is an issue wherever industrial greed prevails and that includes Illinois. I emphasize that child labor is the result of an economy built on the backs of economic slaves, good fathers and mothers who are forced to allow the childhoods of their under-aged sons and daughters to be stolen away by the money-mongers of capitalism.

You may be tired of hearing this, but I never tire of saying it and it can't be said often enough.

There are plenty of fights I could be joining around Illinois, but I think I can do the most good by spreading myself from stump to stump, day by day, as a roaming, evangelizing hellraiser.

But then I receive word from UMW president John Mitchell that I am desperately needed in Colorado. He asks me to meet him in Indianapolis so he can fill me in on the situation out there.

When we get together, we don't waste time squabbling about our personal differences. We get right down to the troubles in Colorado, Utah and Idaho. There is no question that I will indeed go out there and join the battle. It is by far the most outrageous conflict between labor and management I've known so far. It dwarfs the struggles I have witnessed in West Virginia. In fact, I see it as preparation for the larger struggles I predict for West Virginia in the not-too-distant future.

—◆◆◆—

I need to take some time to fill you in on the Colorado story before I tell you about my adventures in that state.

Hard rock mining involves valuable metals from nature such as gold, silver, iron, lead, zinc and copper. In Colorado and other western states, gold and silver were the main events in the mid-1800s, but with the dawn of the Industrial Age, the main event became iron ore as well as lead, zinc and copper. And coal, a soft mineral, also became lucrative as fuel.

Individual prospectors may have had no labor problems, but as soon as gold and silver mining became a business, it led to labor-management troubles.

In May, 1893, forty delegates, representing fifteen unions in six western states, formed the Western Federation of Miners. The WFM was prompted by a strike in Coeur d'Alene, Idaho, where military forces locked up six hundred miners without hearings or formal charges.

The following year, mine owners tried to lengthen the workday for miners in Cripple Creek, Colorado, from eight to ten hours a day without raising pay. Another strike occurred, miners intimidated strike breakers and mine owners raised a private army of twelve hundred armed men.

The sheriff deputized the gunmen. Likewise, the miners took up arms.

The Colorado governor went to Cripple Creek, evaluated the issues and agreed to present the miners' case to the mine owners. The owners agreed to back down.

However, the twelve hundred gunmen remained after the sheriff had dismissed them and continued to abuse citizens of Cripple Creek. Many, for no offense at all, were clubbed and kicked, dragged from the sidewalks and forced to walk or run between gauntlets of gunmen.

The governor called out the state militia to protect the coal miners and citizens. The mine owners were forced to admit they were behind the vigilantes and they agreed to disband their private army. A wage and hour agreement went into effect and lasted nearly a decade.

During that decade, the WFM built power that encouraged unionism beyond Cripple Creek. In 1899 a union newspaper began publication. The unions demonstrated their power by electing union members to public office and creating a new county where the mines were located. The new union county passed an eight-hour law and enforced a union scale. Any business that failed to comply with the county wage and hour laws would be forced to do so through social pressure, boycotts and strikes. Non-union products were forbidden on the shelves of saloons and grocery stores.

All seemed well until the mine owners hired Pinkerton guards to prevent miners from stealing high-grade ore. At one mine, three hundred miners walked out to protest the action. The company negotiated and the Pinkerton guards were replaced by guards nominated by the union.

The new agreement stipulated that miners who were suspected of theft would be searched by a fellow miner in the presence of a watchman. To ensure a cooperative work force, mine managers and superintendents urged all miners to join the union.

Outside the Cripple Creek district, however, things were not going so well. Union strikes were being lost and the WFM concluded that the companies and their government lackeys were once again conducting class warfare.

Meanwhile, the WFM's power continued to grow, having appealed directly to the citizens of the state.

The WFM sought adoption of an amendment to the Colorado constitution requiring a minimum eight-hour day which had been earlier deemed unconstitutional by the state supreme court.

The WFM sought to change that constitution and took the issue directly to the people, received bi-partisan support and an amendment was drafted by the Colorado State Legislature for submission to the citizens of Colorado at the next election. It was passed resoundingly by the Colorado voters in 1902 and needed only to be implemented at the next legislative session in 1903.

But the legislature ignored the results of the referendum and allowed the amendment to die.

At the following WFM annual convention, miners agreed to a proclamation that declared a "complete revolution of social and economic conditions was the only salvation of the working classes."

By the spring of 1903, the WFM was the most militant labor organization in the country.

Also in 1903, Republican James Peabody was elected governor on a law and order platform.

He saw the Western Federation of Miners as a threat to his own class interests, to private property, to democratic institutions and to the nation itself. In his inaugural address he promised to make Colorado safe for investors, and he would use all the power of the state to accomplish his aims.

The pendulum in the mining communities of Colorado was swinging back to management's side.

Chapter Twenty-Eight
Denver, Colorado ~ 1904-1905

This then is the history into which I step on a cold winter morning only to be intercepted by a couple of Colorado state militiamen who inform me that they have an order from Governor Peabody for my deportation from the state. They toss me in the back of a police wagon and haul me across the Wyoming border to Cheyenne.

I trudge over to the Cheyenne train station, my head down like a charging bull. When I get there, the Cheyenne-Denver express is waiting almost as if I am expected. I board her, introducing myself as Mother Jones, when the ticket agent inquires. He knows about me from my reputation as a fighter for railroad unions and gives me a wink and a nod. I have never had to pay for a ticket thus far in my life.

I arrive back in Denver, probably before those militiamen return. I go to a hotel, take pen and paper from the front desk and write a note to Governor Peabody. I give it to a messenger to take over to the governor's office at the state capitol.

"You deported me from Colorado," my letter states, "but it is just a few hours later and I'm back. So what are you going to do about that?" I don't wait for an answer and go directly to union headquarters there in Denver, first to the Western Federation of Miners, then the United Mine Workers.

—◆◆◆—

The WFM was formed in 1893 and has been involved in strikes against Colorado hard rock mining companies and their smelters since 1894. Since there was no union in Colorado representing the soft coal industry, some coal miners joined the WFM but their benefits were limited.

The United Mine Workers was established in 1890 at the national level but was not active in Colorado until 1903. Since then, the UMW has conducted a vigorous recruiting effort among coal miners in northern Colorado with reasonable success.

Recruitment by the UMW of miners in the southern fields has been slower. With less union resources devoted to the southern fields, there has been little union organization and no strikes.

—◆◆◆—

Now, in the winter of 1904, I am sent to the southern field, headquartered in Trinidad, Colorado which is down near the border with New Mexico.

When I arrive in Trinidad, it is like I have entered a totalitarian state. Adjutant General Sherman Bell has appointed Major Zeph T. Hill as commander of the militia in Animas County with headquarters in Trinidad. He has imposed a curfew throughout the region, which allows no one on the streets after nine o'clock in the evening unless a person is going to or from work.

Authorities can identify coal miners through an identification scheme called the Bertillon system, which photographs men and prints their pictures, along with personal information, on identification cards. Miners are required to carry the cards at all times, twenty-four hours a day. A copy is kept on file as if these men are criminals. The Bertillon System continues to be used in Colorado even though last year it fell into disgrace when a man was sentenced to Leavenworth where it was discovered through fingerprints that a prisoner already incarcerated shared almost identical Bertillon measurements. It was obvious that fingerprinting was more exact than the Bertillon System.

Women and children aren't required to carry these cards.

Only men who work in the mines, or are union organizers, are forced to carry the cards and so, when I first get to Trinidad, I do not identify myself as a union organizer except to a few UMW representatives and sympathizers. Instead of carrying a card to identify myself, I wear my usual old lady costumes and keep a low profile, posing as a peddler to get a complete look-see at the conditions there.

I carry a sack of pins and needles, elastic and tape and such sundries as a woman would need to make clothing from feed sacks. I visit with the wives of men who work for the Colorado Fuel and Iron Company which dominates mining in the region. While I quiz the women on work and life, I teach them how to sew.

What I learn is completely familiar to me by now. These people are practically slaves to the company, which owns their houses, the land and the company store.

Miners are paid in scrip instead of money so they have no choice but to pay the high prices charged at the only store in town where scrip is accepted as cash.

Their income is limited by more than the amount of the hourly wage. The coal produced by the men is weighed by a company agent without a union check system to verify that miners are getting full credit for the actual tonnage they've produced.

Union organizing is hampered by the curfew system and getting people to attend union meetings is made harder yet by the fear among the workers and their families that the mine bosses might find out.

If they consider joining the union, it is with the understanding that their membership will *be* secret and be *kept* secret. That being the case, what can I say the benefit is of *belonging* to the union? There is no strength in secret unity.

Knowing all this, and since our union is weak in the southern coalfields anyway, I decide to go back to the local office of the Western Federation of Miners in Trinidad where I talk with their president and secretary far into the night. I describe to them what I have found in the coal camps and say I think it is high time the UMW and the WFM join forces and call a statewide strike. They wholeheartedly agree and encourage me to convince the national UMW.

The next morning I take the train east to Indianapolis and meet with President John Mitchell and three other top officers I know well. They readily agree to join hands with the WFM and call a strike. They pat me on the back and admonish me to hurry back to Colorado to get the job done.

Our joint strike gives the coal miners the courage they need, and manages to shut down most of the mines in southern

Colorado, hard rock and soft coal. But it is very difficult to break the stronghold the government has on the strikers in the southern fields. For example, in May of 1904, eighty strikers in Berwind, Colorado, object to the humiliation of the Bertillon system and refuse to be photographed. They are marched by a detail of cavalry for twenty miles to Trinidad in scorching hot sun. During the march they are given nothing to eat or drink and one man, who falls by the roadside, is left lying in the sun to die.

When they get to Trinidad the government forces them to get registered either with the state or with their company, be photographed and required to carry their ID card at all times. If they don't, they will be subject to arrest and jail.

—◆◆◆—

Late one evening I return to my hotel after working all day and into the night, helping strikers and their families. I have been distributing food and clothing, encouraging families and holding meetings under the cover of darkness.

As I am about to snuff my lamp, the hotel clerk knocks on my door and tells me there is a man on the telephone asking for me.

The Trinidad WFM president is on the line. "For God's sake, we have to go up to northern Colorado," he cries.

"What's this all about?" I ask.

"Oh, Mother, don't waste time asking questions. We can't miss the train. They're having a meeting up there in Louisville, Colorado, and they're proposing to settle the strike in the north."

"Who is 'they'?"

"The United Mine Workers."

"But this is a statewide strike," says I. "They can't settle with the northern mines until there's an agreement with the southern miners. They can't desert their brothers down here."

"I know it," he says, "but the trouble isn't with the Colorado miners. It's with the national headquarters. They're going around

us. They're going to order the men back to work in northern
Colorado!"

He is actually speaking to me from the local railroad station
where he is holding the train until I arrive.

When I get there, the local WFM president has gone out to
talk to the conductor, but the other WFM officers I had spoken
with on my first night in Trinidad are waiting for me.

"Mother," one says. "You must *not* get on that train with our
president."

"Why not?"

"Because you must *not* block the settlement with the northern
miners."

"And *why not*?" says I with indignity.

"Because the national president of the United Mine Workers
wants it, and he pays you."

"Are you through?" I glare at him.

He nods.

"Then I am going to tell you that if *God Almighty* wants this
strike called off for *His* benefit, and not for the miners, I am going
to raise my voice against it. And as for John Mitchell paying me,
I've had him take me off the payroll once before for the same
damned reason, and I'll do it again. It is the hard earned money
of the miners that controls me, not blood money."

I board the train and when I sit down beside the betrayed
southern president of the WFM, the only true leader of the bunch,
I grumble, "Such treachery you are receiving from your own
men!" He grimaces.

We arrive in Louisville, Colorado, just in time to attend a
convention of miners that has been called overnight to discuss
the agreement between the union bosses and the coal company
bosses.

I watch their two slick lawyers discuss their mutual agreement. Standing behind them is UMW President John Mitchell. He has recently been toasted, wined and dined by the Denver Citizen's Alliance and the Civic Federation, fine sounding names of organizations that front for the mining companies.

In the afternoon the miners call on me to address the convention.

"Brothers," says I. "You English-speaking miners of the northern fields promised your foreign-speaking southern brothers that you would support them to the end. Now you are told to betray them, to make a separate settlement, leave them high and dry.

"Regardless of the languages you speak, you are all miners. Your fight is against a common enemy, common masters. Your companies are the same companies that use and abuse your brothers north and south. You have a common enemy and it is your duty to fight to the finish. Not for some. Not for yourselves. For all.

"Or you can let them divide you. North to south, language to language.

"I've seen this before in West Virginia and I can tell you this divide-and-conquer strategy is used by your enemy to defeat your brothers and eventually to defeat you by undermining your unions. I don't understand why our union leaders don't see it."

I look directly into the eyes of John Mitchell as I speak.

"This proposal was kept secret from me down in Trinidad until I was informed by a loyal representative of the Western Federation of Miners." I gesture to my companion by way of introduction.

"I am told that I've been accused by some of the members of the national board of the UMW of being more of a representative of the WFM than of the UMW. As if that was a crime.

"If that means I am fighting for the rights of the working man regardless of which union, then I plead guilty. I know no boundaries when it comes to fighting for the working class."

The audience rises and cheers en mass. A vote is taken. The majority decides to stand by the southern miners, refusing to obey the national president. John Mitchell storms from the hall.

—◆◆◆—

Three times Mitchell tries to make the northern miners return to the mines and three times he is unsuccessful. Finally the UMW withdraws all support from the striking miners and their families in Colorado. The northern miners have to go back to work to survive. There is no shame in that. They fought until they could not.

From the day I went against John Mitchell's authority, the guns were turned on me. Slander and persecution and black shadows followed in my wake. The old story that I once ran a brothel surfaces again, when in truth I had only given assistance to a prostitute. I ignored the claim then and I ignore it now.

But I never stop fighting. The withdrawal of the UMW leaves behind virtual peonage in the south. With the support of the WFM and local farmers I am able to keep the southern coal mining families alive and fighting for another year.

For the first time, however, I have made enemies other than with the industrial slavers. Stories in a Denver paper, *Polly Pry,* called me power hungry, "an old hag" and a "vulgar, heartless creature with a fiery temper and a cold-blooded brutality."

For the first time in my life I am glad my family is dead. I would have hated for my children to have read such vile words and wonder what their mother had come to.

Whether that *Polly Pry* was right or wrong, it *is* true that I am now solely associated with the WFM which has become one of the most violent unions in the country, matching brute force with brute force. I still don't agree with violence as a solution, but you have to understand that when you beat a dog long enough, it becomes mean. I'm feeling pretty damned mean!

The situation, unfortunately, becomes worse, much worse than it has been since I first arrived in Trinidad. Each mine is an armed camp. Armed strikers are clashing with strike-breakers. In the Cripple Creek area, which has been the scene of violence for many years, thirty-three people die in dynamiting and shooting incidents.

At this critical moment I am once again visited by pneumonia and I have to spend several days in the hospital while my boys from the mines stand vigil in the cold outside my window. When I am well enough, I speak to them and a group of strikers from Trinidad.

A few days later, soldiers put me and three other organizers on a train and we are escorted down to the New Mexico border where we are put off in the middle of nowhere. Each of us receives a letter from the governor. I am once again deported.

—◆◆◆—

My fellow deportees take off in different directions. I stand on the tracks where I have been put off until another train comes along. It stops and the conductor jumps down.

"Mother," says he, "do you want to go to Denver?"

"I do," says I, "but I don't want you to lose your job."

"To hell with the job," says he. "All aboard to Denver!"

The train passes through Trinidad, but I keep going. I think the time has come to give it up and move on.

In Denver I wire my bank for money and take a hotel room. After I have rested awhile I sit down and write the governor a letter.

"Mr. Governor. You had your dogs of war deport me again. And again I am back. I hold a letter signed by you that under no circumstances am I to ever return to this state. I wish to notify you, ordinary citizen Peabody, that you don't own Colorado. You just run it temporarily. When Colorado was admitted to the sisterhood of states, my forefathers gave me a share of stock in it. And that's all you have, one share of stock.

"I have rights as a citizen and you weren't elected dictator. The civil courts are open and if I've broken any law, which I haven't, it's up to the courts to deal with me. My forefathers established these courts to keep dictators and tyrants such as you from interfering with civilians. So, if you aren't prepared to follow due process, I'd advise you to leave me alone."

I send copies to the Denver newspaper and then catch a train for Utah where I am also needed and the prospects are better. Looking back, I see that the miners in southern Colorado soon give up and go back to work. One newspaper reports that the coal companies have spent over a million dollars fighting the strike, the unions half of that. All for nothing.

Chapter Twenty-Nine
All Across America ~ 1905-1911

For the next few years, I am once again an independent hellraiser.

John Mitchell wants nothing to do with me and I want nothing to do with John Mitchell. He fooled me once, fooled me twice, but I am damned sure not going to let his treachery fool me again. I'm sure he feels the same way about me because I scuttled his plan.

Meanwhile, I go right on with my crusade against the excesses of capitalism, supported by the Western Federation of Miners and the Socialist Party. They pay part of my expenses, though it isn't necessary. During the past few years while I've been on the United Mine Workers' payroll and expense account, my own bank account has grown nicely. I have not had to rely on my income from my partnership with Jenny Flynn.

Now, I can easily get along without financial support, but it is good to be both independent and supported by a couple of useful organizations.

On the negative side, the WFM admittedly has become one of the most militant unions in the country, which automatically casts me as a harbinger of violence. Certainly, the fight for the rights of the worker has become violent, but not because it is the way of the worker.

To the contrary, it is the way of the pigheaded mine owners and operators.

Labor may be picking the fights, but it is not picking the weapons. Like the Knights of Labor, the WFM continues to try negotiation and arbitration first, but the mine operators are having none of it. Instead, they hire gun-toting thugs to use brute force to control the means of production; that is, to suppress the working men, women and even children who are the creators of the wealth as they bring the coal to the surface.

The wealth lays with the workers, not in the mineral rights owned by the companies. Those minerals have no real value until they are brought to the surface. The capitalists just cannot stand the thought of not owning the means of production — the people — just as they own the natural resources beneath the earth.

I remember how troubled Terence Powderly and the Knights of Labor had been in facing the inevitability of violence. Terence could not overcome his intellectual views and ideals in order to meet violence with opposing force. As a result, they failed themselves and their members and the Knights faded away.

Today I see the leaders of the United Mine Workers on the same downward path. They try to face the obstinacy of the mine owners and operators with non-violent reason.

They put on their pinstriped suits and climb into the opulent caves of the rich industrialists. They wine and dine, and over drinks and delicacies make unconscionable deals like, "Here, here. We understand your problem, Mr. Bossman, and we're here to help you. Let's make a deal. You can keep taking blood from this arm if you take a little less from the other one."

That's the way I see the deals made in West Virginia and Colorado by the UMW, specifically by John Mitchell. Amidst the smoke of cigars I imagine Mitchell saying, "Here, let's make a deal. We'll give you the south if you give us the north." Trading one set of human beings off for the benefit of another.

I hear other wheeler-dealers in the same circumstances saying, "We'll give up on having honest weigh-men if you give us better pay." Or, "We'll give up on safety if you give up on hours."

Honestly, I don't see how union representatives can think they can keep their own integrity intact while trying to outwit the devil himself, bargaining by betraying the ones who are desperately depending on them. And once integrity is lost, I don't know how these union representatives can face their fellow worker, even their fellow man.

So, the Knights of Labor with its high ideals and ineffectiveness faded away. Now the United Mine Workers is failing its members and losing its credibility. The WFM is steadfast and strong. You'll just have to forgive me. Surely you can see why the WFM is becoming my kind of union.

Unfortunately, the WFM represents primarily hard rock miners and only in six western states. Their only interest in coal miners comes because of their support for me. I need a broader base.

And so, in June, 1905, I join a group of radical socialists to form the Industrial Workers of the World. It's headed up by the man I've told you I admire so much, Eugene Debs.

The newspapers start calling them the "Wobblies." The organization certainly does make people nervous and soon the IWW is clashing with business and government even more forcefully than the WFM.

It gets out of hand and soon I am forced to distance myself from the IWW, not because I do not support it, but because the bad publicity is not good for my image as a woman who, though not afraid of violence, preaches against it. And, in case you've forgotten, my image has been carefully crafted to draw sympathy for myself and the American worker.

The Wobblies are making a grievous mistake. They are frightening the American public and smearing the face of labor.

But the IWW is correct to place the blame for the conflicts on federal, state and local governments and their side soon shows it colors.

In almost every disturbance between business and labor, the government takes the side of the capitalist, condones and *joins* the violence the capitalists throw at American citizens who are simply fighting for the rights given them by the Constitution of the United States. Like the rights to life, liberty and the pursuit of happiness. Like the rights of freedom, equality and equal opportunity.

It's ironic, but our inept enemies are improving the image of the working class while our friends are giving us a black eye.

The class war has turned topsy-turvy.

I make speeches at hundreds of meetings of socialists, who are radical but not so violent. I am not in total agreement with many of the socialist views and I'm careful not to let my involvement with them alienate my public.

I see socialism as an alternative to *capitalism*, not an alternative to democracy. In my mind, *socialism* and *capitalism* are at war. *Capitalism*, not socialism, is the real threat to democracy. In fact, I believe capitalism is *destroying* democracy and the principles for which it stands.

I want to lecture on that.

But before a discussion like that can be had, the debaters need to understand that these words are much confused by ignorance, emotion, dogma and propaganda. It is incomprehensible to me that these words and their relationships with one another are so confused by the average American. I am not so surprised they are exploited by the captains of capitalism.

Most of all, I know that to debate these issues is academic. Regardless of how poorly capitalism performs, America will never abandon it. And as positive as democratic socialism can be, America will never embrace it. And so, Mother Jones and the working class will just have to learn how to live with it.

And that's all I have to say about that.

Chapter Thirty
Monongah, West Virginia ~ December, 1907

Much has occurred in West Virginia during these interim years. In the north I have spent a great deal of time rabble rousing among miners in the Fairmont Field, encouraging union membership and urging action against dangerous and desperate practices. A great deal of that work was accomplished with the help of that great socialist leader and friend of mine, Eugene Debs.

In tandem with his work for the socialists, I was successful in organizing a series of UMW strikes against several mines including Consolidation Coal's mining and coking operation in Monongah, West Virginia, located around forty miles south of Pennsylvania's southwestern border.

The atmosphere on the outside of the Monongah mine gave Debs and me just a hint of what it must be like inside.

The company town was covered by a smoke-laden haze, caught between hills surrounding three hundred twenty coke ovens. Air quality had destroyed vegetation surrounding the mine and cabins and shortened the lives not only of the miners underground, but of their families above.

Our list of objectionable conditions was long. Open sewers, foul drinking water, servitude multiplied by debt to the company store and past due rent for meager company housing. Children as young as eight years old worked with their fathers in the mines to help their families make ends meet.

But the press turned a blind eye and our strikes were broken up by court injunctions and brute force.

Consolidation Coal's Monongah mine remained non-union and in December, 1907, it was the scene of one of the worst two mining disasters in American history. Preceded by a horrific explosion at the Darr mine near Jacob's Creek, Pennsylvania, which killed two hundred sixty-nine miners, the Monongah calamity topped that number with three hundred fifty-eight killed, nearly as many widows made and more than one thousand children orphaned.

It was later learned that the Monongah figures were severely understated in an attempt by the mining company to cover up the true number of deaths even before the dead were covered in their coffins below the earth.

Although the cover-up makes it impossible to report the true number, investigators are fairly certain that the number was closer to five hundred.

It was a particularly bad year for coal miners and their families.

Both mine disasters were caused by methane gas explosions, a safety issue Debs and I had warned about throughout the Fairmont District.

Investigators gave a more detailed account. According to investigations by the United Mine Workers and safety and health officials from the federal government, what happened was the underground mine cars broke away from the engine and raced down the slope from the mine entry, taking out the ventilation system which sent coal dust swirling which then forced methane gas into the mine where it had previously been contained.

Now, after it was too late, an analyst finally has concluded that the Monongah disaster was the result of unsafe practices, a tale of corruption, of power and greed by some of the wealthiest men in the nation, including John D. Rockefeller, one of the owners of the Monongah mine and one of the biggest mining magnates in West Virginia and Colorado.

During the days following the disaster, the human tragedy remained prominent in the press and among the conversations of concerned citizens. The press and public had turned a blind eye before the disaster, but I assumed, with all eyes opened, surely these miners would not have died in vain. That it would lead to positive action.

But a week or so after the blast, after the men were buried and the horror of the mental and photographic images disappeared, people closed their eyes again and nothing really changed in Monongah or anywhere else in the Mountain State.

In spite of a lot of political discussion, hellraisers like me and Eugene Debs were the only ones trying to keep the issues alive after the men at Monongah were called back to work. We continued to go unheeded.

Particularly troubling to me was the fact that the mine owners successfully managed to blame the miners themselves, most of them immigrants, for the accident, deflecting any blame regarding defective equipment and substandard safety mechanisms. They were successful in blocking all efforts to impose significant health and safety reforms to reduce the risk that another tragedy like Monongah could happen, even at Monongah.

And, given that nothing had changed, my little voice told me this would not be the only Monongah mine disaster in history.

Chapter Thirty-One
Arizona, Mexico and New York ~ 1911-1913

The issue of non-English speaking immigrants has been weighing on my mind for some time. It is an issue that became evident in West Virginia and even more so in Colorado when the English speakers of the northern mines nearly abandoned their non-speaking brothers in the south.

Back in West Virginia I had already witnessed the disadvantage non-English speaking Europeans faced in the coal mines. Now, in addition, I am seeing non-English speakers from Mexico and Asia in the mines and mills of the West. For them, the language barrier doubles their disadvantages and renders them even more vulnerable to the exploitation of the capitalists and even their labor unions, as the behavior of the UMW demonstrated in Colorado.

The Europeans were lured to this country by glowing reports of an exaggerated American freedom full of opportunity and dreams. When they arrived here they were surprised, shocked and helpless, unable to talk it out with anyone but themselves or the few who could provide translation.

Now the Mexicans are coming from just across the border. These people were not alive when the southwestern United States was the northern half of Mexico, but the culture of Mexico remembers the story and has passed it on to succeeding generations who are now heading across the border as if they are going to northern Mexico.

After all these years they still think of California, Arizona and Texas as part of their Mexican heritage. There are many Mexicans still living in these annexed lands. Many of them have learned English, but those who are coming north now from what's left of Mexico have not.

What they do find familiar here is exploitation and poverty. They are disappointed, but that's life to a Mexican. Disappointment, despotism and desperation.

Those who remain in Mexico also are in the hands of a despot, Porfirio Diaz, who seized the Mexican presidency by frightening and intimidating the Mexican people into voting him into office and now continues in office by the same methods. His administration has become a virtual dictatorship that has lasted from 1876 to 1911.

There is no greedier a man on this earth than Porfirio Diaz. He has found a way to build his own fortune beyond his original dream by enticing American capitalists to expand south of the border where they find in government a master of bribery who, without apology, exploits his own people to line his own pockets. He and the capitalists understand each other. It's a marriage made in heaven.

As Diaz's fortune grows, so does the discontent among his people and by the turn of the century, a revolution is in the works.

—◆◆◆—

I'm holding a street meeting for copper smelters one Sunday night in Douglas, Arizona, which has a border crossing with Mexico. The whole town has turned out.

After the meeting a worker comes running up to me. "Oh, Mother," he exclaims, "there has been something horrible going on at the jail. While you were speaking, a man has been taken to the jail in an automobile. He was screaming about his liberty being taken from him, but the cops choked him off. If you value liberty, Mother Jones, you must help this man."

"Oh, it's probably some fellow with a jag on," says I. The worker tries to explain who this man is, but I'm not understanding his broken English. I'm tired and I'm assuming this is some domestic problem that has nothing to do with me. I push past the fellow and a few of the men with me shove him out of the way.

I give it no further thought and go to my hotel. There I'm discussing mining issues with a few union organizers when the editor of *El Industrio,* the Spanish newspaper, bursts into the room.

"Oh, Mother," says he, "they have kidnapped our young revolutionist, Manuel Sarabia."

I have a faint recollection of a fellow by that name. Sarabia is an outspoken Mexican revolutionary who is widely published in the United States. He is working with the socialists in America to gain support for the revolution against Diaz.

The editor goes on to say that under cover of darkness, Sarabia has been taken from the jail and transported to Mexico where he faces certain death.

"Get all the facts you can," says I. "Get them as correct as you can and I will immediately telegraph the governor and the authorities in Washington. Don't stop for a moment because if you do, they will murder him."

The next day the editor of *El Industrio* fills me in on the details that led up to Sarabia's kidnapping.

While still in Mexico Sarabia had incurred the hatred of Diaz and the forty thieves because Sarabia had called him a dictator. Diaz still fancies himself as president, in spite of there not being an election held, even though it is long overdue.

Sarabia spent a year in Mexican jails and then escaped to the United States to continue his fight for Mexican liberation.

Diaz's hate followed Sarabia across the border in the form of Mexican thugs.

"That's got to stop," says I. "The idea of any blood-thirsty pirate sitting on a throne and reaching across the border to tromp on our Constitution makes my blood boil."

That night we plan a protest meeting. We have a hard time getting the meeting announced in the local papers because they are owned by the Southern Pacific Railway and the Copper Queen mine. Both companies have operations in Mexico and they see to it that the local newspapers are in tune with the pirates in Mexico.

I go to Phoenix to see the governor who I believe to be of the stuff that Patrick Henry, Thomas Jefferson and Abraham Lincoln were made of. The governor orders a captain of the Arizona Rangers to go across the border and bring Sarabia back. It gets done.

The rebels in Mexico finally depose Diaz, and Francisco Madero is elected as a truly democratic president. Right away he sends for me to come to Mexico to help his country organize its workers under a new democracy.

I go to Mexico City and advise the new president and some of his labor leaders on the ideals of American unionism and the difficulties we are having in the face of capitalists and government officials who are opposed to union representation. Madero announces proudly that the government will no longer stand in the way of worker rights in Mexico.

An amendment to the Mexican constitution is passed guaranteeing the rights of unions to organize and the right of workers to belong to a union.

I am asked to remain in Mexico to assist the government in the unionization of its labor force, but I have to decline. I already have my hands full with my commitment to workers back in the United States. All workers, including those who are non-English speaking.

Unfortunately, President Madero is not able to get the workers in Mexico organized. He is hampered by the remnants of the Diaz regime and a new revolutionary movement, which is impatient with Madero because he is not radical enough.

Madero is deposed and executed in 1913.

Meanwhile, I am busy fighting for Mexicans living in poverty right here in the United States. Not just Mexicans, but non-English speaking workers from all over the world: the Germans, Italians, French, Russians, Jewish, Polish, Scandinavians, Austrians, Belgians and Hungarians. As well as workers from English-speaking countries such as my fellow Irish lads and lassies.

The enticement of these people to this country has been expressed through the adaptation of a Greek poem enshrined on the base of the Statue of Liberty:

> Give me your tired, your poor,
> Your huddled masses yearning to breathe free.
> The wretched refuse of your teeming shore.
> Send these, the homeless, tempest-tossed to me.
> I lift my lamp beside the golden door!

But what they find in their new country is ill treatment, not by a dictator as in Mexico, but by Americans who despise non-English speakers, thinking they are ignorant because they don't speak English or don't speak it well; the Americans bitterly resent the immigrants when they compete successfully with English-speaking workers for jobs that are often scarce.

On that account I work for many years with the famous social worker Jane Addams, founder of Hull House in Chicago. In 1909 I go to New York to help the striking shirtwaist workers in New York by encouraging them with many speeches. Most of the shirtwaist workers are non-English speaking Europeans.

The New York strike becomes one of the most proud accomplishments I have ever witnessed. A unified force of working women show the power of their sex and their class. And they prevail.

After a long and painful strike on both sides of the battle, the women return to work with better wages, hours and benefits. And safer conditions.

But, as is often the way in American discourse, there is always an exception. In this case it's the Triangle Shirtwaist Company in the heart of Manhattan, within a few blocks of the den of thieves they call Wall Street.

The citywide strike actually started in the Triangle sweatshop. In the end Triangle refused to settle and is allowed to continue its notorious abuse of immigrant women in the workplace.

Among the abuses is a company policy of locking all but one exit door on the eighth and ninth floors of the multi-use building where two hundred seventy-five girls, many of them not yet teenagers, toil twelve hours a day at their sewing machines. Some bring their infants to work due to the lack of anyone being available to look after them.

The locked doors policy is, according to the managers, to prevent girls from stealing anything of value when they leave work. Needles, threads, material, maybe a shirtwaist or two to sell on the streets to supplement their meager incomes.

But to labor advocates, those locked doors are a hazard to the safety of Triangle employees and the union is on record with its opinion.

On Saturday, March 11, 1910, these girls are gathering their belongings at the end of a long day's work. An explosion is heard and a fire erupts that cannot be quickly controlled with the twenty-seven buckets of water that sit on the floors, the only defense provided by the company in case of a fire.

The fire quickly blocks the only open door and the only fire escape collapses with workers clinging to it. Other workers climb over each other to reach the elevator, which is the only escape left to the lower floors. Those who cannot get on the elevator fling themselves down the elevator shaft in hopes of landing on top of the car. Others jump from windows where firemen and passersby try to break their falls to save them.

Fire hoses are useless because they can only shoot water as high as the windows on the sixth and seventh floors. When the fire is out, the bodies of these poor unfortunate women and children are lined up on the sidewalk, and onlookers file by to get a glimpse of the horror brought on by a capitalist economy out of control. Press photographers are having a heyday.

By nightfall, one hundred forty-six employees of the Triangle Shirtwaist Factory are counted dead.

Chapter Thirty-Two
West Virginia ~ Fall/Winter, 1912-1913

Now, finally, I'm going to tell you the full story of what happened at Hollygrove and Mucklow that eventually landed fifty of us — me, the miners and their wives — in jail at Pratt,

West Virginia. It is in that jail where our journey together — yours and mine — began.

I'm telling you now because you've seen enough to have the perspective you need to fully appreciate the significance of these events and the rest of the story to follow.

I am out west working for the Southern Pacific railroad machinists when I read in the newspaper that the Paint Creek Coal Company in southern West Virginia has refused to settle with the union. The union miners at Paint Creek have voted to join hands with the non-union miners at Cabin Creek who have just gone out on strike.

Remembering that I was unable to unionize Cabin Creek miners in 1903 while succeeding in Paint Creek, this latest news is very encouraging to me. It looks like the Cabin Creek miners have finally gathered some courage.

My estrangement from the national leadership of the United Mine Workers has continued for nearly ten years, but during that time I have been called to West Virginia time and again by the miners and local union leaders, including those in Paint Creek. And so I am very much up-to-date on the situation there.

On my return to southern West Virginia, I've got my work cut out for me.

But it is my good fortune that after several years I've got the UMW back on my side. In 1911, my long-time friend John White is elected national president of the UMW and he asks me right away to again become a UMW employee and return to West Virginia.

I thank him and pledge my support, but I decline the job offer, explaining that as much as I trust him, I want to remain independent. My intention remains to represent my boys in the mines, not at union cocktail parties.

—◆◆◆—

And so it is that I wrap my few possessions into the black shawl I use as a knapsack and head back to the Mountain State. My span of work here is now approaching twenty-five years.

I know West Virginia. I know the people. I've been in these hills, on and off, for decades. And I belong here.

West Virginia miners and their wives are good people of good stock. Strong and proud, unafraid of hard work or hardship. They are accustomed to both because they are the products of generations of pioneering spirits in a land that is not the romantic Wild West of literature, but the challenging Wild West of American history when the West lay east of the Mississippi River, before the West of later history was acquired and settled.

The land is beautiful but unforgiving.

Before becoming coal miners, the men of these hills were gatherers and hunters in the tradition of the native Americans who came before them. These mountaineers carry guns for hunting and for protecting their families. They are fearless, self-assured, confident in their responsibilities.

They have hacked their way through endless forests with giant virgin timber growing so close together that the huge trunks sometimes do not let a man pass.

With not an acre of flat land available, the typical West Virginia family has cleared out enough space for a cabin, a vegetable garden and a few chickens.

They are accustomed to winters that are bitter cold and summers that are insect infested. They are one with the land. They know how to eke out a living and they thank their Lord above for His grace and for their independence.

Montani Semper Liberi. "Mountaineers are always free." The state's motto since its founding in 1863 amidst the Civil War when many, but not all, refused to join the Confederacy.

The great Abe Lincoln admired these people and took steps to make the western side of Virginia the independent state of West Virginia.

Montani Semper Liberi. Words to live by.

But just twenty years later the first carload of coal was transported from West Virginia to Tazewell, Virginia. The Industrial Revolution reached these Appalachian mountains and it began to entice these proud people from the primeval comfort of the woods into the unnatural black holes of coal mines. Independence lost. Pride shaken. Life miserable. Spirit broken.

Now they are joined by hoards of European immigrants whose stories include similar trials and tribulations but few with a past so primitive that it has hardened and adapted them like these hardy native mountaineers. The Europeans are more easily tamed.

Telling you all this breaks my heart.

By 1912, the UMW has lost control of much of the Kanawha-New River coalfields, a decline that began after I had fought so hard to win status for the union in 1903. I still attribute the beginning of the decline to the treachery the UMW, John Mitchell in particular, showed when the union settled with the mines at Cabin Creek, leaving Paint Creek holding the bag at a time when they were on the verge of a much better win.

I'm glad to be back, glad to be ready to settle that score.

News of that treachery spread throughout the state in 1903 and union membership went downhill from there.

Now the UMW is back under a leadership I trust, trying to regain some influence in the state. For the miners in the south, the UMW has demanded wages at least equal to other West Virginia mines, particularly those in the northern part of the state.

This battle has come to a head when I arrive in Charleston in the early morning hours. I go to a hotel, wash up, have breakfast and go to catch a local coal train into Paint Creek country. The train has just returned from Cabin Creek which is up another long valley. The two creeks are just a few miles apart as the crow flies, but separated by a mountain covered by dense forest like I've just described to you. Beautiful. Rugged. And dangerous.

The two camps can't be reached without coming first toward Charleston.

"Little Russia." That's what I call Cabin Creek. The miners there are peons, kept in slavery by the guns of the coal company and ... well, you've got the picture. Same as every other oppressive mine I've described to you.

I already know that the minute the miners at Paint Creek struck in support of their brothers over in Cabin Creek that all civil and constitutional rights were taken away. Company enforcers threw the miners and their families out of the company houses in the dead of winter, dumping their personal property beside the train tracks.

I know they are now camped in tents in the nearby woods called Hollygrove. No one is allowed in the Cabin Creek District without explaining his reason, a brakeman tells me. The crew will have to put me off far short of mine company property.

"Mother, it will be sure death if you go up to the Creeks," says a crewman. "No organizer dares go in there now. They have machine guns along the route and the gunmen don't care who they kill."

"Thank you, my son," says I. "But I have to go to Hollygrove, and I may have to go on up to the mines to talk to the bosses. I'll be all right."

When we reach Paint Creek Junction, I get off. Gunmen are armed to the teeth and looking to use their weapons. Suddenly a boy runs screaming to me.

"Oh, Mother Jones! Mother Jones! Did you come to stay with us?" He rubs his eyes with dirty fists.

"Yes, my lad, I've come to stay."

A guard is listening.

"The hell you say! I think you won't be stayin'," he says as he raises the business end of his weapon.

The boy drops to his knees and grabs me around my legs.

"Oh, Mother. They drove my papa away and we don't know where he is. And they threw my mama and all us kids out of the house and they beat my mama and me."

I ignore the guard's threat. The boy is crying as I lead him on up the creek on foot. He pulls up his shirt and shows me his bruises.

"The guards did this, Mother. And you should see my mama. She looks much worse. Mother, when I'm a man I'm going to kill me twenty gunmen for hurting my mama. I'm gonna kill 'em dead."

I hike up the creek to Hollygrove. The weather is warmer now, the "sarvice" berries are in bloom. The mountaineers call them "sarvice berries" because when they bloom it is a sign that an itinerant preacher will soon be able to come to perform religious "sarvices" for people who have died over the winter or need to be married, even if it's too late.

When I find the boy's mother, she says, "I think the strike is lost, Mother."

"Lost!" says I. "Not until my last drop of blood is lost."

I travel up and down the creek holding meetings, rousing tired spirits. I arrange for three thousand miners from the Creeks … the miners call them "cricks" … to march over the hills to Charleston where I will read a declaration of war to Governor Glasscock.

I appoint six trusty men to continue up and down the Creeks announcing a meeting to be held in Charleston at 1 p.m. the next day.

—◆◆◆—

When the governor meets us on the capitol steps the next day, he looks like a scared rabbit. He sits down in a chair to listen. I wait calmly for my time to speak, checking my hair, which I've tied in a knot behind my head, fussing with the position of my bonnet, smoothing my dress. And yes, calming my nerves. I'm known for rough talk, but for me this is a grave occasion. I have prepared a written declaration of war and I want to read it in a firm and determined voice.

I arise, nod to the governor and address the crowd.

"This, my friends marks, in my estimation, the most remarkable move ever made in the State of West Virginia. This day will mark history for the ages. What is it? It is an uprising of the oppressed against the master class.

I go on like that for a while, then turn to address the governor.

"Your Excellency, William E. Glasscock, Governor of the State of West Virginia, it is respectfully represented unto you that the owners of the various coal mines doing business along the valleys of Paint and Cabin Creeks, Kanawha County, are maintaining in their employ a large force of armed guards, armed with Winchesters, a dangerous and deadly weapon.

"They also possess three Gatling guns which said guards use for the purpose of brow-beating, intimidating and menacing the lives of all the citizens who live in said valleys, as well as those whose business calls them into said valleys who are not in accord with the management of the coal companies.

"We hold that the maintenance of said guards by the companies and the stationing of said guards against the people is a menace to the general welfare of the people and the State of West Virginia."

The miners applaud roundly.

Turning toward the governor I say, "As citizens of this state interested in the public weal and general welfare, and believing that law and order and peace should ever abide, that the spirit of brotherly love and justice and freedom should everywhere exist, we petition you to bring all the powers of your office to bear for the purpose of disarming said guards and restoring the rights of the citizens of said valleys as guaranteed by the constitutions of the United States and the State of West Virginia."

Then I drop the other shoe.

Turning back to the crowd I say, "I am duty bound to make this plea, but I want to say, with all due respect to the governor here, that I doubt seriously that he will do — cannot do — anything. And for the reason that he is owned, lock, stock and barrel, by the capitalists who placed him here in this building."

The miners roar.

To his face I accuse the governor of abuse of power and finally turn to my audience.

"Now, my friends. The day for petting dogs is done. The day for raising children to a nobler manhood and womanhood is here."

"Amen! Amen! Amen!" comes the miners' unified cry.

"I have gone to jail for you before and I will do it again. I have never taken any backwater and I will not do it now. I am here to unfurl the flag of industrial freedom in the tyrant's face and I call you today into that freedom."

More applause.

—◆◆◆—

They say I talk too much and too long and so I won't burden you with the rest of my speech. Certainly, the governor didn't. As soon as my speech took this turn, he was spirited away.

I'll just say my speech was punctuated by happy applause to the finish, which was a while in coming. Those miners were enjoying every minute of this.

"Now boys, this may be a declaration of war. But I want you to be good tonight. I want you to give the governor until tomorrow night. And if he doesn't act, then it is up to you what to do.

"However, if there are people among us with a few coins to spare, let's pass the hat. With the money I want you to go to the Pluck-me Store and get all you can for your families to eat. Then go to the bars and have a few beers. You deserve it. When that's done, I want you to take the food home to your wives and your children.

"Tomorrow we'll see whether the governor is going to help you or shoot you. Tonight, have yourselves a little relaxation."

This gets the greatest applause of all.

Then someone shouts:

"Here is ten dollars. I will go and get more."

"Maybe the governor will give something!" says another voice.

Laughter.

"I don't think he can," says another. "I think he just became sick to his stomach."

"Maybe he went to the hospital," someone shouted.

"All right," says I. "Now let us go home. Be good boys. I am coming back to the camps to see you tomorrow."

The large crowd disperses, but there are a few dozen hangers on. They want more.

I stand in the middle of their circle.

One says, "You know the governor isn't going to run the guards off tomorrow, don't you Mother Jones? So what are you going to do about them?"

"I'm not going to say to you don't molest the guards," says I. "The coal operators are the ones who hire these dogs to shoot you."

Applause.

"I am not asking you to pick a fight with them, but if the mine guards are going to molest you, then you'll have to deal with them in your own way."

Then I pull out a theatrical prop I brought with me. I had decided during the speech not to use it when I toned down my talk with innuendo. But now I cannot contain myself any longer. I hold up a mine guard's coat covered in blood.

"This is the first time I ever saw a goddamn mine guard's coat decorated to suit me," says I.

The shout from the audience tells me everyone in that little group got my meaning!

—◆◆◆—

When the most of the men had left, a member of the local UMW board comes to me and speaks privately.

"Mother," says he, "do you think this is wise? Do you think it is wise to go up there to the creeks tomorrow?"

"No." I speak in a low voice. "I think it's necessary."

"Well, Mother," says he. "If you think someone should go, let me go."

"No," says I. "I think it is better for me to go alone. You represent the local union. I don't. I'm not responsible to anyone. If you go and something happens, the mine operators may blame the union and sue for damages. I am a private citizen. All they can do to me is put me in jail. I'm used to that."

The UMW man leaves me and goes directly to the governor and tells him to send a company of militia up to the creeks the next day because I am going to be up there. Then he goes to the sheriff and encourages the same thing. He is, as I suspected, a Judas. He is the same man who followed me up the New River in the strike of 1902. At that time he was working for the Chesapeake and Ohio Railroad and coal company. How on earth could he be on the local UMW board and hide his true allegiance? I don't try to think up an answer. I've got better things to do.

That night a locomotive nicknamed the Bull Moose Special pulls an armored car past the tent colony at Hollygrove. In the armored car there are killers led by coal mine operator Quinn Morton and County Sheriff Bonner Hill.

Behind the steel plates are several deputies, mine guards who have been deputized as state militia, and one of the company's Gatling guns.

It is the middle of the night and everyone is asleep except one lone miner whose duty it is to look out for mischief and assure safety while the rest of the men and their families get some rest.

One of the Baldwin-Felts guards opens fire with the Gatling gun, sweeping across the tents in a methodical pattern, aiming to wreak havoc with as many families as he can. Indiscriminately aiming at tents full of unseen men, women and children. Continuing his fire when these innocents run for cover. The cracks of rifles join the melee.

The miner standing guard is killed trying to organize a defense, but miraculously, no other resident of the tent colony is injured. Perhaps by divine providence, the miners have previously excavated large dugouts beneath the tents to nest their families in the warm earth below the surface. The dugouts were intended to defend the families from the cold. Now they defend them from the evil of men.

Whether it is connected or not to my speech on the capitol steps, we have our answer. West Virginia has declared war on its people.

Chapter Thirty-Three
Hollygrove and Mucklow ~ February 8, 1913

I collapse on my hotel bed after the confrontation with the Governor Glasscock last night and this morning I awake still in my clothes. It is pounding on my door that awakens me. When I open it I see one of my trusted Paint Creek miners standing there, a mixture of horror and anger on his face.

"Mother, they shot up the tent colony at Hollygrove last night."

"What?" I am incredulous.

"The guards. The sheriff. Maybe it was the militia. I don't know. But the colony took fire from a Gatling gun aboard the train in the middle of the night. We're in a mess up there, Mother. You must come. Now."

"How many are hurt?" I ask.

"Just one, a man. We had posted him to keep watch over the colony. All the other men and the families, they are okay but shaken."

We hurry to the front of the hotel and my messenger boosts me up into the saddle behind another miner who is already mounted on his horse. It is unladylike, but I am astraddle the animal, my dress skirts pulled over me. My arms are flung around the miner's waist and I want to spur the horse myself.

"Let's go," says I.

We ride like the wind, which requires me to readjust my bonnet from time to time while holding on with the other hand.

—◆◆◆—

When we arrive at Hollygrove I expect chaos. But in fact it is deadly quiet. People are milling around with a look upon their faces I've not seen before. What had once been bitter resolve is now replaced by horror and anger. I cannot get a civil word out of anyone, man, woman or child. They talk to me as if they are shouting at the enemy.

Every man carries a weapon or two. I look for some of the strike leaders, but they are nowhere to be seen. Out organizing an army, I suspect.

For the next several hours I talk to the women while sending out messengers to find some of the strike leaders. I want to have a talk with them. I tell the women about the success I have had in the past with marches of women and children and explain how it's done. I'm not sure how I'll use a "women's army" at this point, but I know I need to calm the men down and come up with an alternative to violence.

A woman by the name of Addie shows me a more positive look. I've seen her around but at this point I don't know her last name. Judging from that look on her face I judge her to be a leader. I ask her if she will serve as my lieutenant, recruiting and leading the women's army. That puts a smile on her face, a vindictive smile.

Finally, a couple of the union organizers come in from the woods.

"Boys," says I, "we need to calm these men down. Trust me, an eye for an eye is not the answer. I've seen too much violence around this country to believe it will ever work in our favor."

"That's not the way you were talking last night, Mother."

"Then you misunderstood me. I meant for you to have guns to protect yourselves, not start fights."

"Well, I don't think you're going to stop the men, Mother. The fight has already been started by the other side. The men are getting ready to attack the guards in their den at Mucklow. If I try to stop them, they'll shoot *me*."

"Don't try to stop them on your own," says I. "Just go out there in those woods and spread the word that Mother Jones is opposed to the kind of violence they have planned. And tell them she has a better idea." I explain my plan as it is now forming in my mind. I tell him about my experience with women's marches. I'm adjusting my plan as we speak.

"I've noticed there are several newspaper reporters roaming around here," says I. "Since the guards are holed up at their Mucklow headquarters, they are not interfering with outsiders. As soon as we get our army of women and children together we will march on Mucklow in a civilized protest and those news hounds will follow.

"There'll be no better opportunity to raise public support than now. The women can do it. If the men retaliate with guns, the opposite will happen. If we go in shooting, the public will see us as the bad guys, not the victims. Tell the boys out there they must hold their fire. Tell them to take fire before they give it. Do you understand me?"

"We understand you, Mother. We'll get the word out there and it will spread like wildfire. I know all of the men trust you, Mother, and you can trust them. Even now when they are ready for a fight."

I give my messengers a couple of days to spread the word while I organize the women and children for a march on Mucklow. They gather their dishpans and spoons, their mops. They have a few pep rallies. The changes on their faces are miraculous. They are full of enthusiasm now. They finally have an opportunity to fight back in their own way.

When they are ready, I call Addie aside.

"Addie, you know what to do. My part in this is done and I have other important duties ahead. I want you to lead these women to Mucklow and keep them on the job until I get back from Charleston. While you are raising hell at Mucklow, I'll be talking to the governor about sending the militia to remove the armed guards in order to avoid an all-out shooting war.

"I'll do it." Addie shouts with enthusiasm.

"I know you will, Addie. I have every confidence in you. You're a good girl!"

She heads back to the women and children who are assembling. I watch her march them off down a path into the woods, which swallows them up. Only the clatter of their dishpans remains behind. The men will hear them and know that help is on the way. The guards will hear them and, I hope, be shamed into staying in their hole.

As I step off the train in Charleston, I am accosted by two state militiamen.

"Are you Mother Jones?" one asks.

"Of course I'm Mother Jones! Are you daft? Who else do I look like?"

"I'm just confirming your identity. You are Mary Harris Jones?"

I sigh. "Yes, yes, why do you ask?"

"I am under orders to arrest you and take you to the county jail."

The two soldiers grab me, one by each arm, and take me to a police wagon. A few minutes later I am being hustled into the jail house. With no further word they escort me down a hall to a bull pen where they lock me in and leave.

I remain alone in that stark and bare holding pen the rest of the day and all night. No one comes with food or water. There is a bed pan in one corner. I use it, then sit down on the floor, then lie down, making a pillow of my hat and go to sleep. I am exhausted.

The same two soldiers come the next morning and give me bread and water. I partake of this meager breakfast while sitting on the floor. I feel like some kind of animal. Next thing I know I am back in the police wagon and I can see through the barred windows that I am on my way out of town.

The way we travel is familiar to me and I know we are on our way to Pratt. When we arrive, I am helped down to the ground and before me stands a nattily dressed man in suit and vest, adorned by a watch chain across the front. In a high voice he addresses me.

"Are you Mary Harris Jones, also known as Mother Jones?" Here we go again with the questions.

"Yes."

"Mary Harris Mother Jones, you are under arrest for instigating criminal assault and for the crime of murder. In due time you will be tried by court martial."

"You're joking," says I. "I am an American citizen who has already been arrested in Charleston and if I had kilt anybody it would be my right to be tried in a civilian court. Which is, I am sure sir, open. The military has no jurisdiction over me."

"That is all," the man utters this with a gesture of dismissal and turns to the soldiers. "Take her away."

The two soldiers manhandle me up the steps and into an old shack of a two-room house where a guard stands. The guard opens the door and when I step inside I see a gaggle of women. Addie is among them. The door closes behind me and I hear the sound of a padlock being attached and closed.

"Mother, oh Mother, I am so sorry to see you here, but so glad too." Addie is a-fluster.

"What is going on, Addie?"

"Oh, Mother, you should have been there! I know if you had been there it would have not gone so badly."

"Tell me about it," says I, and we sit down side by side on an old wooden bench. I have no idea what has happened.

She tells me the women's march had arrived at the Mucklow headquarters of the Baldwin-Felts gang which was a large whitewashed building called the Club House by local folks before the guards commandeered it. I know of this place. It is a large multi-purpose facility with a kitchen and a recreation hall. On the second floor there are sixteen bedrooms.

Addie tells me the building was surrounded by hundreds of men when the women got there. She assumed them to be Baldwin guards, all toting guns.

"We immediately set up a racket just as you wanted," Addie says. "The reporters did come as you predicted.

"I don't know how many of our men were up in the surrounding hills, but every once in a while a rifle would go off. I suppose that was to let the Baldwin-Felts gang know they were surrounded.

"All of a sudden the guards made a rush at us and then veered around us, heading for the hills. There was nothing we could do to stop them, Mother. If you had been there I bet you would have stopped them, but they took no heed of us."

"No, my dear girl," says I, "you did all that could have been done. Don't blame yourself. Those thugs were aching for a fight and no one could have stopped them. Did the reporters follow them to witness the fight?"

"They did not. Those cowards stayed to hide behind our skirts."

Addie went on to tell me that before long a terrible volley of gunfire erupted in the hills, echoing down through the valley.

"We all hunkered down, although the bullets weren't flying in our direction," Addie recalls. "The reporters fled to the Club House. It seemed like the battle went on for several hours and we didn't dare move. We didn't dare follow those chicken reporters into the Club House either. We wanted to get back up the trail to Hollygrove, but there was no telling how many bullets were flying between us and our homes.

"Just before dark we began to see guards staggering from the woods, held upright by other guardsmen. We could see their clothes were bloody, but they were alive. Then we saw more guards carrying dead men down to the Club House. We counted sixteen bodies in all.

"We had brought a lantern with us, as you instructed, Mother. I lit it and led the women back up the trail to Hollygrove. Everyone held hands so as not to get lost in the dark.

"When we got there we were met by a bunch more guards who tried to arrest us. We refused to be arrested and some of the women started hitting the guards with their spoons and dishpans."

My jail mates giggle in the background.

"They managed to arrest those of us who fought the hardest and you see them here. We were brought by box car here to Pratt and a man told us we would be court-martialed for the assault of the men because they were deputized militiamen."

"That's poppycock," says I. "Those were private guards employed by the company. They can hold us in this improvised jail if they want to, but they'll not get away with convicting us of military crimes. We're civilians. We're citizens of the United States of America with all the rights thereof. Trust me, girls. We will find justice!"

I didn't believe what I was saying, but it gave them comfort.

Chapter Thirty-Four
West Virginia State Capitol ~ July, 1912

And so it was that I began my five months incarceration, which I've already told you about. As you know, the women of the Mucklow march were officially released and now I've been allowed to "escape" by being discharged from the hospital in Charleston.

I escape all right!

I march right straight up to the capitol and into the governor's office.

"I want to see the governor," I demand of the receptionist. Unlike the man who arrested me five months ago, she doesn't need to ask me who I am.

"Yes, Mother. The governor told me to expect you. He told me he wants to spend more time with you than he has here at the office. He wants you to go back to your hotel and he will call you there to make arrangements to meet him tonight in the Governor's Mansion. Will you do that for us, Mother Jones?"

My mouth drops open. Can't find words. Just nod.

The receptionist turns to the state trooper standing at the door into the governor's office.

"Please take this good lady to the governor's driver and have her taken by the governor's car back to her hotel."

That night, the governor's car returns to the rear of the hotel and, under cover of darkness, spirits me up to the governor's mansion. It is clear the governor wants to avoid the press.

As the driver jumps down from his open air cab to open the door to the enclosed passenger compartment, a military officer in formal dress uniform meets me and offers his arm. I take it and am gallantly escorted up the steps and into the mansion. Inside, he leads me through enormous rooms, through a large dining room and then to a smaller, private room where a small table is set for two. Governor Hatfield is there and he rises to greet me.

"Mother Jones, I am so glad you could take time with me this evening. I have asked my staff to prepare a feast for you."

I start to protest but he interrupts.

"Now, now, Mother. I'm not wining and dining you. I know your thoughts on that. I just think it's time you have a decent meal for a change and you're going to need the energy before this night is out. We have a lot of talking to do, and I know you're good at it."

I have to smile. Then I choose beer over wine and we get down to business.

"Governor Hatfield, I want you to know that I was innocent of all charges regarding the battle at Mucklow and instead of letting me slip out of the hospital, you should have dropped the charges."

I go on to explain to him exactly what I did during the hours before the confrontation at Mucklow, that I had sent word into the woods that I was against retaliation, how instead of instigating the war I had attempted to circumvent it with the women's demonstration, how the women should have been honored, not arrested. And how it was the guards who began the attack, not the miners.

"I believe your every word, Mother. Why, then, did you not defend yourself, defend the miners and the women at the court martial? It would have been over in no time."

"Well, first of all, Governor, I am a stubborn woman. Second of all, to plead anything would be to recognize the authority of that court, and you and I both know it was an illegal proceeding. Especially in my case, being as how I was not even arrested within the zone under military control."

"Yes, but why did you not give in after the trial was over and when I was offering you amnesty or a pardon?"

"Again, Governor, that would have been admitting guilt. I was innocent and I was convicted illegally. I wanted the charges dropped and my name cleared, and so I would not accept either amnesty or pardon. That still stands, Mr. Governor."

"Your stubbornness again?"

I wasn't sure the governor was asking a question or making a statement.

"Not just stubbornness, sir. Over the years I've found no better place to raise public awareness and sympathy than the prison cell. And until the public becomes aware of the injustice hidden in these West Virginia hills, we will have no chance of beating the capitalists and saving the democracy which I am surely convinced is in great danger of losing its meaning.

"When freedom is lost to the almighty dollar, then democracy is dead. When the right to life, liberty and the pursuit of happiness is denied, then democracy is pointless."

"You make an eloquent point, Mother, but I think the solution will not come while the opposite sides are at loggerheads. You've effectively broadcast the problem. Now it's up to me to find a resolution. That's what I'm doing, Mother.

"You may not know it, but I have been using the power of my office to act as a forceful negotiator between the mine owners and the United Mine Workers. I believe that, as governor of the state of West Virginia, it is my duty to be neutral but forceful, to understand both sides. It is my duty not to represent either the mine owners or the union. My job is to help both sides to an agreement that will bring these coal wars to an end."

"I understand, and I'm beginning to believe in your intentions," says I. "But I sense that you will be as frustrated in your work as I am in mine. Getting a solution is not an easy thing."

"Agreed," says the governor. "In fact, I have very little control over the real problem. Our state is as much a victim of the economic system as your miners. Because we have so little control over the situation here, attempts to solve our problems within the state won't be satisfactory to any side.

"The only thing West Virginia has to offer to the economy is the raw resource that drives the wheels of industry. That should mean our resource has great value. But it doesn't. Even though it is of primary importance, it's not an asset in the bookkeeper's account. It's a cost in the industrial process. The workforce who brings it to the surface is a cost.

"To the industrialist, it's pure economics. In a capitalist economy, costs have to be held down to assure profits. And so, our labor force is held down, our mine operators are held down and the State of West Virginia is held down.

"My point is, we all face the same problem — the miners, the mine owners and the State of West Virginia. The problem and the solution may be beyond our reach, but it is paramount that we three — mine operator, miner and state — stand together, fight together, not with each other but with our mutual enemy.

"Our common enemy is the system. Our common enemy is the out-of-state money mongers who use the economic system for their own greed and without regard to the suffering the system causes."

"You know, Governor, that the extreme capitalists have taken the game beyond competing with each other on market price or making a reasonable profit. They are in a selfish and foolish competition with each other to see who can become the richest man in America. That's not economics. That's greed."

"I am aware of that, Mother. And I am aware that our federal politicians are okay with that as long as the result is a thriving national economy and fast growth in the country's resources such as electric power, water, public transportation, communications, roads and schools. It is still the 'Golden Age' outside West Virginia and no Washington politician wants to get in the way."

"I agree," says I. "These very symbols of progress are the very government initiatives that are making the rich richer and the poor poorer. What's good for the country, it turns out, may be good for the upper class, but not for the lower class. That's why I believe we have a class war that is bad for the country."

"Again I agree, Mother. But that's not the deck we're playing with here in West Virginia. The only thing I can get my arms around is the conflict between and among our citizens over who gets the scraps. I will negotiate a fair but unsatisfactory settlement among the forces lined up along the Creeks. Neither side will be happy, but together, perhaps, we can work in unison to survive an economic force that is beyond our control."

We go on like that for hours. A meeting of the minds.

Finally, I look down at my plate. Guilt wells up in me. I have eaten the biggest, juiciest steak and accompaniments I have ever seen. I'll pay penance, I think, in Colorado.

"About clearing me of the charges?" I ask.

"Mother, it is not in my power to withdraw the charges. They were made and that is a matter of record. I can't change the recommendations of the court. They are their recommendations and they stand. All I can do is neglect to pronounce sentence and let you go. Goodbye, Mother Jones, and godspeed."

Chapter Thirty-Five
Denver and Trinidad, Colorado ~ 1913

Even though I have spent mostly idle time the past five months in West Virginia jails, it has been a tense time filled with anxiety and illness. I am too exhausted to move on to an even more violent coal war raging in Colorado. I am beginning to feel my age now. I'm in my late seventies. My body is failing. The bouts with pneumonia have left my lungs in bad shape and now I have the constant pain of arthritis.

And so, instead of going immediately to Colorado, I stay with my dear friends Emma and Terence Powderly who live in the outskirts of Washington, D.C.

You remember my involvement with Terence in the Knights of Labor and during the great railroad strikes of the eighties and nineties. Terence is now a Washington bureaucrat, but a good one, I hasten to say. A rare thing for me to say about anyone in public office. He helped organize the Federal Bureau of Mines in 1910, promoted an eight-hour day for public employees, championed the establishment of the Children's Bureau, and now heads the new U.S. Department of Labor which was created just this year, in large part as a result of his leadership.

We talk a lot about the situation in Colorado where I'm preparing to go.

—◆◆◆—

The unfinished business I left in Trinidad ten years before has erupted into a full-scale coal war. The smoldering fires that burned in the breasts of the miners of southern Colorado then have erupted into the full flame of war. I still blame the withdrawal of UMW support of the miners in southern Colorado as the reason for the protracted violence that has followed.

In addition to the economic conditions the miners have faced there, they work in the most dangerous mines in the nation. From 1884 to 1912, seventeen hundred souls gave up their lives in mining accidents. The death rate in Colorado mines during 1912 has been documented as the worst in the nation, more than twice the national average. By the end of this year alone, one hundred four men will die in Colorado mines and six more in the mine workings on the surface.

These high death rates are not due to major disasters but to the constant risk of explosion, suffocation and collapsing roofs and walls.

Believe it or not, the fault lies in the way miners are compensated. They are paid to produce coal, not make mines safe for themselves or their fellow workers. The companies, and therefore the miners, consider the shoring up of unstable roofs or walls as "dead work," lost time. An ironic term, but the miners aren't paid for non-productive work and so they don't do it, in spite of the risk. Survival is a choice between earning less and starving your family or risking a horrible death. Not really a choice.

The Colorado Fuel and Iron Company is the main mining company in Trinidad, now the largest mining company in all of Colorado. It's mostly an iron and steel producer, owned by two of the biggest robber barons in U.S. history — John D. Rockefeller and Jay Gould, the railroad tycoon. CF&I is in mining primarily to produce iron ore and fuel for the Rockefeller foundries. Gould is in it to produce cargo for his railroads and other transportation interests.

These industrialists don't know or care much about the mining industry. They play the money game from their plush offices in the East. They don't soil their shoes by visiting the mines. To them, mining doesn't produce profit. It's just raw material, a necessary cost of doing business. The business is manufacturing and transportation. Their coal business is focused on keeping the cost down.

By 1912, Rockefeller has taken total ownership of the mining company. I have heard he has turned it over to his son, John D. Rockefeller, Jr., but that doesn't seem to change anything. At this time I don't know Junior, but I do know his old man is the most ruthless capitalist of all time. And, like his father before him, Junior is way off in New York City, pulling the strings from afar, remotely, just as did his old man. I suppose Junior is a younger version of Rockefeller Senior.

Because CF&I is by far the largest operation in Colorado, it sets the standard for the industry. The standard is horrific. The story I'm about to tell you is far worse than the West Virginia wars I've already told you about.

This morning I see in the Washington, D.C., newspapers that Colorado's new governor, Elias Ammons, has invited me to come to Colorado. The exact quote goes something like this, "Mother Jones is not to be allowed to go into the southern field where the strike is raging."

Ammons was in the legislature when I was there before, so I guess he remembers me. But he's forgotten that such a statement is a challenge I won't resist.

I go to my room immediately to pack. That night I board a train for Denver. When I arrive, I go straight to my favorite cheap hotel and then down to the train depot to buy a ticket for the morning train to Trinidad. Things are so dangerous in Colorado I don't want to get my good railroad worker friends in trouble by having them get me onboard for free.

As I approach the front desk, a man who is registering at the same time, stops me and asks, "Are you going to go to Trinidad in the morning, Mother Jones?"

"Of course I am. Why else would you think I would be here?"

"Well, I want to tell you that the governor has his detectives at the hotel and the railway station. They're watching you."

"Detectives don't bother me," I boast.

"Maybe not, Mother, but you should know there are two detectives in the lobby, one up in the gallery and two or three at the station watching who boards the trains going south. I gather from the newspaper that you're safe as long as you stay here in Denver, but if you make a move to go south, they're going to grab you."

I thank him for the information and instead of buying a ticket, I go over to union headquarters to enquire about Addie Thompson. When she last visited me in the hospital in Charleston, she told me that she and her husband had been so inspired by my work they had applied for jobs as organizers for the UMW and were going back to Colorado to restart their lives there.

After I congratulated her, I discouraged her by telling her everything I knew about the situation in Colorado and opined that it was entirely too dangerous an assignment for a woman with so little experience. I didn't know about her husband.

She allowed as how her experience with me in West Virginia was all she needed and, apparently, the UMW thought so too. She was determined and I certainly knew better than to try to change the course of a determined woman.

At union headquarters, after some talk about the Colorado situation and my intentions to go to southern Colorado, I said, "I'm interested in the whereabouts of a young woman from West Virginia who came out here a few weeks ago to be a union organizer. Her name is Addie Thompson. Did she pass by here?"

"Yes, Mother, but I'm sad to have to tell you that she was killed during an invasion by the miners of one of the mines at Trinidad."

I stagger on my feet and the fellow who has given me such bad news leads me to a chair.

"What happened?" I ask after regaining my wits.

"You should be proud of her, Mother. The men had already decided to occupy the mine when she got there. They were assembling for the charge. She tried to change their minds, but they were too stubborn. I was told she decided she would march at the head of the pack, hoping that the mine guards would not shoot a woman and the marchers would be spared.

"But she was wearing miners' clothes and a cap. The guards had no idea that she was a woman and they shot her dead. I suppose the guards thought if they killed the leader, the rest would cut and run.

"But, because she was a woman, it didn't work that way. The miners were infuriated. They opened fire and blasted their way into that mine, drove the scabs out, and now they are in possession of the mine."

I am still staggered. A couple of men help me back to my hotel.

After an hour or so of grief and self-blame, I go on with my plans. While I'm not *afraid* of the detectives, I know I will never make it to Trinidad through the train station. And so, when it gets dark I head for the tracks beyond the station and begin looking for a railway coach that will soon be hooked up to a southbound engine.

"Oh, Mother Jones," a voice says, "is that you who's walking these ties?"

"It's me," says I, "but I'm not just walking. I'm looking for a sleeper that's bound for Trinidad." I explain my problem.

"I don't know which one," the man says, "but you wait here. I'll find out."

He goes off with his lantern bobbing at his side. Presently, he returns with a porter.

"How can I help you, Mother?"

I tell the porter I want to know if the sleepers are made up and if there is one going to Trinidad that can be made available to me.

"There'll be one made up for *you*, that's for damned sure," says he.

A few minutes later, as he hands me up to a sleeper car, the conductor comes by and asks if there is anything *he* can do.

"Yes, sir," says I. "Would you please see to it that the engineer stops the train at the Santa Fe Crossing because I need to avoid the guards who will be looking for me at the Trinidad Station?"

"I'll do that," he promises.

When I offer him the two dollars I have been holding in my hand, the engineer asks, "Are you doing business, Mother?"

"Yes, I am."

"Then put your money in your pocket. Your money is no good to me."

I sleep all night in the berth. In the early hours of the morning the porter awakens me and takes me toward the dining car. I have breakfast in the kitchen.

"Eat hardy," the cook says while he flips flapjacks. "You may not get a chance at another square meal for quite some time because things are rough in Trinidad." I obey while I think of poor Addie whose cold, dead body is prophecy enough that things will indeed be rough when I get where I'm going.

From the Santa Fe Crossing I walk the tracks to Trinidad and I'm there three hours before the company guards and the militiamen who are waiting at the train station find out I'm already in town. I have avoided lunch at my usual place. Instead, I've snuck into my favorite hotel using the back door. But I soon learn that someone has apparently seen me. I guess it's the outfit I wear that gives me away.

General John Chase is in charge of the militia in Trinidad and the word is out that he will have me arrested at my hotel.

Before his men learn of my whereabouts, however, a delegation of miners comes first and offers to defend me.

"Boys," says I, "don't get yourself hurt or arrested on my account. Don't make any trouble; just let them have their way." It's easy to be brave, having just come from such a pleasant and useful experience in Mrs. Carney's "jail" in West Virginia.

The miners leave my room and a military captain enters. As he leads me down the stairs and out the front door, the miners and their friends are lined up on both sides of our pathway. One cries, "Mother, I wish I could go for you!" Tears roll down his cheeks.

I am taken to the Sisters' Hospital where I notice a portion of the building is being used as a military prison. They put me in a small room with white plastered walls, a cot, a chair and a table. There are no decorations on the walls.

Surprisingly, they allow me to keep my possessions. I am locked in there for nine weeks without seeing a solitary soul except for the silent militiamen who stand at attention on either side of the cell door. Once in awhile I can see two more across the hall and two more at the elevator directly down the hall.

Outside my small window, which overlooks the walkway leading to the hospital entrance, I can see a guard walking up and down, day and night. You would think they are keeping an eye on an army, not a little old lady.

The Catholic sisters bring my meals, which are handed to me by one or the other of the militiamen. I am not permitted to speak with the sisters or ask for a priest. I receive not one letter, postcard or newspaper. I am unable to read any news whatsoever from the outside world.

I have a lot of time to think of one thing and another. One thing being that I will never again brag about how useful it is to carry on my battles from jail. I am constantly agitated by the knowledge that I am accomplishing nothing for the cause.

Finally, on my last day there, a colonel comes and says the governor wants to see me in Denver.

He comes back for me that night, bringing a subordinate with him. I notice as we make our way out of the hospital that there are no other soldiers in sight. None outside my door, none in the hallway, none at the elevator and none on guard duty outside.

The motorcar I am put in has all the blinds pulled down except where the driver sits. My escorts leave me to ride unattended.

When we reach Santa Fe Crossing I am put aboard a train for Denver and my driver disappears. At Denver I am met by General Chase whose behavior is as cold as his heart. When we arrive at the aristocratic Brown Palace Hotel, I inquire if I am to stay there. He says I am and I say I would much prefer my usual hotel, which is no palace. Without a word he takes me there and says he will be back to get me at nine o'clock in the morning.

I'm thinking this is very strange. During this whole trip there seems to be no concern that I might escape. But then, why would there be? They know I won't leave Colorado. They know if I'm loose, I'll go right back to Trinidad.

The general picks me up the next morning and takes me straight to the governor.

"I'm sure," says the governor, "you have noticed, Mrs. Jones, that you are free. I have decided to release you but I must ask you not to go back to the strike zone. If you do, I cannot guarantee your safety."

"I have never asked you or anyone else to guarantee my safety, Governor Ammons, and I will indeed return to the miners in southern Colorado to help in any way I can."

"I think you should take my advice," Ammons says.

"Governor," says I, "if General Washington took instructions from such as you we would still be under King George's descendants! If Lincoln took instructions from such as you, Grant would never have gone to Gettysburg. I won't take your orders and I'll return to the coalfields at Trinidad."

I stay in Denver for a week and then buy a ticket on a sleeper back to Trinidad. I notice one of Rockefeller's detectives across the aisle from me and in the early morning two of Rockefeller's guards wake me up.

"Get up," they say. "You're getting off at the next stop."

We are in Walsenburg, fifty miles north of Trinidad but within the war zone.

The engineer and the fireman get off the train when they see the company thugs putting me off. They demand, "What are you going to do with that old woman?"

"That is none of your business," comes the answer from one of the Rockefeller thugs.

"We're making it our business," the engineer says. "Either this woman is put back on the train or we will leave it sitting right here."

"Boys," I say, "I appreciate what you're trying to do, but I want you to go back on your engine and be on your way. This will turn out all right. You'll see."

But it doesn't turn out all right.

I am put in a cellar under the courthouse, a cold, damp, dark place without heat of any kind. I wear my clothes day and night and fight off huge rats with a broken beer bottle I've found. I muse that this isn't much different than the rats I fight off when I'm not in jail. I suppose my jailers left the beer bottle here in the hope I would commit suicide.

My only view of the outside world is a small window up by the ceiling where I can watch the feet of people walking on the sidewalk above.

I watch their feet and their footwear trying to imagine what the rest of them looks like. I see the shoddy shoes of miners, the polished shoes of soldiers, shoes of women in fancy high heels, others in run down flats. I see the bare feet of children.

Sheriff's deputies come and shoo those children away when they scooch down, trying to wave at me.

For twenty-six days I am held in this black hole, Rockefeller's prisoner.

One day a man in a suit comes to me and says my lawyers have obtained a habeas corpus for me and I am to be released. I don't know I have lawyers. He says he'll give me a ticket to any place I want to go.

"Sir," says I, "I can accept nothing from men whose business it is to shoot down people of my class when they strike for decent wages and working conditions. No sir! I prefer to walk." And I walk right back to the coalfields where I should have been for the 13 weeks and a few days I have been held in Rockefeller's prisons.

—◆◆◆—

I link up with the UMW leaders in the area and learn quickly that the operators are bringing in Mexicans to work as scabs in the mines. This operation is protected by the state and federal militias all the way from the Mexican border to the strike territory.

They arrive packed in cattle cars, never having been told the truth about how they will be used. All they are told is that they will find easy work at good wages, which they sorely need.

When they get to the coalfields, they find themselves under the control of company gunmen and soon understand that it isn't good what is happening to them. Hundreds of these poor fellows have been lured into the mines with promises of free land, but when they arrive they are stuffed into company-owned bunkhouses. Those with families find themselves in company shacks, three or four families in one or two rooms. They all have the rent deducted from their paychecks.

If they attempt to leave, they are shot.

This is a battle we cannot win at the mine mouth where the lords of capitalism reign supreme. We try to stem the flow of indentured scabs on the rails into the mine property, but there too we are out-gunned. And so, I decide to go down to El Paso, Texas, to help win this war by firing words, not bullets. I take the battle far away from the company goons of Colorado to the Mexican border and beyond it.

In El Paso I hold meetings around the clock. Some of the meetings I call myself. In other cases I go to meetings wherever Mexicans are gathered. I tell them the truth about what's happening in Colorado and warn them away for their own good. With their help, I send the message loud and clear across the border to their friends and loved ones in Old Mexico. I do everything in my power to discourage potential strike breakers from going north to the Rockefeller mines.

Eventually, with some good Mexicans ready to replace me as a hellraiser on the Mexican border, I return to Colorado. Once again I am not welcome, even though they have a welcoming committee waiting.

Chapter Thirty-Six
Trinidad and Ludlow, Colorado ~ January, 1914

While working down Mexico way, I've been following the news from southern Colorado.

The miners in southern Colorado, who were beaten in their attempt to gain fair wages and working conditions in 1904 when I was there, have grown even more angry.

The United Mine Workers, the very union that abandoned them just ten years ago, has returned. And, even though most of the miners still distrust the UMW and even though they have not rejoined the union to any extent, they are honoring a strike which was first called by the UMW back in September, 1913.

The strikers and their families have been evicted from company housing. Homeless, jobless and struggling against the effects of a hard winter, they have turned to the UMW for help and the union has purchased a tract of land near the Ludlow train station, about 12 miles north of Trinidad. There, the UMW has built small wooden platforms and provided free tents to be placed on them as temporary homes.

The tent colony is located right beside the train tracks that transport scabs to Trinidad. The tent city is not just a place for twelve hundred men, women and children to huddle against the elements. It is a strategic location where the miners can interfere with railroad cars full of scabs headed south to the mines and to prevent coal from being shipped from those mines to the north.

The UMW has issued rifles to the miners who have none. They've exchanged rifles with men who had still been carrying flintlocks, relics from the Civil War.

The tent colony is now an armed camp.

I also hear that the conflict is now centered on a single demand — union representation. I am concerned about this. Before the strike, the UMW had made seven demands on behalf of the miners:

1. Recognition of the union as bargaining agent
2. An increase in tonnage rates (equivalent to a ten percent wage increase)
3. Enforcement of Colorado's eight-hour work day law
4. Payment for "dead work" (laying track, erecting roof supports, etc.)

5. Weigh-checkmen elected by the workers to keep company honest
6. The right to use any store and choose housing and doctors
7. Strict enforcement of Colorado's mine laws regarding safety, scrip and guards

Now, upon declaring the strike, the union has stated only one demand, union representation. In the great battle to come we are not asked to fight specifically for better wages, hours, safety or any of the other noble causes that can earn public support. We seem to be fighting for the union, not the people, and I don't see how the public is going to be inspired by that.

The miners who were abandoned in 1904 don't trust the union. And neither do I. But I don't trust the union for many more reasons than the miners even know about, not the least of which is that it is beginning to look a lot like big business.

The so-called leaders are beginning to draw big salaries, the field workers are also well paid and they all spend too much time and money wining and dining their capitalist counterparts.

Soon, I'm thinking, pretty soon we'll have *big labor*, run by a new upper class more interested in their careers than their responsibilities. In too many situations I have already found myself compelled to fight against organized labor at the same time I'm fighting for the underclass. That just doesn't make sense.

Thus, I have mixed emotions about participating in a war aimed only at gaining union recognition. But on the other hand, I have to admit that the situation does call for big labor. The considerable power of the Rockefeller organization has just gotten bigger. CF&I has joined a new coal mine operators' association that represents all the mining companies in Huerfano and Las Animas counties. The Rockefeller interest, being the biggest of the big, is running the coal association.

The combined forces now command a large army of mercenaries led by a professional military commander, a veteran of the Civil War. Sometimes paid gunmen are issued the uniforms of state militia to pose as legitimate soldiers. All of a sudden, you can't tell the difference between public and private troops.

By now, the State of Colorado has run out of funds to pay state militiamen and so the state has either collected their uniforms and sent the men back to their homes or the troops have been contracted out to fight under the command of the mine owners. In which case, the uniforms are now filled by company men.

On our side, the UMW has prepared to meet force with force, gun for gun.

I don't trust the UMW, don't agree with its bellicose strategy, but it's not a good time for my voice of reason to walk away. No choice, really. Against big business, backed by the government, the only hope miners have is to join the forces of big labor and hope that winning a battle for the union will eventually lead to the wins that count, the ones that will free the workers from economic slavery and mortal danger.

—◆◆◆—

The lines have been drawn, the forces made ready, the decisions made. It's not a fight I want. And so, as I ride the rails back to Colorado from the Mexican border, I ask myself, "What can Mother Jones do?"

Well, some people have referred to me as the "Miners' Angel." I decide that will be the role for me this time when the train rolls into the war zone, Trinidad station.

The militia has other ideas and orders me to stay on the train, keep heading north toward Denver. I get off anyway, which seems to confuse these soldiers. It is like they don't really know what to do with me. First they take me to the telegrapher's office and then they change their minds and escort me to the hotel where they have their headquarters.

I tell them I want to get breakfast and so they take me to the dining room.

"Since I'm in your custody," says I, "I guess you'll be paying for my breakfast."

"State of Colorado will pay for it," one says.

"Well, since I'm the guest of the State of Colorado," says I, "I'll order a big expensive breakfast. I'll have everything from steak and eggs to pie and ice cream."

I am just finishing up when the northbound train to Denver is ready to pull out. My military escorts put me aboard while a delegation of men sings a miners' song at the top of their lungs.

"God bless you Mother."

"God bless you, my boys!"

"Mother, I hope you have a warm coat. It's freezing up there in Denver."

"I'll be all right, my lad." I notice the chap has no overcoat, just a cheap cotton thing with a woolen rag around his neck as a scarf.

"You keep warm, my son. And I'll do the same."

Around the miners a number of militiamen stand. One starts swinging the butt of his gun, hitting miners and trying to goad them into a fight. Others hurl vile epithets at them, but the boys keep cool and I can still hear them singing as the train pulls out.

"Y'all keep right on singing," says I under my breath. "Mother Jones will keep right on coming back."

As soon as my feet hit the streets of Denver I am back on a train for Ludlow to play the role of Miners' Angel. From those bitter January days at the Ludlow tent colony until the horror that is to come, I minister to the needs of the families. My ears burn, not with frostbite but with stories of brutality and suffering that weary me. I suppose I should be in the thick of the fight, but I know better. Once again, the battle has gone out of control."

I help by giving families a sympathetic ear.

"Oh, Mother, my daughter has been assaulted by the soldiers. She is such a sweet little girl."

"Oh, Mother, did you hear how the soldiers broke into Mrs. Hall's house? They wrecked everything and terrified the little children just because Mr. Hall, the undertaker, buried two miners who were killed by the militia!"

"Oh, Mother, did you hear how they are arresting miners for vagrancy and making them work in company ditches without pay?

"Oh, Mother," screams a frantic mother, "my little boy is all swollen up from the kicking and beating he got from a soldier because he called him a name. He called him 'Johnny Rockyfeller.' Now my boy is dying!"

"Oh, Mother, did you hear about poor old Mr. Colner? He was going to the post office and the militia arrested him and marched him out in the woods and made him dig his own grave with a pick and shovel.

"He begged to be allowed to go home and kiss his wife and children goodbye, but one of the soldiers said he'd do the kissing for him when he finds his wife. The other soldiers laughed. Colner fainted and fell right into this grave. The soldiers left him there and went back to town to drink. Poor Colner woke up and staggered back to camp. He wasn't physically hurt but they say he isn't quite right in the head."

I spend long days and nights with sobbing widows who have lost their husbands or their children in the mines. I comfort them and I nurse back to sanity the ones who are driven nearly out of their minds by the inhumanity of war. I solicit donations of food and clothing for the families and keep as many miners as

I can away from the saloons, not for moral reasons but because the saloons are in the hands of Rockefeller interests.

I try to get the word out to the public about the misery of these days, but no one listens. Men who sit in the steam-heated offices of the Rockefeller dynasty on Broadway in New York City cannot hear the sobs of women and children over the racket of ticker tapes merrily reporting the day's profits.

The press is blind to miseries like these. Because the events happen over time, stories like these are not instant news. But when they explode all at once in spectacular fashion, then the word gets out. I saw it in West Virginia. I suppose I will see it again here at the Ludlow camp. Meanwhile, what will be will be, I tell myself. I cannot change what is, but I can help make the misery tolerable.

In addition to ministering to the families, I decide to help the miners deal with the scab situation. Their strategy thus far has been to simply harass the scabs as they are transported past the Ludlow tent city and at the mine sites where scabs wander too close the perimeter of the company lands.

But this harassment does little good. The companies have transformed coal cars into armored cars by fastening thick steel plates to their sides. Aboard the cars, Mexicans huddle on the floor while company guards fire their guns over the armored plates toward the camp to discourage harassing fire from the miners. On the mine perimeters, company guards have been doubled and redoubled to prevent both harassment by the miners and escapes by the scabs.

All of the harassment irritates the coal operators, but it doesn't stop the flow of scabs.

I talk to the miners about that.

"Gentlemen," says I, "there is a better way to hurt the mine operators than by mere harassing tactics. But first, you have to understand who these scabs are and why they are here. They're not bad boys as I'm sure you believe. These Mexicans have been lured into a trap by promises of work and good wages. When they left Mexico they had no idea they were headed for a war zone or that they were becoming virtual slaves.

"I have just returned from a long stay down on the Mexican border where I talked with these poor immigrants and told them the truth and sent word back into Mexico. Most of them took the hint and skedaddled back across the border.

"But the Mexican border stretches across hundreds of miles and I couldn't get to them all with my message. These importers of Mexican slaves are at work all along that border and decent men continue to fall prey, unknowing.

"You should understand this, boys. The same thing happened to you. You became virtual slaves when you went up there in those mines the first time, unaware you were becoming captives of capitalism. And, like the Mexicans, you were unable to get loose.

"Well, here's how you can help these Mexican slaves as well as yourselves. Instead of warning shots, which tell them you are their enemies, why not use your ammunition to help these slaves escape? They don't want to be there. They are desperate to get out of there and return to their families.

"Let's do this. Let's get the word into the mines that we want to be their friends. If the Mexicans want to escape, we want to help them. Let's set up an underground railroad like they had during the Civil War to help slaves escape. If you fellows will agree to do that, I've got friends in the immigration department in Washington and I'll get them up to Ludlow to set up a field office to transport these Mexican boys back to their families.

"In this way, we will help our Mexican brothers and do much more harm to the mine operators than a little harassment can do. What do you say, boys?"

The support is unanimous and they set about making a plan to escort and harbor escaped Mexicans until they can be turned over to immigration for safe transport back to their own country. Meanwhile, I contact my dear friend Terence Powderly in Washington who has been a top official in immigration before founding and heading the Department of Labor. He's still got the connections and he's thrilled to help.

Immigration officials are on the next train from the East. They join me in the same rooming house where I have been staying and set up shop in an empty store in the little community of Ludlow. They are careful not to associate themselves directly with our little underground railroad, but their official duties are to transport illegal aliens back across the border from wherever they find them. They find them waiting at the front door of their shop every morning and there is nothing the mine operators can do about that.

Except get madder.

Every day I've been walking the few miles from the community of Ludlow to the tent colony. Even though the colony is outside company lands and owned by the UMW, I am made nervous by the constant harassment by company guards and state militiamen either on foot or in an armored land vehicle made out of an old automobile chassis and covered with steel plates just like the Bull Moose Special railroad car in West Virginia.

This armored car circles the tent city several times a day, showing off the machine guns and rifles onboard. Once in awhile, when a train is approaching with scabs aboard, the gunmen will fire a few rounds over the tents, hoping to scare off miners who are waiting in trenches to fire their own guns to harass the train. When this happens, I join the families in diving under the wood platforms of their homes into dugouts that have been excavated by the men for their families' safety. With bullets flying overhead, these little cellars may not be necessary as long as it's just warning fire. But, if the company thugs ever get a bit too much to drink, who knows what might happen.

Chapter Thirty-Seven
Ludlow, Colorado ~ April 20, 1914

It is the morning after Easter Sunday and the many Greek immigrants at Ludlow are recovering from their celebration of the day before. The Greeks are skilled fighters, having come to America from the Balkan wars of the years previous.

Three National Guardsmen — at least they are wearing military uniforms — appear at the tent colony and confront the camp leader, Louis Tikas, with the demand that he meet the militia commander at the train station in Ludlow village. As it turns out, the military commander is seeking the release of several escaped scabs who are being protected while they wait for transport on the final leg of our underground railroad to the immigration office in Ludlow.

While this meeting is taking place with Lt. Karl Linderfelt, two companies of militia install a machine gun on a ridge above the camp. Tikas refuses to release the escaped scabs and, expecting trouble, runs the half-mile back to the camp. He learns that the miners, fearing for the safety of their families, have set out to flank the militia positions. Soon, a gunfight breaks out.

I am visiting with one of the families and, like other families in the camp, we seek refuge in the dugout below their wooden floor. Some of the larger families that can't fit in a dugout, run for the hills opposite the machine gun encampment.

Bullets are already flying as we flee and these bullets aren't over our heads this time. They are raining down all around us. We are fortunate to reach safety, but I see several women and children go down as they run to their own safety holes.

We listen all day while our boys fire their weapons from the camp to where the two militia divisions are entrenched. At about five o'clock in the afternoon our boys run out of ammunition. They gather the families who are not in their holes and retreat with them into the hills for safety.

With our riflemen gone, the militia begins spraying the tents with bullets, many of them coming like a swarm of bees from the Gatling gun. Their ammunition rips up the tents and leaves the colony in shambles, many of its citizens still huddled beneath the wooden floors.

We are thinking it is about over when we hear a loud boom, followed by another and yet another. We discover the militia is lobbing fire bombs into what is left of the colony. I suppose they want to drive everyone out into the open so we can all be slaughtered. We stay put.

As the raw wind blows down the canyons where we shiver and weep, we hear the tromp of militiamen, drunk with bloodlust and liquor, looting the colony and using oil-soaked torches to set fire to all the tents that have not been burned out by the fire bombs.

Finally, silence comes. It is dark outside, but we dare not leave our living tombs until first light the next morning. I smell smoke throughout the night.

I am the first out of our hole in the morning and when I look around I see wretched people creeping around, looking for the dead. In a dugout under one burned out tent, the searchers find eleven charred bodies, nine little children and two women who were burned beyond recognition when the blazing timbers of the tent floor came crashing down upon them.

Most of the platforms have survived because they were built out of green lumber. But this unfortunate family apparently huddled under a platform built of deadwood.

The tent city is leveled. The largest of the metal objects that have survived the fire seems to be bedsprings lying askew upon the ground and coal stoves with their flues still reaching for the sky. A makeshift stone chimney stands here and there, others lie collapsed on the ground. They had been used to vent open fireplaces as well as the iron stoves that were provided by the UMW.

Yet, as if there might be something left of value, I see men combing the debris in search of their own treasures or the plunder of others. They are not criminals; they are looking for anything to help them survive.

As the victims wander about, I hear a report that Louis Tikas is dead. Mr. Tikas had remained in the camp for which he was responsible. He and two other men were captured by the militia. It is told that while two militiamen held Mr. Tikas, Lt Linderfelt broke his rifle butt over Tikas' head. Mr. Tikas and the other two men were later found dead. Tikas apparently had not died from the blow to his head. He had been shot in the back.

There were nineteen souls lost at Ludlow that day, eleven of them children between the ages of four months and eleven years.

—◆◆◆—

This is not the first massacre since the beginning of the UMW strike in Colorado.

Six weeks before the Ludlow massacre, Governor Ammons called out the Colorado National Guard troops supposedly to prevent the mines from spreading violence. At first, the presence of the Guard seemed to calm the situation, but before long the miners discovered that the sympathies of the Guard leaders were with company management and the real purpose was to break the union.

Adjutant General John Chase, who had served during the violence of Cripple Creek ten years earlier, was back and in his typical fashion imposed a harsh regime which the miners resented.

On March 10, 1914, the body of a scab was found on the railroad tracks near Forbes, Colorado, and the Guardsmen claimed the strikers had murdered the man. In retaliation, General Chase ordered the Forbes tent colony destroyed. There were no casualties because this attack was carried out while the inhabitants were attending the funeral of an infant who had died of consumption a few days earlier.

Now the Ludlow Massacre. "Enough is enough," cry the miners. Organized labor agrees. The UMW urges union members to acquire "all the arms and ammunition available," and a large-scale guerrilla war ensues. It lasts ten days.

—◆◆◆—

While this is going on, I gather a small delegation together and go to Washington, D.C., to appeal to President Woodrow Wilson to send in federal troops, and to Congress to appropriate funds to support it. With the help of my dear Terence Powderly, we obtain an audience with the president.

A few days later, the president sends troops to Colorado and restores order by disarming both sides, displacing and often arresting Colorado militiamen in the process.

The conflict, now called the Colorado Coalfield War, is eventually deemed the most violent labor conflict in U.S. history.

The Colorado government tries to play it down, claiming the death toll is only sixty-nine lives while an investigation ordered, surprisingly, by John D. Rockefeller, Jr., reports one hundred ninety-nine deaths.

—◆◆◆—

In December, 1914, the UMW, running out of strike funds, withdraws from Colorado once again, having failed to gain recognition as the bargaining agent for the miners.

The Colorado Coalfield War fails to reach its goals and many striking miners are replaced by new workers. Over four hundred strikers are arrested, three hundred thirty-two of whom are indicted for murder. Only one man, John R. Lawson, leader of the strike, is convicted of murder and that verdict is eventually overturned by the Colorado Supreme Court.

Twenty-two Colorado Guardsmen, including ten officers, face court martial proceedings. All are acquitted, except Lt. Linderfelt who is found guilty of assault for his attack on Louis Tikas. He is not accused of murder since Tikas died of gunshot wounds and no one knows who did it. He gets off on the lesser charge with a light reprimand.

Costs to both the mine operators and the union are high. On top of that, the Coalfield War is followed by an economic downturn and many of CF&I's coal mines never reopen. Many men are thrown out of work, and the UMW is forced to discontinue strike benefits in February, 1915, due to lack of funds.

—◆◆◆—

If you think this is a sad end to my tale, think again.

To meet the economic impact felt by the miners in the coalfields, the newly formed Rockefeller Foundation steps in to provide relief programs that are organized by the newly created

Colorado Committee on Unemployment and Relief, an idea promoted by the new governor, George Carlson.

The relief fund does more than give handouts. It offers men work building roads and doing other useful projects. Honest labor for honest pay.

Carlson's too-short administration is noted for labor reforms including the passage of a workers' compensation law and the establishment of the Industrial Commission of Colorado.

The casualties suffered at Ludlow are used by organized labor to mobilize public opinion against unfair labor practices in the mining industry. Congress responds to the public outcry by directing the House Committee on Mines and Mining to investigate the Colorado coal wars and to recommend legislation to assure fairness and safe practices in the workplace.

And, the United States Commission on Industrial Relations conducts extensive hearings singling out John D. Rockefeller, Jr., for special attention. As you will soon see, those hearings produce some amazing results.

Chapter Thirty-Eight
New York City ~ January, 1915

In New York City, just a block or two from the headquarters of the Rockefeller enterprises, I attend the Commission on Industrial Relations' hearings on the Colorado Coalfield War. I testify when called upon.

Also in the audience is Mr. Ivy Lee, a young man who is pioneering a new profession that will be called "public relations." He is an employee of Mr. Rockefeller and I don't think much of the lad. As I recall, he's the one who started the rumor during a hiatus I had taken to be away from industrial conflict. The rumor was that I was running a house of prostitution!

"Mother Jones," he says, as I sit in my seat during a break in the proceedings, "I am Ivy Lee. May I have a word with you?"

He is tall and slender in his tailor-made suit and stands over me in the aisle. I turn and give him my hardest look.

"First of all, I have a few words for you," says I.

"I've had some hateful things said about me behind my back and in the press, but nothing has ever been so outrageous as your claim that I was running a whore house!"

"Well, Mother, that's the very thing I want to talk to you about," says he. "I want to apologize."

"Apologies are cheap," says I. "You'll have to prove to me that you really mean it when you say you apologize."

"I will, Mother. May I sit down?"

"I suppose so."

"Mother, I deeply regret the smear I made on your honorable character and for reasons that go beyond the guilt I feel for having sullied your name.

"I was fresh out of college and in my first job when that happened. I had joined the Rockefeller organization as a publicist and my first assignment was to dig up some dirt on you to spoil your reputation.

"During my investigation you were living at an estate where there was an apartment above a carriage house. And in that apartment, I learned, there was a prostitute living in it. And working there.

"I double checked to be accurate and learned you were in charge of the entire estate, having been contracted as an overseer during the owner's absence. I reported that information to my immediate supervisor and she directed me to get the word out that you were operating a house of ill repute. I did it, and I am ashamed to admit I was damned proud of myself at the time.

"I was so young and naïve then. But time has passed and as I look back, I see that this act that I committed upon you was not only against your ideals but against mine. You see, I am working now on a new approach to publicity that I call 'public relations.'

"As you know from yellow journalism, publicity has nothing to do with the truth. To the contrary, my concept for public relations is to help companies do well by behaving well and making sure everyone knows the truth.

"My philosophy is that doing good work so a company can tell the truth is a sure-fire winner for the company, its workers and its customers. Telling lies to *cover* the truth is a sure loser in the long run."

He falls silent, but I know he isn't finished. He just wants to give me a moment to say something.

I stay silent for a moment, and then say, "I like your philosophy, Mr. Lee, and I wish you good luck with it. If you can convince the robber barons of it, you will do more than all the labor unions in the world."

"As for your lie about me, technically, you were right. I was in charge of the entire estate and I knew that young lady was a prostitute and I found out that she sometimes brought men to her boudoir. And I can't claim ignorance because I knew what she was when I rented her the room.

"You can't be serious, Mother!"

"Indeed I am. You see, I felt sorry for her. No one has a life ambition to be a prostitute any more than a laborer wants to be a slave.

"Like everyone else in the underclass, that poor girl was driven to prostitution by poverty. She was not unprincipled. She was uneducated, unskilled and unwanted. The only opportunity to come her way was to sell what little she had. Herself.

"And so, I took her under my wing. I have no apology to make and I'm not sorry I did it.

"What I *am* sorry of, young man, is that the Rockefeller organization was so mean- spirited as to use this against me and to twist the facts the way you did. And I'm sorry for you, that you were so unprincipled at the time as to agree to do the Rockefeller family's dirty work."

"That's just it, Mother. I *was* principled, even then. But I was weak and I made a horrible mistake. I am so sorry."

"All right, Mr. Ivy Lee," says I, "I accept your apology. Now, it looks like they are reassembling this hearing, but I would like to talk to you later about this public relations idea you have. If you're going to be the 'Father of Public Relations,' then I declare I'm the 'Mother of Public Relations' and you and I need to compare notes!"

Through the biggest smile I've ever seen, this Ivy Lee character says, "Mother Jones, I have long admired your work as the public relations representative for the working class, and I would love the chance to talk shop with you again."

—◆◆◆—

I am about to find out that Ivy Lee's boss has bought into his public relations idea.

John D. Rockefeller, Jr., returns to the witness stand after two days of testimony in which he has already run the gauntlet of labor lawyers. He fields their jabs and parries respectfully and courteously and he does so again today. The answers he gives are so reasonable it's hard to believe. It is hard to believe that he is the son of John D. Rockefeller Senior, the most ruthless industrialist of all time.

But throughout the testimony, Junior admits that CF&I behaved miserably and that the company made a serious mistake in hiring paid gunmen who were encouraged to draw down on striking miners and their families.

He reports that the head of CF&I has been fired, but he doesn't totally shift the blame to the top employee. No sir, Junior says he is guilty of being too remote from the situation, with his offices being right here in New York City.

And, yet, he admits that if he'd had all the facts, he probably would not have changed course while in a competitive wartime situation. He says he was born and bred to be competitive and to his teacher — his father — that meant ruthless.

But he had learned a big lesson in Colorado. Ruthlessness does not earn respectability. And in the long run, respectability is the best policy and he says his family will follow the best policy from now on.

His company, he says, was under siege and it seemed at the time that it was necessary to take extreme action. Under a siege mentality, his top men made the wrong decisions.

His greatest regret, says he, is that unarmed citizens, innocent women and children were killed.

Now, he says, he understands that waging war does not benefit either side and he is moving forward with plans to create a better relationship, a working partnership with labor.

Part of that plan has been executed. With the creation of the Rockefeller Foundation, his family seeks the government's approval as a tax-free charitable organization.

Commissioners express the worry that the Foundation may have more than altruistic purposes and that it might be used as a means of developing public sympathy for the company and against unions.

"For instance," says one commissioner, "might the money not be used to circulate propaganda for or against the workmen's compensation acts that have been passed?"

"Well," says Junior, "I don't see why the Foundation should not have the same legitimate methods of spreading its views as do the unions or the other organizations that have been mentioned during these hearings.

"But our company is changing its views and there will be no conflict of interest between the charitable goals of the Foundation and our positions concerning legislation that will benefit the worker.

"The Rockefeller family sees the futility in conducting labor relations at the point of a gun. We are not proud of it either. My father has transferred ownership of CF&I to me and I have complete authority to change the way we do business."

The chairman then asks, "Where would you draw the line as dispenser of money for philanthropy between your capacity as adviser to your father and as a CF& I director?"

"Your question," says Rockefeller quietly, "is based on the assumption that a man with one interest cannot be loyal to another. Regardless of the beating we have endured on the field of battle and in the press, we still hold our integrity dear. The Foundation will allow us to assume the role we have thus far shunned, the role of social responsibility."

"That's all well and good, Mr. Rockefeller, but I have a hard time having confidence in your pledge."

"I understand. I have no problem if the federal government imposes safeguards to that effect."

I'm thinking to myself, "Isn't this the very change in business relations we've been fighting for?" Yet, at this hearing I observe the labor union arguing against Junior's plan when the labor union itself has no alternative to offer.

They don't trust Junior's plan but they've pulled out of Colorado once again, leaving the workers and their families high and dry. They blame the lack of money for dropping out. But here they are arguing against the money that the Foundation will provide to the workers who are out of work, partially due to the union's strike.

I'm beginning to trust this Rockefeller, Jr., fellow more than I have the unions over the past fifty years! He seems genuine. And my little talk with Ivy Lee has me thinking that just maybe the time is right for good labor relations to make for good public relations and a better way of life for laborers. This could just be the turning point we've been hoping for all these years and I'm thinking I'll grab the opportunity.

—◆◆◆—

My new friend Ivy Lee takes the stand when Rockefeller, Jr., is dismissed. I'll not call Mr. Rockefeller "Junior" from here on.

Ivy Lee is heckled mercilessly by union supporters on the panel over statements and errors made in publications he produced during the Colorado strike. These hecklers are loaded for bear. Those publications presented the company side of issues and events and Lee's being blamed for authoring them. He says he regrets the inaccuracies but refuses to accept blame, saying the material was provided to him by the coal operators and his job was simply to print it.

That answer doesn't ring true to what he has just said to me earlier about how calling me a whorehouse madam was a mistake. Why couldn't he admit that it was also a mistake to publish company propaganda without questioning it? But he's talking in the past, not the present. I hope.

It also occurs to me that business, at least the Rockefeller business, is taking a positive look ahead during this hearing while organized labor is playing games, looking behind.

Ivy is still being grilled when Mr. Rockefeller — notice I didn't call him "Junior" — approaches me much as Ivy Lee did an hour or so ago.

Standing beside me in the aisle with testimony still going on, John D. Rockefeller, Jr., addresses me quietly. "Mother Jones, I am going back to my office down the street and I was wondering if you would be so kind as to visit me there as soon as you can. I know you know the address. You've mentioned it so often." He gives me what seems to be a genuine smile.

"Of course," says I.

—◆◆◆—

Later, I walk down the street to the Standard Oil Building at 26 Broadway, the address I have so accusingly recited often as the place where kings move pawns around on a board connected distantly to the working men and women they exploit.

I'm looking forward to today's game.

During our conversation we talk about another plan Rockefeller has that will be in addition to the charitable work he has proposed through the Rockefeller Foundation.

He is not open to recognizing any union as a bargaining agent, but instead plans to make room at CF&I for a company union with its own board of directors elected by the employees. In this way, negotiations between business and labor can be held in a spirit of mutual interest, each side on the same team.

"Of course, I am immediately suspicious," says I, "just as you have been questioned about the motives of your Foundation at the hearing today. I can't say I would trust your company union any more than I've trusted the UMW over the years, but I'll have to say I might not trust it any less."

He laughs. "Well, that's a good starting point," he says. "What I can say without a doubt is that, organizations aside, my sincere intention is to give a say to the workers in company business that affects them. If I can make that happen, and if it's fair and equitable for all, then my job is done and perhaps you will endorse my efforts. I'm going to work hard for your endorsement, Mother Jones."

"Well," says I. "Like you said this afternoon in the hearing, it depends on integrity. You say you have it. And from what I've seen and heard of you these past days, I'm beginning to think you might have it.

"But I've thought the same thing about leaders of unions such as the UMW. And, too often they've let me down.

"In an odd way though, I can see that you may well have more to gain by being a good employer than union leaders on the outside have in lining their own pockets. If you truly mean what you say, and if you see the value in giving your workers a reasonable share of the benefits from capital gain, then you and your workers have mutual interests that will make your company union work."

"Then you endorse the idea?"

"Yes, I endorse the *idea*," says I. "But I won't be able to endorse the program until it *proves* itself."

He laughs again. "Mother Jones, you would have made a fine industrialist."

We spend an hour and a half together. The next day in the *New York Times* I read what Mr. Rockefeller and I had to say about the meeting.

"Tell us what you discussed," demands a reporter.

"Oh, we've just been talking over everything for the best interest of the nation and the cause of humanity," says I.

"Did you tell Mr. Rockefeller about conditions in Colorado?"

"Yes, I just told him a few things but I've been in jail so long, my head's out of gear."

"Are you going to Colorado with him?"

"Oh no, we would be mobbed."

I didn't want to say too much about our conversation because I believed it was between Mr. Rockefeller and myself. Any other time I would be loving this media exposure and milking it for all its worth.

As I turn away from the reporter, one more thing crosses my mind. I think it needs to be said. I turned back.

"One thing I want you to know," I says. "I just told Mr. Rockefeller one thing. I have been misrepresenting him terribly. He's not his father."

—◆◆◆—

Mr. Rockefeller was more disposed to talk about the interview than I, and I found his commentary very interesting. He received several reporters in his private office. He seemed hopeful that his direct personal contact with me and tomorrow with representatives of organized labor might be the beginning of better things.

He spoke of his desire to gather information from every possible source about the grave problems before him and his company. And he thought the frank explanations he had given on the stand during the hearings would help workers realize he has a real desire to do all he can to improve conditions.

"Now that the strike is over," he was quoted as saying, "I saw no reason why I should not have a chat with Mother Jones. And I have appointments tomorrow with three top labor leaders."

A reporter asked what Mother Jones had to say.

"Mother Jones went over all the main points in the situation. She told me about the schools and the desire of the miners to choose their own teachers. She told me about the company stores. She talked about the right of workmen to bring their grievances to company officials without jeopardizing their jobs.

"I found myself able to agree in principle with all that she said. I was not able to respond as specifically as I should because I do not have direct knowledge of the conditions in Colorado, and therefore I do not know specifically what the company can do. But I'm going there and I intend to have specific answers and solutions as quickly as possible."

"How soon?" a reporter wanted to know.

"Well, right now I have a stack of new questions from the Commission and I'll need to respond to those first. I have more than that on my desk regarding business matters. But I'm intending to get out to Colorado in a few weeks."

With some embarrassment, Mr. Rockefeller heard what I said about him to the reporters and he confirmed that I had praised his testimony and that I had changed my view of him.

He confessed that he was pleased. He said he had similar positive feelings about me and those he had met during the hearings who, until the hearings, he had known only as "the opposition."

"The union representatives are as clean-cut as any fellows you would wish to see," he said. "I'll have to admit I had a rather low opinion of them before we met. That's the ticket, you know. Understanding one another."

In the article, Mr. Rockefeller went on, "I believe it will be for the good of everyone that I can have talks with the three union representatives tomorrow. I want to meet them man to man. I want to talk things over with them. I want to find out exactly how they look on things and I want to tell them what my own views are. I am sure we will understand each other better and that our meetings will have an influence for good."

How many lives, I ask myself, could have been saved by a few attitudes like that?

Chapter Thirty-Nine
Matewan, West Virginia ~ May, 1920

I wish I could tell you that the Colorado Coalfield War was the coal war that ended all coal wars or that it was the biggest of the industrial wars to be fought in America. But in spite of my best efforts to change history, it isn't to be.

Following the Ludlow Massacre, I travel the country telling the story and campaigning for changes in the behaviors and laws of men that will prevent that kind of madness from ever happening again. I use the horror story of Colorado to repeatedly shock my audiences and keep the memory alive in people's minds.

Again and again I remind the public that it is the responsibility of their elected officials and their attendant bureaucrats to see to it that changes are made in public policy that will quell the violence that still seethes in the hearts and minds of working men and women wherever they suffer.

I use John D. Rockefeller, Jr., as an example of the kind of wise and responsible employer who can change his ways and help government reduce the potential for more violence. I call upon all employers to follow his lead.

President Wilson and members of the House Mines and Mining Committee become my allies by proposing to union leaders and mine owners alike that they agree to call a truce and create grievance committees to work out differences peacefully.

There is voluntary, but spotty, compliance by some unions and companies, but I am called upon repeatedly during 1915 and 1916 to assist in various strikes across the nation.

I go back to New York to help in the strikes of garment workers and streetcar workers. While I'm helping the wives of the streetcar workers there, the women fight like wildcats and the police threaten to take us all to jail. To me they say if anyone is killed, they will hold me responsible and they hope I hang.

"If they want to hang me, let them," says I. "And on the scaffold I will shout 'Freedom for the working class'. And when I meet God Almighty, I will tell Him to damn my accusers who blame me and the working class."

Then I'm called over to a place named Roosevelt, New Jersey, to help workers on strike at a fertilizer plant. The strike leaders tell me they are against taking up arms, but two unarmed workers have been shot by company guards. Although the guards have been arrested, they have been let out on bail. Now these guards are back on the job and the workers are afraid for their lives and disappointed in the judicial system.

The men are talking about going back to work and the strike leader wants to organize the wives like I have done in other cases. They ask for my help and I respond.

"Help your husbands stand firm," says I to a group of wives I've gathered. "Don't let them become scabs. Don't let them go back to work. And don't let them resort to violence, no matter what happens. Men have never won a strike by violence and no strike has ever been won without the help of their womenfolk." I tell them of the way I've organized women to fight and my talk inspires them.

I am called to similar strikes for the remainder of the decade, the last one in 1919, a steel workers' strike in Pittsburgh, Pennsylvania.

These and many other incidents continue to forecast more violence on a scale we have already seen in Colorado. I am expecting very bad things to happen and I expect them to happen in West Virginia.

A call confirms my fears. I am wanted in Matewan, West Virginia.

—◆◆◆—

By 1920, the UMW has finally organized most of West Virginia. But the call asking me to help doesn't come from the union. You see, I have once again disassociated myself from the UMW, due largely to my extreme dislike of the new president, John L. Lewis. I think he is much more interested in promoting his own self-image, with his big, bushy eyebrows and three-piece suits, his limousines and his entourage. I think he is more interested in raising the money in his pocket than he is in improving the wages of coal miners.

John L. and his minions are high-paid wheeler-dealers, not cut from the same cloth as the many fine volunteer leaders and low-paid organizers of the past who lived like paupers and died penniless right along with their working class brothers.

No, the call does not come from John L. or any of the other well-healed union men. It comes from Sid Hatfield, the local sheriff of Mingo County.

I don't know Sid, but I think he is a nephew of former Governor Henry Hatfield who was so helpful to me at the end of my long stay in West Virginia prisons a decade ago. Sid is also a former coal miner, which tells me he is sympathetic to the miners' condition.

He was elected sheriff with the help of Cabell Testerman, the mayor of Matewan. I know Cabell as a strong supporter of the union cause and if he endorsed Sid Hatfield, then that's good enough for me. It appears the government in and around Matewan is pro union and this seems like a situation where the miners will get a fair shake for a change. I just cannot turn a youngster like Sid Hatfield down.

I can't in spite of the fact that my age is not on my side. I pause to consider my health before promising to go back to West Virginia. My heart and lungs are bad. It is as if I have miner's consumption, a combination of lung diseases caused by inhaling coal dust over a long period of time. But it is the long-term effects of my repeated bouts with pneumonia in various prisons that have done me in.

I have lived long beyond the normal life expectancy of my time. Like most old women, my bones have grown weak, arthritis is my constant companion and I am bent over and walking with a cane. I am suffering from a long list of old age complaints, not the least of which is fatigue. Even if I can will myself to fight once more, I'm wondering how a pitiful old woman like me can be of any help.

Still, I know my very presence will matter to my boys. And so, I go.

While most of West Virginia has been organized, several pockets of southern West Virginia are holdouts. Notwithstanding my attitude toward the UMW at the time, I think the union is doing the right thing in trying to organize these non-unionized bastions of coal company power. Matewan, with its political sympathy to organized labor, is the right place for a showdown.

The coal operators, without the backing of local law enforcement agencies, use every illegal means to block the union. They fire everyone who is even remotely supportive of the union and blacklist them so they cannot get jobs anywhere else. Of course, they evict them from company housing.

In their neck of the woods, the law is their law and their law enforcers are the same Baldwin-Felts agents that have caused such havoc for so many years.

The attitudes toward the working man are blatant and atrocious. One company lawyer says of the evictions, "It is like a servant who lives at your house. If you discharge him, you ask him to get out of the servants' quarters. It is a question of master and servant."

There you go. And you thought I've been exaggerating about economic slavery. There's the proof, the very viewpoint I've accused the capitalists of for so long.

The union has set up tent colonies like they did in Hollygrove and Ludlow, but the tent cities in this case are massive. By May, three thousand out of the four thousand Mingo County miners have joined the union and a upwards of ten thousand idle and angry coal miners and their families are concentrated in camps throughout the region.

At the Stone Mountain Coal Company mine near Matewan, every single worker joins the union and is subsequently fired and evicted.

On May 19, 1920, twelve Baldwin-Felts agents arrive in the town of Matewan, including the Felts brothers, Albert and Lee. The brothers try to bribe Mayor Testerman with five hundred dollars to allow them to place sub-machine guns on the roofs of the town. Testerman refuses.

The Felts brothers and their gunmen march up to the Stone Mountain Coal Company property where they set about the eviction of a woman and her children who have not moved out because the woman's husband is absent.

They force her and her children out at gunpoint and throw their belongings in the road amidst a steady rain. Word gets back to town and to the camps and the miners are furious. Sheriff Hatfield decides to obtain a warrant for the arrest of the Felts brothers and their gunmen to prevent violence.

Sid Hatfield, with a fellow by the name of Fred Burgraff as witness, and Mayor Testerman meet the detectives on the porch of the Chambers Hardware Store.

When the sheriff tries to serve the warrant, the Felts brothers produce a warrant of their own which they say they previously obtained from a justice of the peace in rural Mingo County. Their warrant claims to authorize Albert Felts to arrest Sid Hatfield. The sheriff declares the warrant fraudulent and a shootout breaks out among the men.

It is still unknown whether Albert Felts shot the mayor, or whether Sid Hatfield shot the mayor. There had been rumors that Hatfield was sweet on the mayor's wife and some people wondered if this incident just gave Sid Hatfield the chance to get Mayor Testerman out of his way.

Nevertheless, the mayor is the first to go down. Sheriff Hatfield fires at the Felts brothers and keeps firing, chasing Albert Felts into the Matewan Post Office where he is shot dead. Brother Lee is already down.

Other men rush in and, by the time the gunfight ends, ten men lie dead including both Felts brothers.

The rumor that Sid Hatfield had designs on Mayor Testerman's wife were never proven, but Sid did marry Testerman's wife soon after the shootout.

—◆◆◆—

The gunfight becomes known as the Matewan Massacre. I've never been able to figure that label out since it was a shootout, not an ambush. Nevertheless, the outcome of the fight provides enormous encouragement to the coal miners in West Virginia because it is the first time the seemingly invincible Baldwin-Felts Agency has been beaten. The deaths of the two Felts brothers is a bonus long celebrated.

The new miner's hero is the man of the moment, the man who made it happen — Sid Hatfield.

While Hatfield becomes a symbol of hope, the unions gain strength from the coal miners' new faith in themselves and make great progress in their recruitment throughout Mingo County. The right to strike becomes a promise.

—◆◆◆—

I remain in Mingo County while a series of non-violent strikes are called up and down the Tug River. I try to encourage non-violent negotiation wherever I speak, and wherever I visit coal operators, but the tendency toward violence continues to grow, due in some part to the behavior of the miner's hero, Sid Hatfield, who struts about, wearing the hero badge boldly, damned proud of himself.

Both sides are building their arsenals and Sid has become the problem, not the solution, not only stirring up an appetite for violence among the miners, but converting Widow Testerman's jewelry store into a gun shop.

The trial of Sid Hatfield for killing Albert Felts begins on January 26, 1921. The good news is that it puts the miners' cause in the national spotlight, but it also continues to boost Sid's standing to a mythical status, further bolstering his bluster and that of his gun-toting admirers. He poses and brags to reporters in a manner that fans the flames of belligerency among the men.

Sid Hatfield and all the men involved in the shootout are acquitted, but in the meantime the union is facing significant setbacks. Eighty percent of the mines have reopened with existing miners signing "yellow dog" contracts. That's what we call miners who give up the strike and become scabs.

In mid-May, the union miners launch a full assault on non-union mines with a three-day battle waged all along the Tug River. Sid Hatfield assists the coal miners by deputizing them and I think the worm turns. Now it's the miners who deputize thugs. The action ends in a "flag of truce" forced under martial law.

Scores of miners are arrested by the state militia without habeas corpus and other basic legal rights, arrested and jailed for the smallest of infractions. The miners respond by using guerrilla tactics to avoid capture and carry on the fight.

In the midst of this tension, Sid Hatfield goes over to nearby McDowell County to stand trial for charges of dynamiting coal tipples. He may have gotten carried away in his support for the guerrilla warfare being waged by his admirers.

He is accompanied by his friend Ed Chambers, a guerrilla leader. The two men are flanked by their wives as they walk up the courthouse steps, unarmed.

A cluster of Baldwin-Felts agents standing at the top open fire and Hatfield is killed instantly. Chamber's bullet-riddled body rolls down to the bottom of the steps and, in spite of Sally Chambers' pleas, one of the agents runs down there and shoots Chambers once more in the back of the head, point blank.

Sid and Ed's bodies are returned to Matewan and word of the slaying spreads through the mountains. The miners assume the Baldwin assassins will escape punishment and they are enraged, promising that they themselves will see that justice is done.

Miners along the Little Coal River are among the first to militarize and begin patrols to guard the striking miners.

On August 7, 1921, the miners from Logan and Mingo counties attend a rally in nearby Charleston held by UMW District 17. This district encompasses most of southern West Virginia. The rally is led by Frank Keeney and Fred Mooney, both local veterans of minefield conflicts who are well read and articulate.

They meet with Governor Ephraim Morgan and present him with a petition stating the miners' demands. Morgan summarily rejects these demands and the miners leave the meeting intent on taking over Logan and Mingo counties by force.

I call on the miners to do no such thing and am immediately accused of losing my nerve. I explain over the derisive shouts from the group that indeed I do fear a blood bath the likes of which they have never seen, but which I have seen in Colorado. I try to describe those battles to them and I mean to explain how, despite the bloodshed in Colorado, the miners gained nothing. But I am drowned out by their shouts of derision.

Thus, they leave Charleston and head out to Lens Creek Mountain near Marmet, a Kanawha County community near the capital city. Thirteen thousand armed men from Boone, Fayette, Mingo, McDowell and Logan counties gather there and on August 24, they begin their march on Logan County.

Impatient to fight, a group of miners in St. Albans, another Kanawha County community, commandeers a Chesapeake and Ohio freight train and renames it the "Blue Steel Special," their answer to the Bull Moose Special of Hollygrove fame. They meet up with an advancing column of marchers from Danville, Boone County.

Meanwhile, Keeney and Mooney want no part of this and they flee to Ohio. They are replaced by the fiery Bill Buzzard. At the same time, the reviled Sheriff Don Chafin of Logan County has begun setting up his positions on Blair Mountain. Chafin has the financial support of the Logan County Coal Operators Association. Together they set up the nation's largest private army, three thousand sworn "deputies." They establish offensive positions along the front.

These converging forces are about to make the Colorado Coalfield War seem like child's play.

Chapter Forty
Blair Mountain ~ August 25, 1921

The first skirmishes occur on the morning of August 25 but the bulk of the miners are fifteen miles from the main battlefield.

By August 29, the uprising is fully joined and the number of fighters has reached twenty thousand by the time they reach Blair Mountain. The miners' army is well organized by veterans of World War I and its solders have been previously trained as soldiers in the U.S. Army.

They are like an Army division with supply units and passwords to weed out infiltrators. Not only do they commandeer trains, but private vehicles for off road transportation.

President Warren G. Harding is threatening to send in federal troops and a long meeting is held in the town of Madison, the Boone County seat. Agreements are made for the miners to retreat, and the miners prepare to draw back. But Sheriff Chafin has spent days assembling his army and he will not be denied his battle.

Within hours of the Madison agreement, Chafin's men are deliberately shooting union sympathizers in the town of Sharples, West Virginia, just north of Blair Mountain. Families are caught in the crossfire, infuriating the retreating miners who turn back toward Blair Mountain.

The two sides engage along a ridge on Blair Mountain and the battle becomes the largest insurrection on United States soil since the end of the Civil War. There is no way to know how many deaths occur.

Private planes are hired to drop homemade bombs on the miners. A combination of homemade bombs and leftover bombs from World War I are dropped on several towns including Jeffery,

Sharples and Blair. One bomb failed to explode and was retrieved for use as evidence later by the miners during the treason and murder trials following the battle.

Governor Morgan sends an urgent message to President Harding who sends twenty-five hundred federal troops including a bomber squadron under aviation pioneer General Billy Mitchell.

Army bombers from Maryland are used for aerial surveillance and the men below are worried that the military planes will also begin dropping bombs.

Gun battles continue for a week. At one point the miners nearly break through Chafin's defenses to take the town of Logan and their ultimate targets, the counties of Logan and Mingo.

Up to thirty deaths are reported on Chafin's side, up to one hundred on the union miners' side. Unreported, and therefore countless, are a number of deaths never made known.

Finally, the U.S. Army troops arrive. Faced with this federal onslaught, the battle quickly comes to an end.

Chafin's troops are disarmed by the federal troops. Most of the miners return to their homes before their weapons can be confiscated. Many hide them in the woods to be retrieved later.

Not all the miners make it home. A total of nine hundred and eight-five miners are indicted on charges of murder and conspiracy to commit murder. Though some are acquitted by sympathetic juries, many are imprisoned for various amounts of time. All are paroled by 1925.

A serious attempt is made to punish William "Bill" Blizzard who is charged with treason. He is tried consecutively and unsuccessfully in three West Virginia towns — Charles Town, Lewisburg and Fayetteville — before the charges are finally dropped.

It is at the last trial where the unexploded bomb appears, not to disrupt the proceedings, but to be used as evidence of the brutality of the local government and the companies during the battle. It is upon this evidence that Blizzard is released.

In the short run, the battle, as I predicted, is an overwhelming victory for management. The union ends up the loser and UMW membership in West Virginia plummets from more than fifty thousand miners to approximately ten thousand.

In the long run, the battle once again raises the awareness of the American people and their politicians of the turbulent causes that continue to lead to violence, not only in the coalfields, but across America where uncontrolled capitalism continues to exploit people and ferment unrest.

As a direct result, the defeat leads to a change in union tactics. Never again will the United Mine Workers, or any other union, engage in gunfire diplomacy. And if I am ever to stand before a gathering of angry laborers again, I expect they will hold their tongues, listen to me and understand that violence is not the answer.

Chapter Forty-One
Washington, California and Maryland ~ 1930

After Blair Mountain I am more of a symbol than a working union organizer or a fighter for the rights of the working class.

I'm a poor, homeless old woman now. I stay for a short time with the Powderlys in Washington, D.C., before Terence's death, then move out to California to stay with friends there.

Death nearly takes me in 1923 and more often than not I take to bed and to writing.

My articles are published mostly in the alternative press and in 1924 a fledgling newspaper, the *Chicago Times*, sues me for libel, slander and sedition. They win what many call a "shocking" three hundred fifty thousand dollar judgment.

I'm not shocked. I call it funny, considering I have no money and will likely be a mere memory before this sum can be collected. My partner, Jenny Flynn, closed our Chicago dress factory several years before her death, due to unfair competition from the sweatshops. All along, we had shared our profits with our employees and, with our factory closing, we shared their loss of income. What little money I have saved from my profits is long gone, spent on the causes of labor.

These final years allow me to accomplish one more of my ambitions. In 1925 I publish my autobiography which I have been writing since I left West Virginia in 1922. My everlasting friend, Clarence Darrow, honors me by writing the introduction.

The battle at Blair Mountain seems to have marked the end of large-scale labor wars, but strikes continue and I receive a steady flow of requests to appear on behalf of aggrieved workers in industries across the country. Incidents continue to occur and lives continue to be lost either in battle or at work, but they are minor compared to the stories I've told you.

My last public appearance is as the guest of honor at a Labor Day celebration in Alliance, Ohio in 1926. From that day forward my boys in the coalfields can only dream of my coming. Unless it is in spirit.

In 1927, Carl Sandburg publishes a book of American folk songs called *The American Songbag*. In it he includes a song that was originally a spiritual in the 1800s called *When the Chariot Comes*. Mr. Sandburg claims it was rewritten with lyrics inspired by the life of Mother Jones and renamed *She'll be Coming 'Round the Mountain*.

> She'll be coming 'round the mountain when she comes (when she comes). She'll be coming 'round the mountain when she comes (when she comes). She'll be coming 'round the mountain, she'll be coming 'round the

mountain, she'll be coming 'round the mountain when she comes (when she comes).

The rest of the verses go like this:
She'll be drivin' six white horses when she comes (when she comes) . . . .
Oh we'll all come to meet her when she comes (when she comes) . . . .
We will kill the old red rooster when she comes (when she comes) . . . .
We'll be havin' chicken and dumplings when she comes (when she comes) . . . .
We'll all be shoutin' "Halleluja" when she comes (when she comes) . . . .

I know it's just a silly children's song, but it brings tears to my eyes. It is often sung by fighting coal miners in the Appalachian coal camps of the south and by railroad work gangs in the Midwest.

My sincere hope is that the oppressed laborers of the world will continue to sing this song long past my death as a plea to the spirit of Mother Jones to help them through their trials and tribulations.

My final days are spent with my friends Walter and Lillie May Burgess on their farm in what will eventually be called Adelphi, Maryland. A gala party is held for me at the farm to celebrate my one hundredth birthday.

Some historians have already discovered I'm really only 93, but no one brings it up. Certainly not me! After lying about my age all these years I don't know why I should start now to tell the truth. And I've added to my fabrication by telling them I was born on May 1, which, of course, is the date established as America's Labor Day. Not a coincidence. Another of my little white lies.

Feeble as I am, I make it to the party and cut the cake. The press is there and a fellow with a great big movie camera follows me back to my room. Lillie May helps me back into bed.

Although she tries to comb my hair, it has become so thin and I just know it looks a mess. I wish I could wear one of my bonnets for the moving picture, but I guess that would look silly in bed.

The cameraman explains that he is there to make a film for RKO Pictures and that it will be shown in newsreels in movie theaters throughout the country. He has big floodlights all around my bed and when they light up, I squint and blink. Then the camera rolls and the fellow says "action." I guess that means I should say something.

"I pray for the day when working men and women are able to earn a fair share of the wealth they produce in a capitalist system, a day when all Americans are able to enjoy the freedom, rights and opportunities guaranteed them by the Constitution of the United States of America."

—◆◆◆—

Death finally comes to me in December, 1930. As I have requested, I am buried in the Union Miner's Cemetery at Mount Olive, Illinois.

Among the tombstones there is the marker of "General" Alexander Bradley who is said to be the most flamboyant figure in labor history. Bradley got his name while serving in Coxey's Army, famous for the cross-country march of unemployed workers which ended with a stroll down Pennsylvania Avenue in Washington, D.C. on my "birthday," May 1, 1894.

It was this march that inspired me to organize the March of the Mill Children a few years later. I've taken you on that journey.

When he returned home to Mount Olive from Coxey's march, he became a self-appointed organizer for the United Mine Workers, which only had around four hundred members in that region at the time. Nevertheless, Bradley and a handful of area miners decided at a secret meeting in the woods to join the nationwide strike of the UMW on July 4, 1897.

With Bradley leading, the miners marched to coal camps in Belleville, Edwardsville, Glen Carbon and Collinsville, Illinois, urging the men to "pour oil on their lamps," meaning open their eyes and join the strike. They did.

Then, on his own, and wearing his favorite outfit, a top hat and Prince Albert coat, with umbrella in hand, "General" Bradley took the train to Du Quoin, seventy-five miles away, to continue his campaign. The miners there also agreed to join the strike.

The unions in and around Mount Olive remained strong for several years after that. On October 10, 1898, four Mount Olive men were killed in a shootout with mine guards as a train carrying one hundred eighty black strike-breakers attempted to pass through a band of armed strikers at Virden, Illinois.

The mine guards were better armed than the miners and the battle only lasted ten minutes. Still, seven miners and four mine guards lay dead. Forty more miners and four more guards were wounded.

Originally the union men were to be buried in the town cemetery, but there was objection from the Lutherans who actually owned the cemetery. They thought the men should not be buried there because they thought the miners were "murderers."

Therefore, the local union purchased an acre of land nearby and the bodies were buried in what became the Union Miners Cemetery.

I liked "General" Bradley, and I liked this story, and so I let it be known a long time ago that I wanted to be buried there.

—◆◆◆—

Since I'm just here in spirit now — I guess I can jump ahead and tell you that a great monument with a statue of two coal miners was erected a few years later and dedicated to me with a plaque at the base of the monument.

Chapter Forty-Two
McDowell County, West Virginia ~ Present

A young black girl lies face down on her bed, crying her eyes out. Her infant child has died of shaken baby syndrome. Her boyfriend is in jail. Child Protective Services has just left with her other two children. She is now alone in her grief. I wish I could comfort her as I did Sarah James one hundred years ago.

I've been keeping an eye on this young lady for quite awhile. I know her story and it reminds me in some ways of Sarah's story when I found her in the jail in Pratt, not too many miles from here. You remember her. She had been charged with child neglect and prostitution. Her young son had been taken from her. Like this mother, she blamed herself for a misery not of her making.

Back then, Sarah was as much a victim of a capitalist system that cares nothing for the human condition as this girl. It is the same capitalistic insensitivity to human need that leads to these sad stories.

I'll call this weeping mother "Angela" because I think she's an angel. Society may condemn Angela for her life's failures, but first hear her story.

She lives in an old abandoned miner's shack outside of the town of Welch which is located in one of West Virginia's southernmost counties, McDowell. That county is the poorest county in one of America's poorest states. It is in the region where the worst of the coal wars I've told you about took place.

During the coal-mining boom of the 1950s, McDowell County produced amazing wealth which lined the pockets of the industrialists but deposited little money or transferable skills in the pockets or the minds of the workers who produced that wealth.

Those miners were mostly the descendants of mountaineers, European immigrants, and freed slaves. When the boom was over, the industrialists closed the mines, sold the majority of the developable land to other absentee owners and pulled out.

The population of McDowell County shrank to nearly one-third its former size and many of the people remaining were poorly educated, unskilled or dependent for a livelihood on welfare or other social programs. Among those who were left, up to thirty percent were unemployed.

Over the years, that number improved, but not because employment rose. No. Unemployment statistics improved because those who were employable finally left McDowell and, more often than not, left the state. Angela's husband abandoned her and her children to start a new life for himself.

—◆◆◆—

At the peak of employment in the 1950s, coal operators as a group were the largest employers in McDowell County. Now, it's Walmart.

Angela works for Walmart. She has worked there since she dropped out of high school to supplement her deadbeat husband's income. In his absence, she has to work a second job at one of the fast food chains because the business model for both her employers is worker exploitation. At both jobs she draws minimum wage or less and receives no benefits. Both employers limit her to thirty hours in order to circumvent employment benefit laws.

And so, this poor mother, the great-granddaughter of freed slaves, is now an economic slave, working sixty hours, seven days a week in order to earn wages that fail to add up to a poverty level existence for her three children who are necessarily left at home alone.

Unless, of course, she finds someone to watch over them for free.

And that's what she does. She is guilty of leaving her children with a succession of unemployed boyfriends while she works.

Conditions like these make it hard to find a worker in McDowell County who is not either hopeless or angry. The boyfriend, who shook her youngest child to death, was angry. And now, Angela is devastated and only momentarily defeated, I hope.

This story is not unique to McDowell County, or to West Virginia.

Walmart has been called the "Welfare Queen" of America. At nearly five hundred billion dollars per year, Walmart grosses the third highest revenue of any corporation in the world. In 2011, Walmart's CEO, a millionaire many times over, received an over eighteen million dollar compensation package. The Walton family is worth in excess of one hundred and two billion dollars, which makes it the richest family in the world.

Most appalling to me, the CEO makes more in one hour than his average employee earns in an entire year!

And before you say "that's not my problem," consider this. The abusive wage and hour policies of retail chains like Walmart increase the reliance of hard working people on government assistance programs as a social safety net. Which, in turn, passes along to you, the taxpayer, with the cost of food stamps. "Huh?"

you say? That's right. Studies show that as many as eighty percent of workers at Walmart stores rely on food stamps.

Thus, its customers and taxpayers end up subsidizing Walmart's profits.

Employers such as these routinely shift the responsibility of providing healthcare for their employees to sick people who don't work for Walmart or some other big box company and who struggle to pay for their own healthcare insurance. When an insured citizen gets sick and goes to the hospital these days, the bill covers not only themselves, but the uninsured patients in adjacent rooms who are employees of companies like Walmart.

This amounts to a sick tax. And a big one — thousands of dollars in premiums per person per year. This is the single biggest reason for the high cost of healthcare and yet irresponsible capitalists fight against a new law to require healthcare coverage for all. And they dupe their employees into trash-talking the idea because their capitalist masters don't want it.

So you should ask me, "If you were able to fight the good fight today, where would you fight it?"

And I would say, "There is so much to address, but I believe I would start in the retail and fast food industries."

Big box retailers and fast food chains are the coalmines and the sweatshops of modern America. Their business models are based on the exploitation of throwaway labor. Not only do they pay unlivable wages, they hire entry-level workers and expect a turnover rate, on the average, of three months.

The work is so simple and so mechanized that no training is required. Even someone who is to run the cash register gets an hour or less of over-the-shoulder training before stepping up to the till.

In three months, any ambitious employee learns there are no life-long careers waiting there. If those employees are lucky enough to have had parents who earn salaries above the poverty level, they just might overcome the system. If not, they will get trapped in economic servitude just like their mothers and grandmothers, just like the coal miners of yore.

A Taco Bell worker explains. When he started at a chain restaurant at age fifteen he was paid seven dollars and fifteen cents an hour. Six years later, as a supervisor, his take-home pay is ten cents higher, seven dollars and twenty-five cents an hour.

Mothers like Angela are tempted to give up on work and go on welfare. Many do. Angela is thinking she might still have her three children if she had simply gone on the government dole, stayed home and cared for her children. But, bless her soul, she was too proud to let the system beat her. I'm not so sure she won't give up now.

I am hoping Angela will keep on fighting. Some workers do. Fewer win.

There are flickers of hope.

A few months ago, workers at a McDonald's restaurant in Harlem, New York, staged a protest and soon four hundred workers in the fast food industry went on a one-day strike to bring attention to the travesty of the McWages that leave them living well below the poverty line, living in basements below the sidewalks.

At the protest, workers chanted, "We cannot survive on seven twenty-five," which is the average hourly wage paid to fast food workers in New York City. In fact, that is the federal minimum wage.

Even if employees were allowed to work forty hours a week, that would add up to less than three hundred dollars before taxes. A little more than two hundred dollars when the employee is restricted to no more than thirty hours. Working two fast food jobs for sixty hours total, a worker can earn up to four hundred and thirty-five dollars in a week, twenty-two thousand, six hundred and twenty dollars in a year. Still slightly below poverty for a family of four in 2012. And does rising up to the poverty level in America spell "the American dream?"

In 2012, the U.S. Census Bureau discovered that more than sixteen percent of the population lived in poverty in the United States, nearly fifty million people. Children in poverty were at the twenty percent level.

The fast food industry is shameless. Burger King brags that its company has provided "an entry point into the workforce for millions of Americans" and McDonalds says its "employees are paid *competitive* wages" (competitive, that is, with other slave labor enterprises) and brags that their employees have access to flexible schedules (meaning clearing their calendar to work another job).

The National Restaurant Association looks for sympathy by saying "if the minimum wage goes up to, say, fifteen dollars an hour as these protestors are demanding, more than thirteen million jobs could be jeopardized." That would be a shame, says they, because "the industry is one of the best paths to achieving the American Dream."

I have to say, it looks like the American Dream has turned into the American Nightmare. Again.

The irony is, most Americans of any class other than the rich have to buy their food and clothing at "the company store" — the retail sweatshop, because it's all they can afford. Unlike the scrip of old, their money is good anywhere but they don't have much of it, so they are forced to spend it at the "company store," which pauperized them in the first place.

They are trapped inside the big box just as the coalminers of old were trapped in the company town. They have no choice but to work at places like Walmart because most of the independent small businessmen who once provided a good living to Mom and

Pop and their valued employees are out of business, victims of unfair competition from the big box.

And when the day is done, they have no choice but to give their meager earnings back to the store for food and clothing. They are limited to cheap clothing produced in some sweatshop or sold in a thrift store because they can't afford anything else. Second hand stuff for second class citizens.

Even the middle class struggles on a budget while the filthy rich buys its expensive toys, wanders around its opulent mansions, reinvests its cash in stocks and bonds, ships its surplus wealth off shore.

I also observe that when American workers cannot be exploited, Congress passes laws that allow for the import and exploitation of what Congress calls "guest workers."

Approved by Congress, these laws provide temporary farm workers and non-farm laborers to a variety of U.S. industries that routinely prey on the vulnerability of these workers and get away with a host of labor and human rights violations. The workers don't report the violations for fear of deportation, blacklisting or other types of retaliation.

Does this sound familiar? Thumb back through my story.

Many among these economic slaves are recent generations of the very illegal aliens I dealt with in my era, the Mexicans we called "scabs." According to the Department of Labor, some one hundred six thousand guest workers were brought into this country this way in 2011 alone. Approximately fifty-five thousand came for agricultural work and another fifty-one thousand were exploited by the forestry, seafood processing, landscaping, construction and other non-agricultural industries.

Far from being treated as guests, these workers are exploited and abused for capitalistic gain without the fundamental protections guaranteed, but often not provided, to American citizens.

I marvel at the duplicity of American public policy. Along the southern border of the U.S., the leaders of democracy build high fences and run border patrols under a social policy aimed at keeping illegal Mexicans *out*. Meanwhile the captains of capitalism support human traffickers who import virtual slave laborers *into* this country for the purposes of exploitation and profit.

Most American citizens resent these foreign workers. Citizen workers are painfully aware that imported cheap labor depresses wage rates and robs unemployed Americans of a job market that should offer employment at a reasonable wage.

And I can't help but notice that we are now exporting the misery and tragedy of labor to the most desperately poor countries of the world. American workers resent those foreign workers because they are taking jobs the American does not want at the wages usually paid.

I can't say that I am shocked, but I am deeply saddened by the tragic news that came to us so recently from Bangladesh. The loss of eleven hundred garment workers in the collapse of a single, shoddily built factory building in that third world country. The tragedy was reminiscent of the Triangle Shirtwaist factory fire in New York City, the one I described to you earlier.

We lost one hundred and forty-seven souls in the Triangle fire for the lack of exits. In Bangladesh, it was due to the addition of more floors to expand a sweatshop already operating in an unstable building and further weakened by the vibrations of the heavy machines used in the factory. Last year it was a factory fire in Pakistan that killed two hundred and sixty.

The greed of capitalism knows no geographic bounds and America's economic system is not too far away from places like Bangladesh to wear the blame.

—◆◆◆—

And so, I ask you, who is fighting against the exploitation of labor in America and abroad? I see that the importers of foreign-made garments in America in the wake of the Bangladesh tragedy are now showing some regret and some social responsibility. But how long will that last? How long did it last after the Triangle Shirtwaist fire over one hundred years ago? Not long, and it's obvious we didn't care enough to fix the problem. We exported the risk of sweatshops to Bangladesh and other countries around the world.

I see the government in Bangladesh now saying it will change its policies. At last it will allow organized unions to form. It is small comfort to me to hear those words when I see that, in America, organized labor has declined so dramatically since the 1970s. In my opinion it's largely due to the weakness and ineffectiveness of the labor unions themselves.

A study published in the *American Sociological Review* shows that union membership among men in the private sector between 1973 and 2007 dropped from thirty-four percent down to eight percent. For women it was from sixteen percent down to six percent.

During that same period, wage inequality in the private sector increased by more than forty percent.

In my waning life in the 1920s, and though I admit our gains were modest, union and non-union companies were beginning to respond to labor's voice in order to avoid the threat of more strikes, more strife, more battles, more wars, more disasters. But I see now that the capitalists have been able to undermine the fighting spirit of their workers by convincing more and more of them to abandon collective bargaining, to give up their strong voices and depend instead upon the promised benevolence or certain whim of a kinder and gentler capitalistic system.

Don't you believe it.

I believe the decline in unions lies as much with the misdirected performance of organized labor as it does with the guile of capitalists. I've told you repeatedly of the danger of climbing into bed with the capitalists, and these statistics and true stories prove it to be so.

—◆◆◆—

I observe that the elderly are now joining the underclass when they retire, even though they may have been the middle class or two-job survivors in the underclass during their productive lives.

Fewer of them are the beneficiaries of corporate retirement programs today and those who have retirement benefits paid for those benefits themselves through payroll deductions at a sacrifice to their substandard incomes.

Many simply could not buy into these retirement programs and so they rely solely on Social Security, which these same workers also funded from their own pockets. And over the years they've again been exploited by their own government which stole money from the Social Security fund to shore up shortfalls in government revenue needed because of the failure of the capitalists to shoulder social responsibilities.

Remember, capitalism is about greed, not social responsibility. And so the captains of government have bankrupted the people to cover the costs that should have been funded by the wealth produced by industry, not workers.

And here's irony again. Since the 1960s, the branches of government, presidents and Congress have reduced the tax burden on the few, the richest Americans, from ninety percent to thirty percent.

First, it was the "trickle down theory" that justified reducing the social responsibilities of the capitalists already at rock bottom to boost the economy. Most recently, it is a government that gives out grants to save banks, not mortgage holders. That, supposedly, to jump start the economy and provide jobs for the unemployed.

Damn right.

My distrust is not with the players, both management and labor. My distrust is with the system. Capitalism is all about the money. To the contrary, democracy is all about the people. Well, democracy *should* be all about the people. There is an inherent conflict between the two and without checks and balances, without vigilance and a strong voice, the economics goes upside down and a state of inequality grows.

It is this way now.

America today is the land of inequality and I can see in the press that people are beginning to get the message. Here is one example.

Apple, Facebook and Google, among others, reinvented the Gold Rush in California's Silicon Valley. A few are earning megabucks while the general population earns an average of about $19,000 a year. Apartment rent alone in the Valley can average more than $20,000 a year.

One long-time journalist there recalls how Silicon Valley was once a land of orchards, farms and ranches. Now it is a place of the incredibly wealthy and the incredibly poor. Homelessness and hunger are rampant. And, just a few miles down the road in San Jose, the homeless are building tent cities. Sound familiar?

And are these poor people simply uneducated and unskilled? No. These knowledge workers are college educated, a new underclass once populated by mineworkers and textile workers. They are people whose brains are being exploited by the high tech industry to produce the highest profits in all history. And yet, its greatest natural resource, the human resource, goes begging.

—◆◆◆—

The stock market crash of 2007 is the best lesson yet regarding the status of American labor and its relationship with the economy.

Immediately the capitalists began laying off employees and within a single year Wall Street had recovered. But employment didn't recover. It remained in the double digits for years. Full recovery for the working class is not yet in sight. Will it ever be?

It has long been a fact on Wall Street that the way to drive the stock market *up* is to drive employment *down*.

Part of the 2007 stock market recovery came as a gift from the Federal Government. Congress bailed out the banks while the families who were "qualified" by those same banks for low down payment, low interest, high-profit loans were being put out on the streets. It's reminiscent of coal mining families of old, exploited and then evicted.

Corporate profits are now at record highs. Are those corporate capitalists investing any of it in jobs? No. Do they at least hand out some modest pay raises? No. Do they pay more in taxes to help bail out the social structure? No. Do they step up to their own social responsibilities for healthcare and decent wages? No. Instead, they successfully lobby for lower taxes which is supposed to spur the economy.

If it does, it is the capitalist's economy that is raised and the working stiff's economy that gets "spurred."

The Public Interest Research Group recently issued a report showing that corporations are now sitting on one point seven trillion dollars in cash, ninety billion dollars of it sitting in offshore tax havens. PIRG said that we average citizens will eventually make up for that money which is sitting offshore and not here at home.

Meanwhile, people take up the slack. Subsidize the greed of capitalism from their own pocketbooks and their own lives.

—◆◆◆—

The other day I read an article in my favorite periodical, *Mother Jones* magazine, which presented charts with a headline I really liked: "It's the Inequality, Stupid." Using charts, it showed how a huge share of the nation's economic growth over the past thirty years has gone to the top one-hundredth of one percent who now make an average of twenty-seven million dollars per household while the average income for the bottom ninety percent, the rest of us, is just a little over thirty-one thousand dollars.

People are finally awakening to this fact and they're mad as hell about it. I'm ecstatic! It's high time the American people woke up to what I've been saying since the Civil War.

It's the inequality, stupid.

Now, what are you going to do about that? First of all, you can stop fighting each other over the scraps. Another way we can both help is to keep the spirit of Mother Jones alive and raising hell. I know I will.

Afterword

While this is a work of fiction, I have generally remained true to the actual history of Mother Jones with a few exceptions.

All the major characters are actual with the exceptions of Jenny Flynn who was invented as Mother Jones' business partner, Sarah James and Addie Thompson who were Mother Jones' jail mates in Pratt, West Virginia.

All of the other characters are real and, where full names are used, their roles are true to history. Where characters have only a first name, the characters are real but not specifically identified.

All of the events are real and true to history except, in some cases, actual episodes have been consolidated or moved in time and place to capture the flavor of some of the events not otherwise included in this book. If every event Mother Jones either witnessed or participated in were to be covered in a single book, it would be a monstrous tome.

A few of the stories are either pure fiction, or conjecture based on historical facts and fabricated for a reason. Some are fabricated from probability because there are so many gaps in the records.

Mother Jones did have a business partner in Chicago at the time of the great fire, but her name is unknown to me. I made the name of Jenny Flynn up and extended the story beyond the fire.

Mother Jones and her partner did not rebuild after the fire as a full-fledged dress factory that became the source of the money Mother Jones used to sustain herself through more than sixty-five years as a labor activist.

I made it all up to fill one of the many gaps in Mother Jones' history. Among the mysteries is the question of how Mother Jones supported herself during times when she had no income, which was more often than not. The answer is pure conjecture on my part, not only to solve the mystery, but as a device to imagine what kind of industrialist Mother Jones would have been had she become a full-fledged capitalist.

Further, the Chicago factory gave me a chance to help Mother Jones demonstrate how capitalism *ought* to work in her opinion.

The stories behind the tragic mothers, Sarah James at the beginning of the book and the unnamed mother at the end, are pure fabrications although they represent thousands of such stories and the actual and emotional impact unchecked greed has on the American family.

I used the fictional character of Addie Thompson, especially her violent death in Colorado, to demonstrate the vulnerability that Mother Jones faced without killing off our real life hero prematurely.

—◆◆◆—

Much of the dialogue is made up. Some of it is based on actual records, some of it is pure conjecture. But all of it is in the spirit of Mother Jones and her associates.

The words of Mother Jones presented in this book are true to the history but either made up or slicked up. For example, we can only imagine the dialogue that went on while Mother Jones and her family were quarantined in Memphis, suffering from yellow fever.

We can only imagine what was said during the months she was incarcerated in Pratt, West Virginia.

We can only imagine what passed between Mother Jones and Terence Powderly as they sat on that hill above the railroad yards in Pittsburgh.

Many events involving Mother Jones are well chronicled, but without dialogue. When her actual words were recorded, it was done by a stenographer because there was no electronic means of voice recording. In most cases, the stenographer was being paid by the capitalists for the purpose of using Mother Jones' purported words against her, and thus suspect to interpretation.

Even the words Mother Jones wrote down were often suspect. Her own autobiography was dictated by her when she was quite old and feeble. Even if her memory were unimpaired, Mother Jones was reckless with the facts throughout her lifetime, remembering and reporting events to fit her purposes. Her little white lies about her age are a good example.

While Mother Jones is noted in history as being an effective speaker at rallies and in head-to-head confrontation, her dialogue does not come off well in print except for those colorful quotes that are so often repeated today.

She did give a great deal of thought to what she was going to say in advance of speaking, but she did not organize her thoughts well, did not follow notes and usually rambled a great deal when she got on stage. She skipped around and repeated herself, especially when a catch phrase in a workman's vernacular proved itself popular with the crowd.

Mother Jones' speaking style was more showmanship and energy than it was oratory.

All that having been said, make no mistake about this — Mother Jones was as intelligent and well read as she seems in this novel. She often quoted the classics and referred to current events. If her persona were anything less, it was because she fit herself into the environment in which she lived and worked.

I want to give praise to the many historians who have produced the huge collection of Mother Jones stories and facts which were so valuable in the writing of this work of fiction. First and foremost, my hat is off to Charles H. Kerr for publishing the *Autobiography of Mother Jones* in 1925.

Also to Judith Pinkerton Josephson for *Mother Jones, Fierce Fighter for Workers' Rights,* 1997. Dale Featherling, *Mother Jones, The Miners' Angel,* 1974. Edward M. Steel, Jr., *The Court-Martial of Mother Jones,* 1995, also *The Speeches and Writings of Mother Jones,* 1988 and *The Correspondence of Mother Jones,* 1985. Philip S. Foner, *Mother Jones Speaks,* 1983. Madelyn Horton, *The Importance of Mother Jones,* 1996. And Elliott Gorn, *The Most Dangerous Woman in America,* 2002.

These are but a few of the serious histories available in book form.

I also want to thank the many contributors to the history of Mother Jones on the World Wide Web. Principle among them are those who contribute so freely to Wikipedia, as well as Creative Common for the words of Eugene Debs. Also of great value are the hundreds of articles to be found online.

And finally, I tip my hat to *Mother Jones* magazine for keeping the name of Mother Jones alive and her spirit in action.

My thanks also go to a few of my friends, some of whom took on the task of reading chapters as they were produced and giving me feedback even before editing. Principle among them is a dear friend who was a legislative research assistant during the time I served in the West Virginia State Senate. Allen Hager's eyes literally lit up when he got to talking about the dynamics, revelations and powerful lessons he found in the draft pages of *Hellraiser* as it unfolded. With the exception of Mother Jones, he was my greatest inspiration and he kept me from falling into a blue funk when my words weren't flowing.

Allen is now a successful "capitalist" located in Omaha, Nebraska.

Also valuable among my loyal draft readers were Gary Adams, also a former legislative assistant now located in Sacramento, California; Walt Kinsey, an old college buddy and friend for life, Cross Lanes, West Virginia; Homer Womack, a fellow retiree and tennis player here in Sun City Center, Florida; Diana Huber, retired tractor-trailer driver and teamster, Ruskin, Florida; and, Ardena Forster, retired school teacher in Island Heights, New Jersey and forever friend of my wife Michele. Unlike the most of us, Dain is not a flaming liberal.

Last but not least, to my best friend, wife and partner Michele Ash, I give my highest praise for standing with me through the good times and bad for more than 40 years. She is a talented journalist and graphic designer who edited this book, designed its cover, chose its typography and laid it out in a fashion that is easy to read in print and in e-book. I am just one of her many clients.

—◆◆◆—

And, last but not least, I want to thank you, the reader. As Mother Jones knows, there are two vital parts to communication — the sending and the receiving. Without the latter, the former is of no value. Thank you for taking part in this book. I'd say we've had a fine conversation.

About the Author

Jerry Ash has written eight books ranging from histories to business management. *Hellraiser* is his first historic novel intended for the mass market.

He has completed a novel titled *Latent Images* that is planned for release in 2014.

A coalminer's son, he is a native of Bridgeport, West Virginia, located in the center of the northern coalfields referred to in this book.

Among his published books is *West Virginia USA*, 1976, which was co-authored with AP feature writer Strat Douthat. It was a chapter written by Douthat that introduced Jerry to Mother Jones.

Jerry holds a masters degree in journalism from West Virginia University and was an assistant professor of journalism there for seven years.

In the 1970s, he was editor and co-publisher of a small town weekly newspaper in Terra Alta, West Virginia, *The Preston County News*, which won forty state and national awards during those years. At the same time he co-founded the *Pioneer Press of West Virginia*.

In the 1980s he was elected to two terms as a West Virginia State Senator. After leaving the Senate he became vice president of the West Virginia Hospital Association and then president and CEO of the Nevada Hospital Association.

After a stint as executive director of Lifegift Organ Donation Centers in Houston, Fort Worth, Lubbock and Amarillo,Texas, in the 1990s, he worked as an independent business consultant and became known worldwide for his expertise in the field of knowledge management. He was editor of *Inside Knowledge* Magazine in London, England, before retiring in 2010.

He and his wife Michele live in Sun City Center, Florida, where Jerry rides his motorcycle to bluegrass music concerts and jamborees all over the state. He is a competitive tennis player and avid reader.

Although he prides himself on having had an eclectic career, he says his most satisfying accomplishment has been the writing of *Hellraiser* and he believes it will ultimately be his most lasting legacy.

Please join
MOJO's *Hellraiser* Club

Now that you've read *Hellraiser*, please join Mother Jones's *Hellraiser* Club, a blog dedicated to keeping the spirit of Mother Jones alive forever, or until equality and justice prevail in the workplace. Whichever comes first.

Hellraiser's author, Jerry Ash, will be your host.

Mother Jones will be your guide. She makes a good case for continuing her fight in the last chapter of *Hellraiser*:

"It's high time the American people woke up to what I've been saying since the Civil War. It's the inequality, stupid. Now, what are you going to do about that?"

One way, she says, is to keep her spirit alive and raising hell.

www.jerryash.com

—◆◆◆—

Support a modern *Hellraiser*
Turn the page to find out how

—◆◆◆—

—◆◆◆—

Please support the
Mother Jones Investigative Fund

To make a donation to Mother Jones and the Foundation for National Progress, a 501c3 new organization that specializes in investigative, political, and social justice reporting, you can mail a check to Mother Jones Investigative Fund, 222 Sutter Street, San Francisco, CA 94108, or visit the website at www.motherjones.com/donate.

—◆◆◆—

Printed in Great Britain
by Amazon.co.uk, Ltd.,
Marston Gate.